Totally Bound Publishing books by Gloria Herrmann:

Single in Seattle
Reeling in Love
Puppy Love
A Latte of Love

I0680791

Single in Seattle

A LATTE OF LOVE

GLORIA HERRMANN

A Latte of Love
ISBN # 978-1-78686-327-0
©Copyright Gloria Herrmann 2017
Cover Art by Posh Gosh ©Copyright October 2017
Interior text design by Claire Siemaszkiewicz
Totally Bound Publishing

A LATTE OF LOVE

Dedication

For Wendy, my sister from another mister, my best friend in the whole wide world, and my inspiration for the *Single in Seattle* series.

I wanted to write a story that celebrated all the aspects of true friendship—the good, the bad and the not so pretty bits in between. You've been there by my side, a witness to my times of struggle and strength. We've learned many lessons in love and friendship along the way. The greatest thing I've learned is that it's rare to meet someone who honestly has your back, who is standing in your corner, someone who isn't afraid to say the things I often don't want to hear, but who is also the first one to be my cheerleader.

Thank you for always being there through the good, the bad and everything in between.

Prologue

This is just too much. Mackenzie was beyond overwhelmed. Weddings and pregnancy — all the celebrations for life events she was pretty certain she'd never experience. The planning of these were over the top and quite frankly ridiculous. *It's way too much.* She had somehow survived Molly's nuptials, but with the wedding happening in Hawaii, she'd tried to view it more as a much-needed vacation than an actual event. Mackenzie was happy for Molly. She was. It was just that Mackenzie didn't exactly have warm n' fuzzy feelings about the whole wedded bliss crap. Mackenzie had even gotten through Tiffany's stupid stunt in Hawaii without saying too much on the subject. Leave it to Tiffany to not be satisfied with just simply being married, regardless of the fact that she'd had been drunk and wound up tying the knot with Colin in Vegas. Bridezilla wanted the wedding of the flipping century, which meant Mackenzie would be forced to endure another round of vows and lovey-dovey bullshit.

Mackenzie just couldn't wrap her head around any of this crazy nonsense. It hadn't been all that long ago when the three of them had all been single and just living their lives in Seattle. *Friendship Fridays* had meant so much more then. It hadn't been the same for months now. If she were to be completely honest, Mackenzie could admit it was because she was a teensy bit envious of her besties. At one time she had been engaged, even had the perfect dress, the six-tiered cake ordered, a ridiculous number of flowers bought — and what in the hell had happened? Gideon. That was the who *and* the what. *Men. They screw up everything.* Gideon had ruined what was supposed to have been the most perfect day of Mackenzie's life. *Their life.*

"You sure you don't want to grab dinner with us?" Tiffany asked as she pulled up to the curb outside Mackenzie's house.

"Nope. I'm exhausted. You two have fun." Mackenzie faked a yawn from the back seat.

Molly twisted around from the front passenger seat and threw her a curious look. "You okay?"

"I'm fine," Mackenzie answered.

She wasn't the least bit *fine*. Mackenzie'd had all the shopping she could handle, even though retail therapy usually did her a world of good. Today there had been too many reminders of what she could've had — what she should've had.

Mackenzie hopped out of Tiffany's shiny new SUV — one of the perks of being hitched to a millionaire. She waved goodbye as her friends pulled away. Mackenzie hung her head and rifled through her large bag in search of her keys. Her game plan for the night was simple — a well-deserved adult beverage, pajamas and a book — anything to take away the sting of having shopped for baby shower decorations, party favors for Tiffany's epic wedding and remembering Gideon.

She found her keys and looked up to find that her plans for the evening had just changed.

Shit.

Chapter One

Why? Why did Gideon have to show up on my doorstep after two years? No communication of any kind. Not one *damn* word. There hadn't been any texts, calls, not even an email or letter. *Not a thing.* Two whole heartbreaking years, missing him and wondering what she could've done differently to have made things work. *Nothing, that's what.* Sometimes there were no answers, no reasons for why things happened. She, of all people, had learned that hard lesson and wore the emotional scars to prove it.

Mackenzie blinked back the blur of tears that had been threatening to fall for the last several hours. He'd already left her...again. *Would there be a next time?* Mackenzie wasn't sure she even wanted there to be. A torrential downpour of feelings raged inside her. *Why me? Why now? Because life must have it out for me.*

Today had already been exhausting enough, not that she'd minded spending time with her besties, Molly and Tiffany. So much had changed over the course of spring and summer that it had left her questioning where she was in her life. *Where do I fit in now? What am I even doing with my life?* Career-wise, Mackenzie was good. She was a teacher, a noble profession. Granted, most of the time it was a day filled with her watching booger eating, being patient with whining and rattling off ABCs to five-year-old kids, but it filled her maternal void. Love-life-wise, she was lost, floundering in a vast sea of loneliness. Okay, perhaps that was a little dramatic, but when her two best friends in the entire world had both gotten hitched within what seemed like minutes and she hadn't, it made her a tad grumpy, to say the least.

The three of them had been single off and on over the course of their long friendship. The girls had seen her with Gideon and they'd seen her without him. It hadn't been a pretty scene, either way. So much could change in a moment, from being engaged to the man of her dreams to being dumped only a few days before the ceremony. It had gotten a little more than ugly. *Why did he even bother coming back? What could he possibly have to say after all this time?*

It didn't matter because Mackenzie had experienced enough heartbreak only a few months ago to last her a lifetime. The hurt Gideon had caused didn't even compare to the pain and grief she'd been left with when her sister had been killed. Nothing could replace her. A man could be replaced. A new love could fill the hole where it had once been cut and carved out her heart, but losing a sister? That chunk of her heart could never be replaced. She didn't give two flying fucks what he'd come there to say. At least that was what she told herself.

She cinched the waist of her most comfy pajamas and padded barefoot into her kitchen. It was vodka time. Mackenzie snatched a lemon from her overflowing fruit bowl. She couldn't help but laugh as she gave it a hard squeeze.

When life hands you lemons, screw lemonade. Just add vodka.

* * * *

The next day, a slightly hungover and irritable Mackenzie had agreed to join Molly at the waterfront. Mackenzie crossed her long, jean-clad legs as she sat on a weathered bench and stared out at the murky water. Boats bobbed on the surface as seagulls cried overhead. The Seattle sky, an ugly gray filled with thick clouds, matched her mood. Her bestie, Molly, was seated next to her. Her friend had been going on and on about the plans for her baby shower that they would be having soon. Mackenzie's mind couldn't be further away. She sipped on the pumpkin-spiced latte in her cardboard cup. The spicy blend of flavors announced that fall was officially there. Trees had already begun to change. Bold colors of red, orange and yellow could be seen in every direction. There was a chilly bite to the air and Mackenzie was thankful for the warmth of her delicious coffee drink. She cradled it in her hands and stole the heat from the small cup.

"If Owen would just let us find out what the gender is, this whole planning would be much easier. You know?" Molly complained as she rubbed her belly.

"Life is only full of so many wonderful surprises. Let this be one of them," Mackenzie countered. *Do I even believe the crap I'm feeding Molly?*

Molly huffed. "What's going on with you? You seem so down in the dumps."

Mackenzie hadn't shared much of what she'd been feeling lately. Of course, her friends knew she was still mourning her sister's death. They'd been incredibly supportive and patient with her as she tried to navigate through the confusing waters of loss. What they didn't know was that Gideon had returned. She wasn't sure how supportive they would be when they did find out. To say they were angry with him was a mild understatement. Utterly livid and wanting to cause physical pain… That was a more accurate description of their feelings toward a man whom Mackenzie had once loved with all her heart and soul — and still sort of did.

"It's just been rough," Mackenzie replied. It was a simple answer and she hoped it would suffice.

"I know, Mac. It's gotta be hard." Molly frowned, her face full of sympathy — not an ounce of pity, just genuine concern and love. She reached for Mackenzie's hand and gave it a strong squeeze. It was almost enough to unleash the tears Mackenzie had worked to hold back all day.

Molly was quiet then spoke, "Owen wanted to know when you planned on scattering her ashes."

Mackenzie wasn't anywhere near ready and she wasn't sure she ever would be. The wooden box sat on a shelf in her bedroom and she looked at it every single day. Each one that passed was supposed to get easier, yet it hadn't. Instead, Mackenzie wondered each time why her baby sister had died that day. *How could something so awful happen to someone so sweet and kind?* She knew traffic accidents occurred all the time, but when it was a family member who had been killed due to another's stupid error in judgment, it was brutal. Mackenzie had always been against drinking and driving. She'd never allowed herself behind the wheel in that state, even after only two cocktails. It gutted her to think that someone had decided they were okay enough to drive when they obviously were not, and now her sister was gone because of it.

It was nice of Owen to offer to take her out to sea where Mackenzie could scatter her remains, but it was too soon. "I appreciate the offer. Please tell him that for me. But I'm just not quite ready."

"It might help you move on," Molly added. "We're all here for you. You know that, right? We're just concerned and want you to be okay."

"I'll be fine." *I will be, right?*

Mackenzie focused her attention back out on the water and it took everything she had to not break down. She'd save that for later when there was no one to watch.

* * * *

It'd been two whole days since Gideon had sat on her porch. For two days, her mind had replayed their entire history together, over and over again—the good, the bad and what might've been. It didn't matter if she was driving, brushing her teeth or shaving her legs. She was constantly thinking about him.

Mackenzie was done with Gideon. She needed to be for the sake of her sanity. *So why is it so damn impossible?* Every time Mackenzie closed her eyes she saw him— his handsome face with the strong jaw that was always clean shaven. She could thank years of military service for that. His green-blue eyes were like deep pools, sparkling and inviting. Then there were those great lips she had once loved kissing, the same lips that had whispered some of the naughtiest things she'd ever heard spoken, but those that had also told her it was over. Mackenzie'd never thought she'd see his face again—had even hoped she never would—yet she had and now her whole world was more of a mess. *How is it possible for shit to get worse?* Seeing him had thrown her for a loop, flipped her world upside down and when she'd heard his voice, it had been her total undoing. Mackenzie had ordered him to leave but now regretted not at least finding out what it was that he'd wanted. It had eaten away at her, gnawed at her all day and night. She'd attempted to put on a happy mask at work and tried to tell herself that it didn't matter what he had come to say. There was nothing that could take back the hurt he'd caused her. No words could replace the two miserable years without Gideon. *Or can they? Does he have a valid excuse? Has something changed?* Mackenzie mentally slapped herself. *What is wrong with you, woman? This man left you days before your wedding.* No, there was nothing he could say to make that okay.

Mackenzie sighed. No, he didn't have that right anymore. He'd lost that privilege. She needed to take her mind off Gideon. *Now.* Mackenzie looked at the screen of her cell phone and hesitated. *Should I bother with this one?*

"Hello?" a sexy voice on the other line answered.

"Hey, Jason." Mackenzie smiled at the masculine sound of his voice. She had promised herself that she was done with him, too, but figured a sexy distraction couldn't hurt right about now. Mackenzie just wanted to combat her boredom with a little conversation and one that wasn't with one of her girls. They would only pester her and ask if everything was okay.

Jason… Now he's a story all in himself. She and the girls had traveled to Vegas shortly after her sister had died. She'd needed to escape Seattle, to drown her troubles and to let loose. What better way than dancing on tables? That was where Jason had come in—a hot, muscular and beautifully inked bouncer. Mackenzie, little Miss Conservative, would have never considered a possible fling or romance with someone like him. Yet, she'd found herself attracted. She'd known they couldn't be more different, but there was just something about him that had made her pulse quicken and had gotten her all hot and bothered. Maybe it was his strong, alpha-male presence. Perhaps it was the way his lips felt against hers. Or maybe, just maybe, it was because poor Mackenzie hadn't gotten laid in over two years. No matter how much she'd tried, though, nothing had happened between them — physically speaking, anyway. Mackenzie and Jason had texted, called and even visited each other a few times. Again, nothing. Her own insecurities made her believe it had everything to do with her, that something must be terribly wrong. Mackenzie just couldn't figure out what. *Is he not attracted to me? Am I getting to be too old? Does he think I'm boring and not the fun girl I tried so hard to pose as?*

"Hey, babe, what have you been up to?" he asked.

"Nothing much, just work. You?" Mackenzie tried to think of what topics they could cover. Their last visit had ended with Tiffany getting hitched to her lovely, extremely wealthy and Irish boss, Colin. Things hadn't gone so well the last time she had been with Jason. *Why am I even calling him? Desperate times call for desperate measures, cupcake.*

"Same. When are you coming back to visit me, sexy?"

Such a tease. Does he miss me? The silky sound of his voice made her desire him. There was no doubt that she'd drop her panties if he asked. *God, who am I?* This was not like her at all. *See what happens when you become desperate to get laid? You become stupid, weak and are willing to do just about anything to fulfill that ache.* And at that very moment, Mackenzie would do anything to sleep with that very hot bouncer from Vegas.

"I could say the same for you," Mackenzie replied slowly. *Would I welcome Jason back into my life? Hell, yeah, if it meant I could finally quench this ridiculous lusty thirst — to end the drought, as Tiffany named it. Two years of celibacy.* Mackenzie was practically a nun or a born-again virgin.

He laughed then his voice went rough. "I just may need to." Mackenzie's ears perked up at the change in his tone when he asked, "You alone, babe?"

Mackenzie swallowed and nodded. *You stupid, horny idiot, answer him.* "Yeah," she managed.

"God, baby, I've missed you so much," Jason growled. "My cock is so hard right now just at the sound of your voice."

She'd never heard him talk dirty. *Where exactly did this come from?* Not that she was complaining.

"Are you wet hearing me?" Jason asked.

Uh. Mackenzie inhaled deeply and decided to see where this was headed. "Maybe a little," she lied. Mackenzie had no flipping clue. *Maybe I should check?*

"Are you touching yourself?" Jason's voice was heavy. "That would be fuckin' hot if you were."

She wasn't good at this whole phone sex stuff. Mackenzie had no clue how to talk dirty or play the role of a sex kitten. She was beyond out of practice and found herself fumbling as she tried to undo her pants. After finally having loosened the fuzzy pink pajama bottoms, her hand rested on her crotch on the outside of her plain, terribly ordinary cotton underwear. Did she dare play along with Jason? She didn't feel the least bit sexy.

"I wanted you a lot when you were here, sweetheart."

Then why in the hell didn't you do something about it? Mackenzie breathed into the phone, "I wanted you, too." She let her finger dip past the elastic of her underwear. That felt naughty and so good. *Oh, shit.* Mackenzie'd had no idea this conversation was going to head in this direction but she decided to just go with it. This was going to be one helluva distraction. Mackenzie circled her finger around her clit. She enjoyed the soft, moist feel of her sensitive nub.

"Tell me what you're doing right now. I'm squeezing my cock and thinking of how sexy you are," Jason described. "I'm so hard right now. I just want to bend you over and give you all of it."

Yes, I need this. Mackenzie licked her lips. Oh, what she'd give to see his cock. "I'm playing with my clit. I'm imaging it's your tongue, baby. That you're sucking on it and licking every single inch of my wet pussy." Mackenzie felt brazen and figured after the shitty week she'd had, she'd more than earned this moment of lusty distraction.

"Fuck, yeah. I'd love to eat that juicy pussy and make you come all over my face." Jason's voice had become ragged. Mackenzie closed her eyes and pictured his dark goatee covered in her juices. She could hear him stroking himself. The fast, steady movements carried across the miles through their phone. Jason whispered, "Damn, this is hot."

She had to admit Jason was right. This was extremely hot by Mackenzie's standards and it turned her on fiercely. Mackenzie plunged one finger inside to find herself warm and slick. *God, I need to get laid.* Her fingers weren't going to cut it. Her dildo barely handled business whenever she'd felt the rare urge to pleasure herself. What Mackenzie needed was true human contact, someone to love her. She wanted to be pounded and she pictured Jason hammering into her. She drove her fingers deeper while she worked her clit with her thumb. *This will just have to do. Better than nothing.*

Jason moaned then the line went quiet. Mackenzie froze. She stopped her fingers. "Hello?" she asked, fearful they'd been disconnected.

"Thanks, babe. Damn, I needed that," Jason announced. "Hey, I gotta run. You know, work and shit. Maybe give me a call tomorrow."

Silence again. Jason had ended their call. *What?* He was already done. *What about me?* Mackenzie was so pissed off that she removed her hand. She threw her head back and cried out in frustration. *Did he forget that I needed to get off, too? What a selfish prick.* She hated men. Men sucked.

Chapter Two

Misery loves company. But misery also loved vodka —
or at least Mackenzie did. She had somehow managed
to get through the rest of the week. It was a downright
miracle that she had made it to Friday. Fridays had
always been special, but she wasn't sure for how much
longer. *Friendship Fridays* were something that she,
Tiffany and Molly had done for years. It consisted of
food, booze, a dumb movie and lots of laughs. The best
part was that it was like an adult slumber party —
pajamas, no makeup, junk food and, most importantly,
booze.

"I hate you both right now," Molly said as she eyed
the glasses Tiffany poured more vodka into.

"Hey, you got yourself knocked up," Tiffany pointed
out as she took a sip of her cocktail and closed her eyes.
"You're so missing out, by the way. This is delicious."

"Gimme," Mackenzie ordered as she held out her
hand. She swallowed a large gulp of the fruity

concoction and couldn't even taste the slightest hint of alcohol. "Damn, this is good."

They all stood in Molly's kitchen. Mackenzie stared lovingly at the tall bottle of expensive vodka, care of her now very rich bestie, Tiffany. The vodka was smooth. Why they'd even bothered to cut it with the fruit juice was beyond her. She'd happily guzzle this over the rocks or straight from the bottle. She wasn't picky as long as it got the job done.

"So, what's everyone been up to this week?" Tiffany asked, peering over the rim of her glass with her big brown eyes.

"I finished a shoot this week. Ugh, that model, though." Molly rolled her eyes.

She worked with them all—the good, the bad and the very pretty. Molly was becoming a legend in the industry. Bestselling authors wanted her images on their book covers and that was the simple definition of it. Molly was an incredible photographer, naturally talented, and was finally being recognized for it. If the stunning high-rise studio in downtown Seattle with the most spectacular views didn't already give that away, Mackenzie didn't know what did.

"Just too sexy for ya, huh?" Tiffany teased.

"More like too much ego. The thing is he wasn't even that hot. Like, we just shot his abs for the cover because…well, that's all that was attractive. But he was pretty certain he was God's gift to women—even pregnant and married women," Molly said in disgust.

"Hey, look at the positive. At least that means you're still considered hot, even in your current condition," Tiffany tried to point out.

"Not even. I'm a full-fledged cow," Molly argued as she rubbed her belly.

Mackenzie rolled her eyes. "You're gorgeous, Moll. Pregnancy is a beautiful and wonderful thing." It was also one of the most painful things.

"Thank you. I can't see my feet, and that is *not* so wonderful. What is, though, is the size of my boobies. Have you guys seen these new knockers?" Molly squeezed her breasts together.

"Wanna share a little?" Tiffany asked as she grabbed her slightly smaller breasts. Leave it to Tiffany to be the one who would ask for more than what God had already gifted her with, which was more than enough.

"Gladly." Molly pretended to scoop them toward Tiffany.

"Hey, don't forget about me," Mackenzie teased as she wiggled her flat chest.

She had the smallest boobs of them all. *Thank God for padded bras and those plastic cutlets.* She'd once considered going under the knife and buying the perfect set. But after watching far too many botched surgeries on talk shows or having a few friends show her their less-than-perfect outcomes, Mackenzie decided it was better to stick with the push-up bras.

"Where's Owen?" Mackenzie asked as they all ventured out of the kitchen and into the large living room.

"Fishing." Molly rolled her eyes. "I swear that man lives and breathes the damn ocean."

"Just like you live and breathe photography?" Tiffany countered and winked.

"Yeah, but mine doesn't take away from the time we could be spending with each other."

"But you're spending time with us right now," Mackenzie pointed out as she swallowed more of her drink and began to feel the onset of a happy buzz.

"I'm not talking about tonight," Molly explained, attempting to get comfortable on the couch. "I worry that maybe me being pregnant has something to do with it. Like, what if he's avoiding me?"

Mackenzie and Tiffany shook their heads in unison.

"No way," Tiffany said. "If anything, he finds you more attractive. We've both seen how much he adores you."

Molly twisted her hair into a loose knot and pinned it to the top of her head. "Well, he's not acting like it."

"I'm sure it's nothing. Every couple goes through stuff like that, especially when everything happens so fast," Mackenzie said. She knew better than any of them that sometimes couples didn't make it, though. Mackenzie prayed that Molly and Owen were a lot stronger than she and Gideon had been. *Why do women always have to second-guess their relationships?* It just didn't seem fair. *When did life get so tough?*

* * * *

Rain. Seattle was well known for it. Rain and coffee went hand in hand, a truly perfect union, and that was why Seattle was awesome. Mackenzie tried to warm her fingers that frigid morning. She had survived the weekend and was now tucked safely in her classroom on this very wet and gloomy Monday. Bright and cheerful colors covered every square inch of her school space. She had two large windows that offered a view to an empty playground. Puddles were everywhere and rain splattered hard against the foggy glass. Rainy days meant muddy carpet, wet children who would complain and an awful hair day. However, the coffee she held in her hands would make the morning tolerable, then an afternoon pick-me-up would be needed. That was her routine — caffeine in the morning and afternoon. Without it, *adulting* wasn't even possible.

She sipped the warm mocha and savored the creamy, rich chocolate flavor. It soothed her. Calming wasn't what was expected from coffee, but it had that weird effect on her. It relaxed her nerves and made false promises that everything would be okay, like thinking about Gideon for over a week. She wondered if he'd show up again. Part of her wanted him to, the other — the rather bitter side — not so much. She had reflected on the reason for his unexpected visit all weekend. She couldn't fathom what he could possibly have wanted. *Do I dare call and ask?* Too much vodka on Friday had nearly caused her to do just that. Thank God for her besties. Drunk texting or calling was never a good thing.

Mackenzie closed her eyes as she heard the shrill of the school bell. That meant the students would start trickling into the building, then they would stampede into her classroom and it would be time to shape these little brains into future scientists, doctors, lawyers, teachers or people who would have absolutely no clue what in the hell they were doing with their lives. *The joys of teaching.* Mackenzie downed the last sip of the caffeinated warmth and prayed that it would work its magic soon.

The clock moved at a snail's pace for the remainder of the day and she knew her pent-up irritation at Gideon was to blame. Mackenzie tried to put him out of her mind but it just didn't seem possible. Relieved didn't even begin to describe just how happy Mackenzie was to hear the loud shrill of the bell as the school day ended.

"Don't forget your raincoat," Mackenzie called after one tiny blond-haired boy. She sighed as he ran off with the shiny plastic blue slicker in his hand. Her classroom was now empty. It had been a long and very soggy day and recess had been canceled. That had meant a full day with youngsters, which also meant unrestrained energy that she'd love to bottle up and market. It would rival any energy drink or triple-shot espresso. *Youth is definitely wasted on the young.*

Mackenzie started to put the small sunshine-yellow chairs on top of the round tables when she felt eyes on her. The hairs on the back of her neck went wild. She turned around slowly, deciding to keep hold of one of the chairs, just in case. Mackenzie was shocked, to say the least, when she saw Gideon standing there. His jacket was splattered with wetness. His hair had droplets of rain clinging to it. His eyes almost appeared to shimmer with the fluorescent light as he looked back at her. There was a mix of pain, hope and something else that she couldn't quite place. *Love? No, it surely isn't that. That left long ago, right?*

"Mac."

She spun back around and tried to catch her breath. Her chest felt dry and empty, starved of oxygen. *Just breathe.* Hearing him say her name was too much. Time paused then began to rewind, like an old VHS tape, quick and distorted. Happy times. Sad times. Mackenzie couldn't keep up with all the images and emotions that her brain fed her. *How dare he come here?* Anger surged inside her. He had no right to be there in her classroom.

"Gideon, what do you want?" Mackenzie asked. She kept her back to him. Facing him wasn't an option until she got a handle on her turbulent emotions.

"Mac, I want to talk to you. I need to." Gideon's voice was still the same — a little rougher perhaps. It carried a sound that Mackenzie had missed more than she'd care to admit.

"I don't know what there is to say. I think you said all you needed to two years ago."

"I know this has to be a shock. I don't blame you for not wanting to talk to me, but please," he begged. "Mac, at least look at me."

Mackenzie shut her eyes, willing the strength to face him. Then she felt hands on her and she flinched.

"Do *not* touch me," she ordered him.

"Then look at me."

Fine. She released the chair onto the table and shifted her stance to face him.

"What?" Mackenzie crossed her arms and tried to ignore the stinging tears that flooded her cheeks. Tears for Gideon. Tears for their love. Tears for her sister's death. Tears for life being so damn shitty sometimes. Oh, yeah, she had plenty more where these came from. Crying had sort of become her thing lately.

"Oh, Mac," Gideon said and smoothed a tear from her cheek.

Mackenzie quickly pulled back. "Didn't I just tell you not to touch me?" she spat.

"But you're crying," he countered.

"So? I cry a lot." Mackenzie didn't care. There was no use pretending she was stronger than she really was. *Honesty is the best policy, right?*

"I hate seeing you cry."

"Well, pal, I got news for you. This isn't the first or the last time I will shed some tears," Mackenzie answered. *Doesn't he realize that* he *is the reason behind them? Does he think that I've been all dried-eyed since he abandoned me when I needed him?*

"Look. I'm sorry. I didn't think showing up here would upset you so much," Gideon said. He shoved his hands in his jean pockets. He was uncomfortable and didn't know what to do with himself. She'd known him long enough to read his body language and what he was feeling. Her heart sank. *I just never quit loving someone, no matter how hard I try.*

"Fine," Mackenzie relented. "You want to talk? Go for it. Talk."

"Here? Now?" Gideon's eyes darted around the room. He seemed confused.

"Why not? You got a better place in mind?"

He looked around the room again. Gideon was too large for miniature chairs and tables. The man who wore a somber face with eyes that had seen far too much cruelty in the world, didn't belong in the bright, rainbow-colored room. "You hungry?" Gideon asked.

"Is this going to take long? I can't even begin to imagine what you want to talk about. Two years, Gid, two long years. Nothing, not a single word from you." Mackenzie shook her head and threw her hands up in disbelief. She'd hit the point just beyond her wall of sadness — that pissed off area she'd visited more times than she could count. It lived in a gray and dying area of her heart, a hopeless land where her soul seemed to simply exist.

He frowned. His movements were slow and Mackenzie could almost see the gears in his head turn, like he was choosing his words. Gideon wasn't a stranger to an angry Mackenzie. *Been there, done that.* She wasn't interested in sharing a meal with him. Her stomach had been threatening to spill out onto the floor since he'd entered her classroom. Mackenzie's nerves were raw, to say the least. There was a part of her that couldn't help but feel like no matter how much she denied it, it was wonderful having Gideon so close to her again — to feel his presence and share the same air. That part was eager to run away to anywhere he asked. It was the same part that wanted to know what he had to say. Mackenzie begged that side of her to shut the hell up.

"Please," he begged again.

"I just don't want to make a scene," she explained.

"And here is better?" Gideon raised his eyebrows and gave her a knowing look.

"You have a point. But at least we're alone right now."

Gideon nodded. "True."

Ah, the man of few words — one of the things that had always aggravated Mackenzie during the course of their relationship. She was the talker and he was the silent type, not a good pair for communication. Mackenzie also knew why he was silent. Why words didn't come easy for him.

"Okay, let's just go somewhere." Mackenzie walked away and started to gather her coat and purse. Gideon was right on her heels.

"Here. Let me help you," Gideon offered as he took her coat and started to assist her in putting it on. "It's pouring out there."

"No shit. It's Seattle, Gid."

Once outside the school, Mackenzie insisted on driving herself. Gideon was less than thrilled and asked her to follow him. He had the nerve to advise her to drive carefully. As she buckled up and looked through the rain-splattered windshield, Mackenzie wanted to scream. The man infuriated her. *Why did I agree to this?*

Gideon navigated the streets of Seattle like he'd never left, his SUV finding every well-known local shortcut. Then she saw where he had brought her — their favorite Chinese restaurant. Mackenzie was half tempted to keep driving. *How could he think it's a good idea to come here with me?* There were too many memories inside that red building with the fake pagoda by the large, ornate doors. The place had the best pork fried rice anywhere, crappy karaoke and a bar that served the cheapest drinks in all of Seattle. They had the best fortune cookies, too. One time she'd gotten one with a beautiful engagement ring in it. It had been two years since Mackenzie had eaten there. She'd refused to go inside after Gideon had left. This was *their* place. It was where they had met, where they'd fallen in love over egg drop soup and where he'd proposed. It was also where he'd broken up with her. This was the last place he should be taking her to talk. *What a clueless asshole.*

"You going to get out of the car?" Gideon asked after he'd tapped on her window.

She was pissed. A fire raged inside her broken heart. "Why, Gideon? Why here?" *Damn, more tears. Who cares?* She swatted them away and searched for a tissue from her glove box. Her car's registration, a few tiny salt packets from a fast food place but no tissues. *Damn.*

Gideon frowned and answered, "Because this is the place where we come when there's important stuff that needs to be discussed."

Mackenzie spotted an old wrinkled tissue in her cup holder and tried to dab her eyes. With all the bouts of uncontrolled crying she'd been doing, it seemed logical that she'd have tons of Kleenex handy.

He opened her door and Mackenzie remained in her seat.

"Come on," he urged.

She let out an exaggerated sigh and climbed out of her small, compact car. Mackenzie looked up at the sky. The rain had stopped but the clouds were waiting to unleash more. They mirrored her emotions. Crying one minute, dry the next…rain, tears, was there much of a difference?

She inhaled sharply and walked in front of him, leading the way inside. *Be the one in control here, girl.* As she opened the heavy door, Mackenzie was immediately hit with the delicious scents of food and bombarded with countless memories. A booth where they'd shared their first kiss, a stool up by the bar where they'd laughed and flirted, the dark hallway where they'd almost had sex but thought better of it and there was the other booth where he'd proposed. Then she saw it, the table tucked away in the far corner. They'd never eaten at that one before until that night. It was where Gideon had told her it was over, just days before they were to get married. *Yeah, this place is like a graveyard with too many ghosts.* She was haunted enough and had no interest in revisiting this place. *Just hear him out then leave.*

They were greeted and guided to another booth, one that she didn't associate with any memories. *Thank God for small favors.* Mackenzie was pretty sure a new memory was about to be made and she wasn't quite sure it was going to be a good one.

The egg drop soup sat in front of her in a giant white bowl. Bits of cabbage bobbed in the clear broth. She added some black pepper and a little soy sauce to it. Mackenzie sipped delicately off the large scooped spoon and sighed. *Yes, it still tastes the same after all this time.* Mackenzie focused on her soup and tried to ignore Gideon's blatant stare.

"Still any good?" he asked.

She nodded. *Why is he trying to act normal?* Nothing about them sitting there together was *normal*. Too much time had passed. Things were different now. For starters, they weren't a couple. Hell, they weren't even friends. *How can he be so clueless?*

God, she didn't want to be there right now, stuck in that booth, seated across from a man who she used to love who was now nothing more than a stranger. If she were truly honest with herself, Mackenzie could admit that she still loved him very much. That was why she couldn't make any new relationship work. Her heart belonged to Gideon. She feared it might always be that way.

"We need to talk, Mac," Gideon said almost in a whisper.

"Do we? I mean, I don't know what's going on or why you're back, but I don't see how it involves me." Mackenzie felt those familiar tears getting ready to make another appearance. "You made it clear that you were done." *Done with me. Done with us.*

Gideon clenched his jaw shut. A tiny muscle ticked as he looked away in frustration. "I don't think you understand why I broke things off."

"Well, enlighten me," Mackenzie snarled at him.

"I loved you so much, Mac, but I knew that our relationship couldn't survive another tour," he started to explain.

They had survived several of his tours of duty before the breakup. *What was one more?* It wasn't the dreaded 'D' word. Deployment was *not* the reason. But Mackenzie knew the real reason. They both did.

Gideon took a sip of water and started again. "I saw what it did to you — the constant worry when I left then how you were every time I came back and again when I had to leave again," he rambled but failed to mention what they both knew was the truth.

Even though he did have a point, every time Gideon had suited up in camouflage with his matching green pack and headed to the airport, it'd felt like someone had carved her heart out with a blunt butter knife. It had hurt so, seeing him leave. Then the worry would move in and stay with her until he'd returned. Yes, it had been hard, but she had made her peace with it. Mackenzie accepted that it was how life with a soldier was going to be. She'd signed up for it because all she'd wanted was him. Whether it was for weeks or months, Mackenzie wanted to be his wife.

"We were getting married, and you ended things just a few days before." Mackenzie dabbed the wetness from the corner of her eyes. Gideon reached across the table and tried to touch her hand, but Mackenzie pulled back. He looked away, disappointment filling his stare.

"I know I hurt you. I'm so sorry, Mac. I hope someday you can find it in her your heart to forgive me."

"Why did you come back, Gid? This is so damn hard — seeing you, talking to you, just being around you."

"I'm back for good now and I want you back," Gideon said. "I want us to fix this. I never stopped loving you, babe."

Mackenzie hadn't stopped loving him either, but that didn't mean she was ready to forgive him just yet. She had battled through so much pain and suffering that Mackenzie wasn't sure she could endure that all over again. Her heart wasn't nearly as strong as it had once been. With the loss of her sister, Mackenzie's emotional state was even more frail. Her mind shifted to Jason — then there was that. A big piece of her wanted to explore the new romance...sort of. He was different. He wasn't some ghost from her past coming back to haunt her and making her revisit old feelings. Yet, the other night Jason had left her hanging after he'd gotten what he was after and he'd never really seemed that interested in making a commitment to her before. She still fumed about that. Horny and sexually frustrated was not a good look for her.

Mackenzie peered down at her soup. *Everything is so complicated now. Why can't life be simple, like this soup? Just a few key ingredients, perfectly blended to create something delicious. No, instead it's full of all sorts of bullshit.*

"I need to tell you something else," Gideon added.

She almost didn't hear him. *What more can he possibly have to say?* Declaring that he still loved her should've been plenty for one day. Mackenzie was still having trouble digesting that bit of news.

"I have a daughter."

A daughter? So, somewhere in the last two years he found the time to make a baby with someone who obviously wasn't me. Yet, here he is back and trying come into my life. No, thanks.

Mackenzie didn't know how to respond. They had been going to have babies together. That had been the plan. They had almost been parents. The pain

Mackenzie had experienced when she'd lost their baby came back to her full throttle. That was why they'd really broken up. They had kept the pregnancy a secret, which in the end had eaten at Mackenzie. She had wanted to tell her girls, to share the amazing news. But when she'd miscarried, a huge part of her was grateful she hadn't told them. Mackenzie felt the air leave her lungs, causing them to burn from the lack of oxygen. Panic filled her veins. *This is too much.*

"Mac, it's not what you think." Gideon gave her a sympathetic look as he attempted to calm her. He grazed the top of her hand with his and her heart raced. She flinched at his touch. The thought that Gideon had a child with another woman when it should've been her made her stomach ill. *What did I expect to happen the past two years? For him to remain celibate? He isn't as pathetic as I am.*

"Really? Because I could've sworn you just said you had a daughter." Mackenzie glared hard at him. The anger and disappointment burned her insides. It was as though acid was tearing right through Mackenzie's body.

"I wasn't given much choice." His voice had lowered again and was filled with a brittle sadness.

"Um, you had to have had some. Just sayin'." Mackenzie shook her head. *Unbelievable.* He wasn't even taking any responsibility for bringing a baby girl into this world. *Maybe I dodged a bullet.*

"It's not like that, Mac. When I left two years ago, I befriended a family while stationed in that godforsaken desert. They became my family. I had lost you and…our future. I was so far away from home. But like so many people over there, they were all killed." Gideon looked up toward the ceiling and Mackenzie saw his deep aquamarine eyes grow wet. "Except one did survive and now she's my daughter."

Mackenzie's anger dissipated but confusion replaced it. "I'm so sorry. But, Gid, I don't understand. You adopted their child?" None of this made sense. *Why would Gideon offer to raise a baby, let alone on his own?*

He exhaled and took another sip of water as Mackenzie reached for her glass. Her throat wasn't dry. She just needed to something to do with her hands as she wrapped her mind around this new information.

"Yes, I adopted their baby."

Mackenzie choked on her drink, water sprayed out of her mouth as she tried to catch her breath to stop the coughing fit before it got out of hand.

His eyes lit up. "I love her and I just couldn't leave her there. Oh, Mac, she's the cutest little thing," Gideon gushed.

She had so many questions and didn't even know where to begin. Seeing that Gideon had a heart of gold, him doing such a wonderful act of kindness and love was not completely surprising. However, she wasn't quick to forget there was that other part of him, the one that had destroyed her dreams for a happy future. The guy who didn't want marriage or family — at least that was what he'd told her. *So now, all of a sudden, he's ready to be a daddy?*

Then it dawned on her why he had come to her. *His little girl needs a mother.*

* * * *

The rest of the week was a blur. Thankfully, it was Friday, and Mackenzie couldn't wait to eat and drown her troubles. Molly and Tiffany would be over soon and Mackenzie had just gotten home from work. The kids had been rambunctious all day and the bell couldn't have rung any sooner. She was finally in her jammies and waiting for her girls to arrive. She'd just washed off all her makeup when she heard the doorbell ring.

"Just come on in," Mackenzie hollered. She hurried to greet them, drying her face with a towel as she jogged to the door. Tiffany entered first. Molly waddled behind her.

"Hey, guys," Mackenzie said as met them in the foyer that led to the kitchen.

"I don't smell anything amazing. What's up?" Tiffany asked. "You do know I come here for the home-cooked meals, right?"

"Hey, you're a married woman now. You should be cooking for your husband," Mackenzie countered.

"Uh, luckily he cooks, otherwise we'd probably both starve."

Molly laughed. "No, you wouldn't. You'd hire a chef or something. Remember, you're all sorts of fancy now."

Tiffany scratched her head. "How come I never thought of that?"

Molly and her growing tummy went to go sit at the kitchen table. "So, what *is* for dinner?" she asked on her way over.

"You guys want a pizza?" Mackenzie suggested.

"Can't do pizza. Heartburn," Molly answered.

"Chinese?" Tiffany shrugged as she joined Molly in the dining room. Mackenzie trailed close behind her.

The thought of Chinese made her think of Gideon. Mackenzie quickly replied, "Nah, not feeling that tonight."

"So what then?" Tiffany asked with a grumpy scowl. "I need food."

After much debate, they ended up just raiding Mackenzie's cupboards. They made do with cheese, crackers and a few cut-up veggies.

"How have you been feeling, Moll?" Mackenzie chomped down on an apple slice, the juice flooding her mouth.

"Pregnant."

"Meaning?" Mackenzie smirked back at her.

Tiffany added, "Like, how is it? Lots of movement and stuff? We want the deets, our little pregnant princess."

"So many questions. Why? Are you thinking of getting pregnant, Tiff?" Molly raised her eyebrow.

"Not anytime soon, even though Colin pretty much brings it up on a daily basis. I told him we need to get through this wedding first."

"Yeah, that way didn't quite work out for me." Molly reached for a square piece of Tillamook cheddar cheese.

"Oh, but it all did. The ceremony was lovely, you were beautiful and it didn't matter that you were preggers," Mackenzie added.

"Thanks, but it would've been nice to not have been pregnant." Molly frowned.

"Aren't you excited about this little bun in the oven?" Mackenzie asked as she bent forward and kissed Molly's round stomach. "Hey, little baby, it's your Auntie Mac."

Molly giggled at Mackenzie. "Of course, but I'm also completely terrified," she admitted.

Tiffany smiled with a longing in her dark eyes. "I think you're going to be an amazing mom, Molly."

"You just wait, Tiff. Colin will get his way sooner or later," Molly teased.

"Is that such a bad thing?" Mackenzie asked. "It's sort of the natural order of things, isn't it?"

"I guess. I just went completely out of order." Molly laughed. "I'm happy about it, but it's just weird to think that in a few months this baby will be here."

"Speaking of which…the baby shower. We seriously need to finish planning it and do all the rest of the shopping," Tiffany pointed out. "Have you decided on the guest list yet?"

"I thought you were taking care of everything," Molly countered with a huff. "I hate planning stuff."

"This is for your unborn child, Molly. Quit being so difficult," Tiffany said.

"It's to celebrate you and that lovely unborn child. We want it to be special for you, Moll," Mackenzie added.

With all the baby talk, Mackenzie couldn't help but think of Gideon. She was torn about whether or not she should mention to the girls that he was back. They hated the way he'd left her and Mackenzie didn't know if they'd ever forgive him. Hell, she wasn't sure if she was ready to forgive him.

"Ugh, more shopping? Don't you have a wedding to plan?" Molly shot back.

"Yes, but your baby shower is first. Also, Colin and I are thinking about getting married somewhere special." Tiffany wore a sly grin.

"Where?" Mackenzie asked. "Come on. Out with it. I hate surprises. I need to know now."

"Mac's right, tell us now," Molly added then popped a shiny black olive into her mouth.

Tiffany spoke with an exaggerated and terrible Irish accent as she asked, "Do you lovelies fancy a trip to Ireland?"

* * * *

Mackenzie woke up feeling refreshed for the first time all week. She peered over at her digital alarm clock on the dresser to find it was almost noon. Sleeping in had been wonderful and apparently much needed. Last night had been great with her besties. It had almost felt like those old *Friendship Fridays*, except for all the wedding and baby shower planning that had gone on. Mackenzie could look beyond that and wanted to focus on the fun they'd had.

It was crazy to think that they'd be going to Ireland for Tiffany's wedding — well, second wedding. It didn't matter to Mackenzie. The very thought of traveling there was pretty darn cool. She'd be able to finally check that off her bucket list. Being of Scottish descent, she'd always planned on popping over to Scotland to explore her roots and now she could while she was across the pond. She couldn't wait. Too bad they were putting off getting married until the spring. Mackenzie had tried to convince Tiffany that a holiday wedding would be amazing, but for some reason, she wanted a spring or even a summer one. Mackenzie didn't want to have to wait that long. She was more than ready to escape to the land of rolling green hills and ocean-torn cliffs to go to the land of leprechauns, myth, luck and magic. Ireland, to her, sounded like a fairy tale and when Tiffany had returned from her trip there, she'd only confirmed it.

Mackenzie stretched in her warm and comfortable bed. She was reluctant to leave and could easily have wasted the entire day in it. She needed coffee and probably some food in her belly. Mackenzie scrambled off her bed and folded the comforter back. She was half tempted to leave it unmade, just in case she changed her mind about wasting her day.

Coffee. She liked her coffee sweet and creamy, much to Molly and Tiffany's disgust. They were coffee purists. Not Mackenzie. She wanted that caffeine but loved all the flavors of creamers that were out there. There were so many choices that it made her head spin. But she had made it her goal to try just about every single one out there, and Tiffany and Molly hated it.

She inhaled the scented flavor of her coffee today — Mexican cinnamon vanilla. It promised a hint of spicy with sweet and it delivered. Mackenzie savored the first taste. *Now, time to find something edible.* She searched her cupboards and nothing appealed to her until she remembered there was some yogurt in the fridge. In a pinch, that would have to suffice. She saw a mango sitting all alone on a shelf. *Why not invite it to the breakfast party?*

With her coffee, yogurt and now happily cut-up mango, Mackenzie sat outside on her deck. It overlooked her small back yard. The yellow and gold canopy of trees was stunning. Leaves of orange and red were being tossed around by the gentle wind. It was a gorgeous fall day that was quickly ruined by Mackenzie's cell phone beeping. Her dumb ass should have left the stupid thing in the house. She peeked over at it as it vibrated against the glass patio table. *Gideon.*

Should I answer it? Do I even want to? Her mind was still trying wrap itself around the whole Gideon being a dad concept.

"Hello?" Mackenzie's stomach felt queasy as she held the phone to her ear. *Why do I answer my phone and subject myself to this kind of torture?*

"Mac," Gideon said on the other end. His voice was frantic and Mackenzie could hear intense wailing in the background.

"Everything okay, Gid?" Mackenzie became more alarmed as the crying grew louder. She had to pull the phone away from her ear. For some reason, Mackenzie had assumed this baby was a lot older, but the one she heard screaming its lungs off sounded very much like a newborn. *So, this dad thing is sort of new then?*

"I don't know. That's why I'm calling you. I need your help." Gideon paused. "I'm scared, Mac."

"Okay. First thing, just calm down. We'll figure out what's wrong with her." She tried to take charge. It was best to keep a cool head. Granted, she knew he had to be freaking out a little. *Who wouldn't be?* Her motherly instincts went into overdrive. "How long has she been crying like that?"

"Uh, I don't know… For the last hour or so. I'm not sure what to do."

"Gid, how old is she?"

"Just turned four months, right as we returned to the states."

God, they were practically dealing with a newborn. She hoped nothing was seriously wrong with the baby and started to ask Gideon a series of questions. Had he changed or fed her? Did the baby feel warm or cold? Mackenzie hoped she could help with him over the phone and avoid going to Gideon's home. She knew it was futile. This called for a hands-on intervention. "I'm coming over," Mackenzie announced when she wasn't satisfied with how things were going. "You still live at the same house?"

"Yes, and thank you, Mac."

* * * *

She'd broken several traffic laws, but Mackenzie didn't care, especially now as she cradled Gideon's daughter.

"Shhh," Mackenzie hushed the tiny bundle swaddled in pink.

The baby's face was no longer an angry beet red as it had been. It had taken a while before Mackenzie had found out what the precious little girl had needed. Mackenzie had fed, burped and changed her. Nothing had quite cut it. She'd tried rocking her to sleep but it wasn't until Mackenzie started to sing that the baby had calmed down. She'd sung every lullaby she knew. Mackenzie had figured out that she didn't know all the words and she'd had to improvise. That had made it more fun anyway. Her heart wasn't prepared for the unexpected flood of feelings that took over. She also didn't realize just how strong her mothering abilities were. *Damn, this could've been my daughter.*

"You're a natural. Thanks so much for coming, Mac," Gideon said as he stood near her in the small nursery. It was decorated in pale pinks and purples, the epitome of femininity.

Mackenzie put her finger to her lips. The baby was asleep and she placed her into the crib. Mackenzie hovered over her for a moment to take in all her tiny features. She had lots of dark curls and her skin was a caramel color. Mackenzie stroked her chubby cheeks and marveled at the longest lashes she'd ever seen. She was quite jealous of those gorgeous lashes. There would be no mascara in that little girl's future. The worst thing above all else was that Mackenzie had fallen in love with her.

Chapter Three

Mackenzie hadn't heard from him all week. *Surprise, surprise. Should I expect anything different?* This was Gideon, the man who'd disappeared from her life only to show up again unannounced. What did Mackenzie think, that everything was going to go back to how it had been before? So what if he proclaimed that he wanted her back. Gideon sure had a funny way of showing it. Mackenzie was really beginning to hate men. She hadn't heard from Jason. No real surprise there either. *Men are selfish bastards, plain and simple.*

She plopped down on her couch and stared at her television. Should she try and find a movie to watch or finish that book she'd attempted to read the past week? Mackenzie released a heavy sigh. Why couldn't she stop thinking about Gideon—or even Jason, for that matter? *Because you're a sexually starved, nearing-middle-aged, desperate fool. That's why.* It sucked being alone. The house was too quiet, her mind too loud. *Maybe I should get a cat? Then I'd be a crazy cat lady on top of what I already am. Damn.*

Mackenzie closed her eyes when her phone began to chirp, interrupting the annoying silence that was her life.

"Hello?" she answered without looking to see who was calling.

"Hey, lady," Molly's cheerful voice replied.

"Hey, Moll."

"What's wrong with you?"

Everything. "Nothing. I was just thinking about heading to bed. What's up?" Mackenzie lied as she made herself yawn.

"Bed? It's not even seven. Wow, being a teacher must be incredibly exhausting," Molly teased.

"You have no idea." Mackenzie laughed as she peered over at the clock on the wall. *Dang, it is only seven.* It felt so much later with the evening sky being dark earlier. Summers were long and the nights were light until late. The days of fall and winter were short and filled with darkness by the time she left work. All the rain didn't help matters either.

"I wanted to discuss something that just may liven up your boring life a little," Molly begun to explain.

"Oh, no, I know where this is headed. No, thanks."

"You won't even hear me out?" Molly whined.

"No." Mackenzie didn't need to add another prospective man into her life. Molly had good intentions but there was not a snowball's chance in hell that she was going to go on a blind date.

"You suck. You know that?"

"Molly, you can't possibly expect me to go on some ridiculous date," Mackenzie countered firmly.

"Would it be so bad if you did? I mean, shit, you're stuck in a rut, woman."

Maybe now was a good time to explain the latest happening of last week.

"Moll, I need to tell you something," Mackenzie started.

"What?" The concerned sound of Molly's voice made Mackenzie change her mind.

"Never mind. Just know that I'm okay with being single, okay?" Mackenzie lied again. *Who do I think I'm fooling?*

"That's stupid."

"It's not. I just really don't think dating is something I want to deal with right now." *Liar.*

Molly huffed on the other end. "Mac, how else are you going to get laid?"

Maybe I want more than just a good fuck? Having held Gideon's daughter in her arms had sparked a maternal desire that had been dormant for a while.

"I'm good, Moll."

"Your vibe isn't going to handle business forever, you know," Molly snapped back.

"They always make new and improved models." Mackenzie laughed. "I'm sure I can just upgrade."

"On a serious note, this guy would be perfect for you," Molly said.

"The blind date? Yeah, I highly doubt it."

"Why are you so difficult?" Molly asked.

"I'm not trying to be. I promise."

"It's like you won't even try. I just don't get it. You see, Tiffany and I—"

Mackenzie cut Molly off, "Are what? All happily married and shit? Pregnant?" Mackenzie fired at her. "Maybe I don't want any of that. Maybe I'm not like you guys. Maybe I'm perfectly fine with my life the way it is and don't need some *man* to determine my happiness, unlike you and Tiffany."

"Bullshit. You better watch yourself, Mac. You're beginning to sound like a bitter bitch."

Molly's words stung.

The truth hurts, doesn't it, you lying, bitter bitch?

* * * *

Mackenzie sat across from Molly, who acted as though were everything was fine and dandy. Tiffany eyed her.

"So, Mac, how was your week?" Tiffany asked as she dunked a tortilla chip into the brightest guacamole Mackenzie had ever seen.

It was technically *Friendship Friday*, but they weren't hanging out at one of their homes. Instead, they had opted to catch dinner and possibly a movie.

"Long," Mackenzie answered as she helped herself to a chip.

"This craptastic weather sure hasn't helped," Tiffany replied as she bit into another chip. "Have you heard from Jason?" she asked and wiggled her perfectly tweezed brows.

"No, I told you that was over," Mackenzie answered. "I don't have time for senseless games."

"I think you have oodles of time," Molly added. "Time that could be spent dating." She glared at Mackenzie. *There it is.*

Mackenzie shook her head. "You wanna do this again?" she challenged Molly.

Tiffany's mouth hung open. "Uh, what am I missing here?"

"Nothing, just people being stubborn...and bitter," Molly said.

"Exactly, *nothing*. Just someone sticking their nose where it doesn't belong," Mackenzie countered as she reached for her strawberry margarita. She swallowed too fast and the pain was instant. *Brain freeze.*

"I'm going to go out on a limb here and say you two had a mild disagreement," Tiffany said. "Look. There's no point in fighting about Mac's love life. She'll date when she's ready."

Whoa. Is Tiffany defending me?

"I had offered to set her up. Owen has this buddy —" Molly started when Mackenzie hushed her.

"Let's not ruin tonight by rehashing this." Mackenzie smiled at Tiffany and avoided Molly's icy stare.

"It's sort of funny," Tiffany said.

"What is?" Mackenzie asked as she ventured to take another chilly sip of her drink.

"Well, I was going to tell you that I also had someone in mind for you — one of Colin's friends. But seeing how prickly you are, I figured I better just keep it to myself," Tiffany explained.

Prickly? Is that better than bitter? "I appreciate that you respect my boundaries," Mackenzie said.

"Tiff, here's the thing. Mac is becoming a bitter chick. I asked her the other night why she won't let us set her up and she was very bitchy."

"And you said I was becoming a *bitter bitch*," Mackenzie fired back. "Just because I don't want what you guys have," she lied.

Tiffany looked at her with concern. "You don't want what we have. What does that mean exactly?"

"You know," Mackenzie answered.

"Uh, I'm afraid I don't. Enlighten me," Tiffany pressed with an intense stare that left Mackenzie feeling guilty.

Mackenzie shot Molly an irritated look. *Why are we even discussing this?*

"She doesn't want to be married or have kids," Molly answered for her. "Apparently, she doesn't want those things."

"What! That's ridiculous. Of course Mac wants that. It's all we've talked about for years." Tiffany shook her head, clearly in disbelief.

"My point exactly," Molly said as she kept her eyes trained on Mackenzie. "She's just being difficult."

Mackenzie let out a throaty laugh. "Here we go again. You just don't know when to let shit go, do you?"

"I could say the same for you," Molly muttered as she reached for her glass of water.

"Mac, where is all this coming from?" Tiffany asked. "This isn't you."

Maybe they don't know who I really am? Hell, there were times when she wasn't so sure who she was anymore. Mackenzie rolled her eyes and paused to stare up at the brightly painted tangerine ceiling. This was one of her favorite Mexican restaurants. The vivid colors and delicious food always put her in a good frame of mind—except for tonight. Mackenzie dug into her purse and retrieved her wallet. "I think I'm going to go. I'll pay for dinner," Mackenzie offered after she waved down their waitress.

"Seriously?" Molly huffed. "It's like we can't say anything without you getting all pissed off."

"Maybe it's the grief, Mac," Tiffany explained. "But we're your friends. We're here for you."

Her vision grew blurry as all the events buried her. "Gideon came back," she blurted out. She wanted to reel the words back in the moment they'd left her lips.

Molly and Tiffany exchanged shocked looks and said in unison, "What?"

"He was on my porch after you guys dropped me off from our shopping trip," Mackenzie answered as she dabbed her now thoroughly wet cheeks.

"You've got to be kidding me." Tiffany's expression grew tight and angry. Mackenzie had known Tiffany would react this way.

Molly's mouth still hung open when she asked, "And we're barely hearing about this now? What the hell, Mac?"

"I don't know," Mackenzie admitted as relief washed over her. "The last two weeks have just really sucked. I don't even know where to begin."

"How about from the beginning?" Molly said. "This explains why you've been acting the way you have."

"I know, and I'm sorry. I'm just so overwhelmed."

"I can only imagine," Molly whispered as she reached across the table for Mackenzie's hand.

Tiffany had grown quiet. She was like a volcano—like she was stewing and would eventually erupt and unleash a fiery anger. Mackenzie felt bad for Gideon, because hell hath no fury like a pissed-off best friend.

Mackenzie decided to backtrack a tad and share her less than satisfactory phone sex call with Jason.

"Oh, my God, seriously? What a dick," Molly commented as she giggled. "Here I was teasing you about your vibrator. I feel sort of bad now."

"I know. It hit a little close to home," Mackenzie joked.

Tiffany hadn't said much. She just nodded and listened.

"Tiff, you okay?" Mackenzie asked.

"I'm fine." Then she turned her head away. "You know what? No, I'm not. How dare that stupid fucker come back?"

"Oh boy," Molly whistled. "I think we better order you guys another pitcher of margaritas." She signaled the waitress. "Damn, if I wasn't preggers right now, we'd be getting shitfaced."

"It's complicated, Tiff."

"Is it? I don't think so. You're not thinking about seeing him again, are you?" Tiffany asked. Her brown eyes grew wide and a disgusted smirk played across her red-stained lips. "Oh shit, you are."

Mackenzie replied, "No, not at all. I do need to explain what happened, though."

"There's nothing that can excuse the shitty thing he did to you," Tiffany added coldly.

"Let's hear what Mac has to say," Molly urged. "What did our darling Gideon have to say for himself after all this time?" she asked in a sickly sweet voice. She played with the straw of her iced tea and waited.

Mackenzie knew Tiffany could be hot-headed and quick to get angry—not much different from herself. Molly, on the other hand, was a tad more evil. She plotted ways to make people suffer but it was more talk than anything. It was fair to say that both of their barks were worse than their bites.

"Come on. Out with it," Molly ordered as she stabbed the ice in her glass. "What was it like seeing him again?"

"Like being buried by a ton of bricks. I couldn't breathe, wanted to puke and hug him all at the same time. Damn, it was so weird. I didn't realize how much I'd missed him."

"Is he still hot?" Molly asked and Tiffany threw her a nasty look. "Not that it makes the slightest bit of difference. He's still an asshole and we hate him." Tiffany nodded in solidarity.

Mackenzie admitted, "Gideon looks the same." She wouldn't even bother lying. The man was still absolutely sexier than hell. His athletic build from all the years of military training was the same. She knew that perfectly sculpted abs and pecs were hidden under his shirt. But his alpha persona mixed with the newly sensitive daddy version of Gideon added a whole other element, one that had Mackenzie all wound up.

"Too bad," Tiffany added. "What did he want?"

Mackenzie inhaled deeply as both of her friends waited with anticipation on their pretty faces. *Should I come clean about everything?*

"Ooh, this must be good," Molly said as she sipped her water.

"Gid told me he still loves me."

"He wants you two to get back together," Molly said.

"So? He had his chance," Tiffany spat. "He messed up. There's no way she's taking him back."

"There's more," Mackenzie added. She had their undivided attention now. "He has a daughter." They both looked like a bomb had been dropped on them.

"Excuse me? Oh, hell, no," Tiffany said. "Gideon thinks he can just waltz back into your life and ask you to play mommy? Fuck that." Tiffany threw her hands up in the air.

"Calm down," Molly said in through her teeth. "Please don't make a scene, Tiff."

"Are you fucking kidding me? That loser has some nerve." Mackenzie could see how pissed off Tiffany was. In some ways, she sided with her feelings. That was basically what Gideon had asked. He did have some mighty big balls to think he could just come back and ask her for help. Little did her friends know that Mackenzie wished Gideon had truly meant what he'd asked. They were supposed to be parents…together.

"She's not his biological baby," Mackenzie said.

"What do you mean?" Molly asked.

"He adopted her," Mackenzie explained the entire tale that Gideon had shared with her. She continued to tell them about how she'd even helped calm the baby girl. Mackenzie didn't leave out a single detail.

"Wow, that's all I can say." Molly wiped the tears from her eyes. "He's a good guy for doing that."

"Oh, please. Yes, it's nice that he adopted the baby, but it doesn't change anything," Tiffany argued.

"It changes everything," Molly countered. "That's a big commitment. Maybe he's ready for the whole family life. Mac, this might've all happened for a reason."

Guilt bubbled in Mackenzie's stomach. *Should I share everything – every last terrible thing?* She'd already come this far. There was no point in holding back anything else. These were her girls and Mackenzie felt like a fool for not having shared what was one of the saddest things she'd ever survived.

"Guys, I need to share something rather important with you," Mackenzie said through a veil of tears.

"There's more?" Tiffany asked in surprise. "I'm still in shock over this stuff." Tiffany grabbed her drink and begun to chug it.

Molly threw her an irritated glance. "Mac, you can tell us anything."

"I know, but this is really hard," Mackenzie sobbed. "I wanted to tell you both when it happened."

"When what happened?" Tiffany scowled with confusion.

Molly grabbed Mackenzie's hand. "Whatever it is, we're here for you." Tiffany joined in and placed her hand on top. "We got you, girl."

"I lost our baby."

* * * *

There was no denying that the next morning Mackenzie felt better all the way around. The sun was shining, she was sipping her favorite coffee on her small backyard deck and the burden of way too many secrets was now gone. She was content for the time being, relieved and grateful. Her friends had proved to her the previous night that she should never fear telling them anything. They had her back through thick and thin. Molly and Tiffany would always be by her side for all the good, bad and not so pretty moments in between. Why had she even doubted them? Because Mackenzie was terrified of all the changes that were happening in her life. First, it had been losing their baby, then Gideon abandoning her, next her sister dying. It had been one thing after another, pummeling her into the emotional mess she now was. Life didn't just hand Mackenzie lemons, it chucked them at her...hard. Mackenzie wasn't sure how much more she could take. However, today felt *okay* for the first time in a very long while.

Mackenzie listened to several birds chirp at one another in a tree that shaded her home. She relished the warmth and quiet of the moment. Dare she say that she felt relaxed? *Better not jinx it.* Then Mackenzie's phone buzzed in her pocket. She dug it out of her skinny jeans and found Gideon's number blinking at her. Life was tossing out lemons again. Maybe she could duck out of the way and just not answer. But what if that precious little girl needed help? *It isn't my baby. Why should I care?* Because contrary to popular belief, Mackenzie wasn't a bitter bitch.

"Hello?" she answered.

"Hi, Mac." Gideon's voice made her tummy flip-flop and heart beat a little faster.

"Is something wrong with the baby?" Mackenzie listened for any wailing and heard none.

"Nope, she's sleeping...well, like a baby." Gideon laughed.

"So, what can I help you with?"

"Dinner."

"Oh, doesn't she just drink formula?" Mackenzie asked.

"Not her — us," Gideon said. "I want to have dinner with you."

"I don't think that's a good idea."

"Why not? Scared?"

Is he honestly challenging me? Who does he think he is? Be witty, Mac. Think of a good comeback. Nothing came to her. "I just don't think we should."

"We need to talk, Mac."

Mackenzie groaned. *Isn't this what I want? An opportunity to finally lay all our cards on the table and hash this bullshit out?*

"I'm sorry, but didn't we talk already?" Mackenzie asked.

"I'm not sure I'd say it was really productive. I know two years have come and gone, but I'm the same guy. I'm not a stranger, Mac."

"I think you're upset that the conversation didn't go how you wanted it to. And you're right. You are the same guy. Thank you for reminding me of that," Mackenzie shot back.

"Good. When do you want to have dinner?" Gideon's tone had turned cocky.

"Oh, it won't be happening. You're the same guy who walked out on me. I have no desire to revisit any of that."

"Mackenzie, I already apologized for everything."

"That doesn't mean I forgave you." Mackenzie ended the call.

Things don't change overnight. Gideon was a father now. Maybe he was truly sorry for having hurt her the way he did. But did he realize just how terribly hard it had been? She needed to remind herself how badly she'd been hurt. It didn't help that her body was attuned to Gideon. That only proved even more that things hadn't changed, even after two years. No, Mackenzie needed to keep her distance from Gideon — once and for all.

Chapter Four

"You're not pulling our chain, are you?" Tiffany asked.

"She better not be. This is awesome, but Tiff's right. Are you really serious?" Molly added as they walked along the quiet beach of Carkeek park with their late-afternoon lattes.

"I'm dead serious," Mackenzie replied. There was only one way to move on and finally get over Gideon. She wasn't happy about it, but her friends seemed to be. Maybe their excitement would become contagious. One can only hope.

"Okay, so which of us gets to set you up first?" Tiffany asked.

"I asked first, remember?" Molly said as they picked up their pace. "I get to set her up first."

The day was gorgeous and warm—the kind of day that made her fall in love with Seattle that much more. At least, that was how it made Mackenzie feel. Fall was a beautiful but very soggy time of the year, but sometimes there were days like today when the weather couldn't be more perfect. They made her appreciate the strange weather that constantly changed in her city. It wasn't unusual for it to be clear with blue skies one minute then a torrential downpour a few minutes later. The joys of living in the Pacific Northwest.

The water slapped against the shore that was littered with washed-up seaweed. That familiar pungent Puget Sound scent was heavy in the air. The giant bleached driftwood begged to be used as benches, just the right spots to sit and stare out into the dark water. Mackenzie loved Seattle for so many reasons. First, this was her home, but it was also where she belonged. This place had defined and shaped her. The culture, the tucked-away little pieces of heaven, the incredible coffee... It all made Seattle the awesome place that it truly was. The one and only thing Mackenzie couldn't quite figure out was the men. Sure, Seattle had tons of them. Why is it so difficult to meet the right one? Mackenzie had thought she'd found her perfect guy. She'd obviously had no sense of what made a guy the one. Mackenzie hoped that by allowing her friends to set her up, maybe she'd get her chance at that whole happily-ever-after nonsense she so wanted.

"This is so great," Tiffany said as she sipped from her paper cup. "When can we set up the first date?"

Mackenzie kept her gaze forward and cradled her nearly empty cup. You asked for this, girlie.

"I think we should do like a dinner, make it a little less awkward," Molly suggested. "We can all be there."

"I was kind of thinking the same thing," Tiffany agreed. "Once Colin and I find a house, I plan to do a lot of entertaining. Get ready for tons of dinner party invites."

"And what's wrong with your magnificent condo?" Mackenzie asked.

"Nothing. It's just still not home yet." Tiffany frowned. "I swear that finding the perfect house is almost more difficult than finding the perfect guy."

"I highly doubt that," Mackenzie countered.

Molly nodded. "Mac's right. I love our house."

"You didn't have to go hunting for it. Owen already had it. And your home is amazing," Tiffany commented. "You totally lucked out and got the whole package deal—great guy and great house."

"I'm tired of walking," Molly complained and stopped.

"You okay?" Mackenzie asked.

"I'm just worn out. Everything wears me out now. I want frozen yogurt," Molly whined as she rubbed her belly. "This kid is getting heavy."

"I'm just glad that you're still working out. They say it makes labor easier," Tiffany said as she stretched her arms and moved them in small circles. Tiffany had always been gym obsessed and was even more so now.

"I just want to sit on the couch and eat all day," Molly countered. "Do you know that Owen made us go kayaking? Who makes their pregnant wife do that?"

"Did you have fun?" Mackenzie asked.

"Maybe a little," Molly admitted. "The point is, this is my lazy time—the time when I shouldn't give two fucks about what my body looks like. I'm baking a baby."

"Baking a baby? Not sure I've heard that expression before," Tiffany said as she erupted into giggles.

"You know what I mean." Molly threw her an annoyed look.

"See? That's how chicks get fat, babe. They think they can just sit around and eat, using the excuse that they're preggers to gorge themselves on whatever they want," Tiffany explained.

"I agree this is a time to feel comfortable with your body, to enjoy that extra slice of cheesecake, but like with everything in life...moderation," Mackenzie stated.

"Okay, Confucius," Tiffany teased.

"I'm serious. It's all about balance."

Molly nodded. "Mac's right, and that's why we're going to go get frozen yogurt now."

They all laughed and started to head back to the car.

* * * *

Mackenzie waved goodbye as Tiffany pulled away after dropping her at home. Her tummy was full of mango frozen yogurt and she'd agreed to two dates for the following week. She was nuts. It was as simple as that. Mackenzie couldn't deny that she felt a little okay about this whole blind date thing. It was a step in the right direction. She needed to find a way to move forward and leave her past where it belonged...in the past. That meant Gideon, their baby, the wedding that had never happened and every craptastic thing that had occurred over the last few years.

One realization had come through crystal clear during the night, though. Her besties only wanted her to be happy. Molly had even said that if Gideon made her feel that way, she could learn to accept him. Tiffany, not so much. She'd encouraged Mackenzie to view her relationship with Gideon as a huge lesson in love and that she needed to learn not to repeat the mistakes she'd made. This, especially coming from Tiffany, was a little unexpected and deeply profound. Tiffany was the last person who'd had all her ducks in a row. One doesn't just wake up married with no recollection of the nuptials. Tiffany had. She had been their hot mess, their beautiful disaster who was now all proper and suddenly had her shit together. Somehow, within the last several months Tiffany had become a full-fledged grown-up and Mackenzie couldn't be prouder.

Tiffany had also explained how Mackenzie's relationships would always suffer if she stayed so bottled up. Mackenzie couldn't believe how dead-on her friend was. Tiffany had hit the nail on the head, but more importantly, she had opened Mackenzie's eyes to one of the major factors in why her relationships failed. Mackenzie needed to say what was truly on her mind, loosen up a little and shake away the fears that had kept her heart guarded for so long. It was time to take a chance and see who was out there. Her perfect man might very well be right in front of her. She just needed to be open to learning to love again, and Mackenzie knew the process wasn't going to be an easy one. *Love is never easy. It's messy and complicated. How does one even survive past the first few dates, let alone marriage?* Marriage had changed her besties. Deep down she wanted the same thing. Maybe she needed a little help from her friends. Mackenzie had to swallow her pride and admit that she wasn't exactly an expert when it came to love. *Is anyone, really?*

Mackenzie bounded up the wooden stairs to her front door. Today had been a good day. She'd take it. It wasn't as though she'd had a lot of them lately. *Maybe things are going to start turning around?* Step one in her brand spankin' new positive attitude—believe that anything is possible. Again, another lesson from Tiffany. Maybe her bestie needed to write a love-advice blog instead of being a fashion blogger with an English bulldog. Granted, Sir Paul McCartney was the cutest thing on earth. *Maybe I should get a dog?*

Mackenzie tossed her oversized bag on her couch and walked to her bedroom. She began to strip out of her clothes and change into comfy pajamas. She bubbled with positivity. It was as though a door had been opened and she'd been invited to walk through. She'd been sealed shut in her dismal world for way too long, trapped in a self-imposed prison. Mackenzie felt liberated. *Is this how grief works? One day you're drowning and the next you're like okay…almost normal again?* Then Mackenzie spotted her sister's ashes. She waited for the overwhelming sadness to hit like it had all the other times, but it didn't. She smiled and went up to the box of cremains. Mackenzie ran her fingers over the smooth wood. Her sister had always been the optimist, a little ray of sunshine on the cloudiest days. *God, I miss her.* Yet Mackenzie knew that her sister would always live on in her heart and memories. She might not be ready to spread her sister's ashes yet, but she was ready to start living again.

* * * *

Her phone buzzed. It took only a quick glance for Mackenzie to see who was calling. *Not today, Satan. Not today.* As tempted as she was to answer, Mackenzie couldn't allow herself. Tonight was the start of a new and very scary chapter in her life. Blind date *numero uno.* She applied another coat of mascara on her lashes and recalled how long Gideon's daughter's lashes were.

Quit thinking about him or this will never work.

She'd been good for most of the week, if only he hadn't continually tried calling. Now she was curious as to what he wanted. Mackenzie was looking forward to this dinner date Molly had arranged and wanted her mind clear of any distractions. Tiffany and Colin would also be joining them. She just hoped that it wasn't too much pressure on her blind date. It was hard enough to go on a date with a complete stranger and maybe even a little more awkward when hanging out with married couples. There was that extra unspoken pressure, the kind that makes her feel like she should be married, too. Then she'd start getting desperate — or drunk. Mackenzie had made sure to purchase some wine for the dinner party just in case things weren't living up to the expectations in her head. She was going into this tonight with an open mind. *Maybe this guy will be awesome.* Will he be *the one*? Probably not, but it was worth a shot.

Mackenzie shoved all her worries about tonight aside and puckered her lips in the mirror. The soft shade of the pink lipstick suited her skin tone. Overall, Mackenzie was pleased with how she looked. The smoky eye shadow she'd used brought out the deep brown tones of her eyes. Her blonde bobbed hair was freshly trimmed in preparation for the date. It looked sharp and framed her face.

Not too bad for an old broad.

She smoothed the short black dress with her hands after a double-take in the full-length mirror. It highlighted her best attribute. *Legs for days.* Something

Gid had said often. He had always loved them. There was no question that Mackenzie was blessed with some gorgeous ones. Her sister had always envied them because she hadn't been gifted the long, slender gams from their mother. Mackenzie slipped on one black pump then the other. She studied herself in the mirror. Mackenzie was a single warrior, fighting the battle of loneliness, dressed in her uniform to go to war and looking damn hot. Her feet were already beginning to feel the pinch of the designer pumps. *This guy better be worth it.*

The drive over to Molly and Owen's place left her with a great deal of time to think. At one point, fear had almost gotten the best of her and she'd been tempted to turn around and go home. To make matters worse and adding to that fear, Gideon had called again. *What does he even want? Haven't I made myself perfectly clear?* They'd had their chance. It was now someone else's turn.

Why did I even agree to this whole blind date nonsense? Why would anyone willingly sign up for this kind of torture? Because Mackenzie knew that if she didn't do something, she would no doubt end up a crazy cat lady. Mackenzie spotted Molly's house and pulled into the driveway behind a shiny black BMW. *My date's?* That was some car. *Maybe this won't end up being so bad after all.*

Mackenzie gripped the elegantly designed wine bags. She'd purchased two bottles—one red because God knew she was going to need it and the other was sparkling grape juice because Molly'd had to go and get herself knocked up and Mackenzie didn't want her to feel left out. After she'd pressed the doorbell, Mackenzie stood there and tried to calm her nerves.

This is a good thing, she kept reminding herself. *I can do this.*

"You made it," Owen said as he stood in the now-opened door. Mackenzie must have been daydreaming.

"Oh, hi, Owen."

"Molly's busy in the kitchen and ordered me to answer," Owen explained. "Come on in."

"Thanks. But before we go in, can I ask you a question?"

Owen tilted his head and wore a curious expression in his stormy gray eyes that Molly had fallen absolutely in love with. "Shoot."

"This guy—you know, the blind date, my potential suitor," she rambled.

Owen laughed. "What about him?"

"Like, can you tell me anything about him?" Mackenzie asked.

Owen gave her a gentle smile and grabbed the bag from her white-knuckle death grip. "He's a nice guy, a very good friend of mine and I think you'll like him."

"Owen, that doesn't tell me anything."

"It should tell you everything," he countered. "Molly and I wouldn't set you up with just *anyone.*"

"I know, but you can imagine I'm a little curious to know what I'm getting into before going into this battle."

"It's not war, Mac. It's dinner." Owen ushered inside. *Thanks for nothing.*

Mackenzie inhaled deeply. The aroma of lasagna filled the air. At least the food was going to be tasty. Owen led the way to the kitchen and Mackenzie followed him.

"You're here," Molly said cheerfully as she tried to reach dishes from the cupboard.

"Here, babe. Let me get those." Owen quickly came to her aide and retrieved a stack of forest-green plates.

"Thanks, sweetie," Molly said as she rewarded Owen with a kiss on the cheek.

It warmed Mackenzie seeing Molly in full-blown wedded and domestic bliss. *God, I want that, too.* Owen and Molly were perfectly matched and they just looked darn good as a couple.

Then a handsome man entered the kitchen. *Handsome is really an understatement. This guy is damn gorgeous* — jet-black hair trimmed short and espresso-colored eyes that didn't seem the least bit nervous. Mackenzie was usually a sucker for guys with light eyes, but his were soulful and had a hypnotizing effect. He wore tailored dark-gray slacks and a blue dress shirt without a tie. His black shoes reflected the canned lights in the ceiling. He carried himself in a confident manner that was incredibly sexy and a huge turn-on.

"God, I'm so sorry. Mac, this my good friend Marcus," Owen introduced her to the wickedly delicious-looking stranger.

"It's wonderful to finally meet you," Marcus said as he extended his hand. Mackenzie smiled and shook it. Before she could remove herself from his grip, he brought her hand to his mouth and kissed it. *Well now.*

Molly wore a Cheshire-cat grin and appeared to be very pleased with herself as she handed Mackenzie a cocktail.

"Here. You look like you may need this," she whispered.

Mackenzie leaned in and added, "Oh my God, Molly."

"I know, right?" Molly replied.

The doorbell buzzed and Owen excused himself to answer it. Molly claimed she had to finish getting dinner ready and ordered them to take their drinks out onto the deck until it was time to eat.

Marcus offered her a gentle smile and his hand. He was quick to lead the way. Once outside, the air had a distinctive fall bite to it — crisp, with the hint of a damp sweetness, not much different from the apples Washington state was so famous for.

"This is a tad awkward, isn't it?" Marcus said as he sipped his drink.

"Kind of, huh?" Mackenzie sat on one of the deck chairs that Marcus had pulled out for her. *At least this guy is a gentleman.*

"Honestly, I was worried that Owen was going to set me up with a hideous troll, but he really outdid himself. You're gorgeous."

Mackenzie could say the same for him and laughed. "Thank you, I think." Mackenzie flushed, but hadn't cared for his 'hideous troll' comment. At least he was being honest. It had just come off a tad shallow to her.

"So, what is it that you do, Mac?" Marcus asked while he continued to check her out. She felt as though he were inspecting the goods. Being under the proverbial microscope wasn't something she cared for. *Nothing like being back on the meat market again. The joys of single life and trying to date.*

"Mackenzie," she corrected, "and I'm a teacher." He raised his dark eyebrows and frowned slightly. Marcus seemed to ignore the correction of her name. Only her close friends and family called her Mac.

"That's right. I recall Owen mentioning that." Marcus looked out toward the bay where the sun was casting a tangerine glow on the water. "Was it always a dream of yours to teach? Is it something you plan to do for the rest of your life?"

"Well, I do love what I do. Is it my dream job? I suppose in some ways it is," Mackenzie explained. Why did she feel like this wasn't just breaking the ice and that it was more of an interrogation?

"I see. Would you ever consider giving it up?" Marcus asked as he leaned back in his chair and crossed one leg over the other.

"Why would I want to do that?" Mackenzie countered. "Do you love what you do?"

Marcus let out a throaty laugh and appeared to enjoy this mild battle. "I'm an ER physician. I save lives every single day. So, I guess you could say I very much love what I do."

Wow. That explains the slight cocky air about him, and that Beamer in the driveway. Mackenzie took a long sip of her cocktail and was half-tempted to drain the entire drink right there. So, maybe this whole blind date thing would take some getting used to.

Finally, Molly appeared with Tiffany, who gave Mackenzie an encouraging wink.

"Tiffany, meet Marcus," Mackenzie said as she continued to work on her drink.

Marcus stood and shook her hand. There was a wicked smoothness in his voice as he said, "Pleasure to meet you." His gaze seemed to stay a little too long on Tiffany and Mackenzie made a mental note. *He likes beautiful women and makes no effort to hide it.*

"Lovely to meet you, as well," Tiffany replied with her signature flirty smile. Mackenzie cast a warning glare in her direction just as Colin appeared. He shook Marcus' hand then wound his arm around Tiffany to mark his territory.

Men.

Marcus turned his attention back to Mackenzie. He eyed her like a hungry wolf. She could've sworn he'd just licked his lips. *Good grief, does he have no shame? Then again, maybe it's a good thing that he knows what he wants and isn't afraid to show it. I'm tired of games. This might be a nice change of pace.* Mackenzie took another long sip of her wine.

"It's cold out here. Let's all go inside. Dinner's ready," Molly announced. Colin ushered Tiffany back into the home. Marcus rose again and offered his hand as Mackenzie stood.

"Wanna get out of here?" he teased.

Mackenzie laughed. *Too much too soon. Not a chance in hell, buddy.*

Dinner was as delicious as Mackenzie had assumed it would be. She was proud of Molly and her new wifely skills. Now, if only Molly could pick a better match for her. *Marcus.* That man was more stuck on himself than anyone Mackenzie had ever met, yet oddly enough, she found herself attracted to him. *What the fuck is wrong with me?* It was easy to like and hate him, all in the same breath. He knew he was fine as hell and seemed to use that to his advantage, yet he possessed charm and carried himself in a way that turned her on. The precise and seemingly calculated movements Marcus made as he commanded the room caused an awareness inside Mackenzie. *Don't even get me started on the silky tone of his voice when he shared a few jokes that had everyone laughing but me.* Mackenzie was too focused on studying him, searching for his flaws. Arrogance was one trait Mackenzie could live without and this guy appeared to be quite full of it. He bragged about his amazing career and his many fantastic and over-the-top travel adventures, all while he stared at her. She wasn't impressed. *Okay, that is a complete bullshit lie.* Mackenzie was maybe a little bit impressed and enamored with Marcus. *Maybe this is just his nervous way of coping with the awful concept of a blind date.* Was Mackenzie so desperate that she'd allow herself to *like* this guy in order not to be alone? Or was she just looking for any excuse to dislike Marcus?

"Mac, you've been excited about the Ireland trip," Tiffany said, bring Mackenzie back to reality.

"Uh, yes, very much so. I've always wanted to travel there," she managed to spit out. Her brain was still stuck on Marcus. *How can he already have such a hold on me?*

"Scottish roots?" Marcus asked her. He sat directly across the table from her and that made Mackenzie insanely nervous. "I sort of figured...with your lovely name."

She nodded. "I'm hoping to visit while we're over there," Mackenzie explained as she reached for her wine glass.

"It's an absolute must," Marcus said. "Any special reason why you're headed overseas?"

Mackenzie smiled at Tiffany. "Her — and him, I suppose," she teased. Marcus wore a confused expression. "They're getting married," Mackenzie clarified.

"I thought you two were already married?" Marcus asked Tiffany and Colin.

"We are, but we're having a ceremony for his family," Tiffany explained.

Colin winked at Marcus. "She wasn't satisfied with just one wedding." Tiffany playfully slapped him. "I couldn't be more thrilled to do it all over again with my beautiful bride," Colin said as he stared at Tiffany like she was the only one in the room.

Mackenzie couldn't help but see how happy they both were. *Wedded bliss... That newlywed happiness just oozes from them. I want that, too.*

"Yeah, we're all going," Molly added as she shoveled more lasagna onto Owen's plate. "I've traveled just about everywhere, but I think Ireland is right up there with one of my favorite locations—except for the lighting. That tends to be pretty challenging."

"It's such a magical and gorgeous place. I can't wait for everyone to go with us," Tiffany said as she rested her head against Colin. "I was able to meet Colin's family and just fell in love."

"And they fell in love with you," Colin replied as he kissed the top of her dark head. "But I fell in love with you long before we went back to my home."

Marcus kept his gaze trained on Mackenzie. As nice as the dinner was, it was impossible to get to know him—the real him, not the pretentious, sexy doctor who was well-traveled and more refined than any man she had ever met. Mackenzie wasn't entirely sure she wanted to take any more time finding out who Marcus was—like, what was his favorite color? Did he like going to the opera or museums? However, if she wanted a chance at what her besties had, then she had better get with the program.

Molly must have sensed that Mackenzie was growing uneasy and asked if she could help her get more bread. Tiffany popped up quickly to join them.

"Dinner's super delicious, Moll," Mackenzie complimented her as she leaned against the counter. "Good job on the lasagna."

"Thanks. But let's get to the heart of the matter here," Molly countered as she removed bread from the oven.

"Exactly," Tiffany added. "So, what do you think of Marcus?"

Molly and Tiffany waited for her to answer. Mackenzie wanted to choose her words. "He seems nice enough, I suppose."

"Nice?" Tiffany's perfectly arched eyebrows rose on her pretty face. "That's it? He's fine as all hell and is a doctor, Mac. They don't get much better than that."

Mackenzie rolled her eyes. She didn't crave material things like Tiffany. Mackenzie wanted to fall in love with a man for more than his wallet. "He's a little cocky, to be honest."

Molly moved closer. "He can seem that way. I noticed it when I first met him, too. Marcus is seriously a sweetheart when you get past the smarty-pants-douche-bag attitude. I think he's just sizing you up."

"Why? I'm not in his league," Mackenzie stated. "I'm not sure we're a match." The truth of the matter was that Mackenzie felt she lacked anything special to offer a gorgeous doctor. She wasn't exactly young anymore. Most physicians, at least the ones she'd seen on television, were always going for women significantly younger and hotter. Perky little nurses.

"Don't start that shit, Mac," Molly ordered. "Just give Marcus a chance. If not him, we'll find someone else."

"Someone who isn't Gideon," Tiffany added with a sassy flick of her hair. "You haven't heard from him, have you?"

Mackenzie nodded. "He's tried calling, but I've ignored him."

"Good girl. Now, let's go back out there and get you a doctor," Tiffany said as she grabbed another bottle of wine. "This will help," she added and shook the expensive bottle of Chianti at Mackenzie.

"I hate you both," Molly teased.

"Soon enough," Mackenzie commented as she rubbed Molly's growing belly. "Girl, you're starting to look super pregnant."

"I know." Molly peered down and frowned. "I can barely see my feet anymore."

"Oh, Moll, just enjoy it." Tiffany led the way back to the dining room.

The men were laughing and appeared to be having a good time. *If I could learn to like this guy, at least he'd get along with my girls' hubbies.*

The rest of dinner went well. It was comfortable and the conversation flowed. Mackenzie had to give Molly some credit. Marcus did seem to grow on her more, but that could have been because of the wine. After all the plates had been cleared from the table, Molly served a late evening coffee then everyone prepared to go home. Everyone said their goodbyes and Tiffany and Colin were already out the door as Mackenzie hesitated. She asked Molly again if she needed any help cleaning up. Owen was quick to answer and shooed Mackenzie away, claiming it was his job.

"Can I walk you to your car?" Marcus asked as he helped Mackenzie with her coat.

"Sure," she answered. *No harm in that.*

Marcus held the door open for her. The air was frigid and caused Mackenzie to shiver.

"That was a lovely dinner," Marcus began. "Molly is really a wonderful woman. I'm glad she and Owen are together."

"Yeah, he's not too shabby himself."

"Owen and I have been buddies for only a few years. He was one of my patients, and we sort of hit it off." Marcus laughed. "Molly has nothing but amazing things to say about you, Mac. I'm so glad she introduced us."

"It was really thoughtful of her," Mackenzie said.

"Would you care to have dinner sometime or maybe just go for drinks? I'd really like an opportunity to get to know you a little better and maybe without so many spectators." Marcus stood close to her with his hands in the pockets of his slacks. It was as though he were fighting the temptation to touch her.

Mackenzie inhaled the cold air. It burned her chest as it filled her lungs. *Do I want to see him again? Are there any sparks?* She exhaled. "You know what? Sure," she answered.

"You don't seem all that *sure*," Marcus countered.

"No, I am. I just—" Mackenzie began to explain when Marcus stopped her.

"Aren't looking for anything serious right now?"

"No. I was going to say that I'm sort of getting over someone."

He nodded. "Then let's just take this slow. Drinks first, then we'll work our way up to dinner...maybe even dessert," Marcus suggested with a sly grin.

Mackenzie gave a nervous laugh. "Sounds like a plan. I'm sorry. I'm just not really good at this whole dating thing."

"You're doing just fine." Marcus leaned in and kissed her.

It completely threw her for a loop. Hadn't she just told him that she was a little gun-shy? But she couldn't deny that the warmth of his lips felt nice on hers. Okay, more than just *nice*.

Marcus remained close as if waiting for a signal from her then he pulled her even closer. She didn't know what to expect next and found herself frozen as her mind moved in so many crazy directions. Marcus stood just a little taller than she and it felt sort of wonderful being held by him. His arms were muscular but way different from the bulky muscle Jason had. Gideon was strong but had more of a slender and athletic build. Mackenzie felt like Goldilocks and the Three Bears. Jason had too much muscle, Gideon not quite enough and Marcus was just right. She nearly giggled at the analogy. Mackenzie relaxed further into Marcus' embrace and breathed in his scent. Expensive aftershave tingled her senses. *This feels nice. Maybe not totally right, but it could be if I'd just quit thinking about Gideon.* It was as if he'd ruined her for all men.

Chapter Five

"What are you doing right now?"

Mackenzie looked at her dining room table that was littered with her lesson plans for the coming week — her Saturday morning ritual. "Umm, the same thing I do every Saturday."

"Why do you even need a lesson plan? All they do is eat glue and color," Tiffany said.

Mackenzie chose to ignore her comment. No one understood why she taught kindergarteners. "Where are you?" The background noise was loud in Mackenzie's ear. She pulled the phone away and turned the volume down.

"I'm in the car, but they are doing some road construction. Sorry. Let me close my window. I had it open for Pauly," Tiffany explained. "I'm headed over to your place."

"Why? Everything okay?" Mackenzie asked. She hoped that Tiffany and Colin hadn't fought — or worse, that Tiffany would be dragging Mackenzie to go wedding shopping.

"Everything's great. Pauly and I wanted to come visit."

"You want to dish about Marcus, don't you?"

"Maybe. I have someone else in mind for you — a guy who I think might be just perfect." Mackenzie could hear the excitement in Tiffany's voice.

"I barely met Marcus yesterday. I thought you loved him. Remember, he's a doctor?" Mackenzie said.

"I know, but I didn't want to step on Molly's toes. The guy I have for you is even better," Tiffany explained. "I'm bringing tacos, so you can't say no."

"Well, if tacos are involved... And you're bringing that cute, slobbering bulldog, right?" Mackenzie teased.

"He's my shadow. Like, seriously, this guy follows me everywhere. Don't you, my precious little meatball?" Mackenzie heard Tiffany coo to Pauly.

"Uh, meatball?"

"Yes, he's my chunky ball of cuteness."

They both laughed. Tiffany used to hate animals, except for Mr. Sprinkles, her fat and grumpy cat, but no one could resist Pauly's charm. He made Mackenzie consider getting a dog.

"Drive safe. I'll see ya when you get here," Mackenzie said as she hung up. She needed to get out of her pajamas and clean up a little. *No lazy day for me.*

After she took a quick shower and dressed, Mackenzie was in her room making the bed when she heard a car pull up.

"Your favorite best friend is here," Tiffany called out. "I come bearing tacos."

Mackenzie left her room and followed Tiffany's happy voice to her living room. "You're right. My favorite best friend is here." Mackenzie bent down and greeted the chubby bulldog.

"I was talking about me." Tiffany shook a white bag.

"I can't choose you to be my favorite, but you do rank pretty high up there." Mackenzie winked. "I am starving," she commented as she led the way to her kitchen.

"And just why can't I be your favorite best friend?" Tiffany asked as she pulled out hot sauce from the fridge for the tacos.

"Uh…Molly? You two are both equally my favorite people."

"I'll soon be your most favorite after you hear about who I'm setting you up with," Tiffany replied with confidence.

Mackenzie laughed as she brought plates to the now-cleared-off dining table. "You're killin' me. Spill it."

"Well…" Tiffany said as she sat and began to unwrap a taco from its wrapper, "I've found someone really amazing for you. Okay, so Colin did."

"Really?" Mackenzie cradled her taco, but even as she took a bite, a ton of lettuce and meat spilled from it.

Tiffany wiped her mouth and ignored hers. "Ian is his name."

"Okay, go on," Mackenzie urged as she continued to eat.

"I know Marcus seemed nice enough, but he's not really your style, now is he?"

"I guess not. He did text me about getting drinks sometime this week."

"Well, cancel," Tiffany said.

"I can't do that." Mackenzie almost dropped what was left of her taco.

"Yes, you can, especially after we go out to dinner and you meet Ian."

"Tell me more about this 'Ian' character you're so certain I'm going to love."

"Mackenzie, do you love food?"

"That's a dumb question," Mackenzie countered as she held up her taco.

"Well, Ian is a chef and he owns this trendy hot spot called 'Blu'."

"So, he cooks? That's cool." Mackenzie retrieved another taco from the bag.

Tiffany groaned. "He's like a fuckin' rock star, Mac. He's a little bit of a bad boy, which seems to sort of be your thing right now, judging by your mini-relationship with Jason."

"And that worked out," Mackenzie countered.

"Jason was all wrong for you. Ian, on the other hand, is very polished and he's Irish!" Tiffany squealed. "Not only does he have the same sexy accent as Colin, but he's wickedly successful. He owns several restaurants around the globe and Colin has even invested in a few. They go way back, those two."

Mackenzie nodded as she munched on her second taco. She was hearing what Tiffany was saying but just didn't find herself super intrigued with this Ian guy.

"Aren't you the least bit curious about him?" Tiffany studied her for a moment. "You're not having second thoughts about dating, are you? Oh shit, you're seeing Gideon again," she accused.

Mackenzie shook her head and swallowed her food. After she wiped her mouth, Mackenzie stated, "No, nothing has changed since last night, Tiff. I'm *not* seeing Gideon."

"Good." Tiffany seemed satisfied with her response. "I can't wait for you to meet Ian. We were thinking of going to his restaurant unless you'd like to have dinner at our place?"

Mackenzie shrugged. "Either way is fine by me. When did you want to get together?"

"You don't seem very enthusiastic about this," Tiffany pointed out.

"It's moving sort of fast. Just last night I met Marcus and now you're ready to set me up with someone else. I feel like I'm about to become a serial dater," said Mackenzie as she reached for another taco. Tiffany quickly removed it from her hand.

"No stress eating." Tiffany unwrapped the taco and placed it on her own plate next to her barely touched first one. "As for Marcus, I'm not so sure."

"You seemed pretty sure last night," Mackenzie countered as she stole her taco back. "You're right. He's not my type, but obviously, my type isn't working out so well for me. Marcus is an adventure-seeking ER doctor. Maybe he's looking to settle down now."

"What gives you that impression?" Tiffany tilted her head to the side and waited for Mackenzie to explain.

"He asked if I planned to teach for the rest of my life," she answered.

"And somehow you got a marriage proposal out of that? Maybe he was just concerned about having a teacher for a girlfriend." Tiffany started to laugh. "Babe, trust me. I have no doubt that Marcus would be all for marriage and have you as his trophy wife, but I don't think that will stop him from screwing all the nurses."

"Gosh, you really think he'd do that?" Mackenzie gasped.

"Um, you've watched *Grey's Anatomy* or any hospital soap opera. That's the kind of shit that goes on. 'Stress relief' is what he'll call it. Just watch. He has that predator look and you, my dear, are the prey. He was undressing you with his eyes last night and he didn't care who noticed."

"Wow." It wasn't as though the thought hadn't crossed Mackenzie's mind, but Marcus seemed interested in her and he smelled nice. Smells had always been important to Mackenzie. That would explain her enormous candle collection. She owned an insane variety of candles. Lilac, vanilla and honeysuckle were among her favorites.

"Now Ian, on the other hand... He's also rich, so that's a win," Tiffany pointed out. "Don't tell Colin, but I think Ian's incredibly hot."

Mackenzie didn't like this shallow side of Tiffany and wanted to make it clear that was not how she operated. "I don't care if a guy is loaded or not, Tiff," Mackenzie explained. "It's a bonus that Marcus is a doctor, but it's not something I'm searching for. I seem to be making ends meet just fine on my own." She extended her arms to encompass the room.

"Look, Miss Independent. That's all fine and dandy. I'm not saying you should only be looking for wealthy dudes, but it's just as easy to fall for a rich guy as it is a poor one."

"I know, but I just want to be clear for any of these future dates you so desperately want to set me up on. I'm not necessarily looking for a wealthy guy."

"So, a broke-ass bum is more your style?" Tiffany joked.

"No, I'm not looking for a deadbeat either. I just wanted to be clear that I'm not a gold digger."

"Are you calling me one?"

"Honey, we all know you wanted to end up with a rich guy and you did. By the way, that's the nicest knockoff designer bag I've ever seen." Mackenzie motioned toward the large Louis Vuitton bag that hung on the back of Tiffany's chair.

"It's real."

Mackenzie was shocked. Tiffany had always loved fashion and one of her thrills was to hunt down great designer knockoffs. "Like, really real?"

Tiffany smiled and nodded. "See what having a rich guy does for a girl?"

"You are a gold digger, you know that? I still love you, but you are so terrible," Mackenzie teased.

"Maybe a little. I love Colin with every fiber of my heart," she gushed. "I simply can't imagine not being with him. He's the best thing that's ever happened to me."

Mackenzie laughed. "This coming from the girl who lost her shit in Vegas when she found out she'd married said 'best thing'. I love Colin. He's perfect for you…and you're perfect for him."

"So, you'll go on this date with Ian?"

Mackenzie slouched back in her chair. "I guess so. What do I do about Marcus?"

"It's not like you're going steady. You don't have to date just one guy. It's not the fifties. You're a modern woman and it's okay for you to be a bit of a lady stud, too."

"You mean *slut*?" Mackenzie countered.

"I prefer lady stud. You're *not* a slut. If anything, you're like a born-again virgin. When was the last time you got laid?" Tiffany asked.

Mackenzie released a heavy sigh. "Like forever ago."

"So, no boning happened with Jason?" Mackenzie shook her head. "Damn, Gideon seriously ruined you."

"I wouldn't go as far to say that," Mackenzie argued but knew it was the truth. *How else can I explain being celibate for two years?*

"What else do you call it? Because, sweetie, this isn't just a dry spell. This is a goddamned drought. There's a whole lotta love out there just waiting for you. Don't let Gideon be the reason you are scared to try again."

Maybe Tiffany had a point. *Why haven't I been able to get my freak on in over two years? Because Gideon has ruined me for all men.* Besides being an incredible lover, the dynamic chemistry they'd shared had made every sexual encounter sizzle. Even a quickie was scorching hot. Each and every time they'd had sex, it had been nearly soul shattering. *How can another guy ever live up to that?* Gideon had set the bar to unrealistic levels. It was his way of marking her for life. She could never find anyone who would make her feel that way again. *How could one guy have that ability?*

Or was she the one who had created that imaginary bar? Was it her who'd made it impossible for any man to be with her except Gideon? Maybe she had ruined herself all on her own.

* * * *

Mackenzie was suffering the worst case of the Mondays. After her impromptu lunch with Tiffany on Saturday, her mind had been a mess the rest of weekend. Gideon had tried calling again and even Marcus had sent her a text message. She'd ignored both and instead had opted to stay in bed all day. *So much for that whole positive outlook.* Upon her realization that she'd self-sabotaged any future relationships because of Gideon, it had made her want to hide. She drowned herself in hot tea, far too much junk food and sappy chick-flicks in hopes they'd lift her spirits. Then Monday happened. Nothing particular or over the top was going wrong, but it was just one of those days when Mackenzie simply felt blah. The children were their usual cheerful selves with endless energy. This was normally contagious, but Mackenzie just couldn't shake her bad mood. The day wasn't over yet and she'd hoped that somehow it could be salvaged. She was glad she had no dates scheduled. If there had been, she would've canceled.

The final bell rang and her students were all lined up to go home for the day. Mackenzie said goodbye and made sure they all had their backpacks as they left the classroom. She stood there to make sure they behaved themselves as they walked down the hall that was filled with other students.

After they were gone, she went back to the desk and surveyed the quiet room. It was neat and orderly, much like how she would prefer her life to be. The happy colors throughout provided a perfect learning environment for the young children. All the bright posters and bulletin boards symbolized the many wonderful things about education. She had created this space for her students and was the one who was responsible for shaping these minds at the start of their educational journey. These kids would someday be running the joint. They would be the future teachers, engineers and doctors. Having thought more about what Marcus had said the night they'd met, Mackenzie began to question why he'd even asked that. *Does he not respect my profession or is he looking for a stay-at-home wife and mom? Am I over-analyzing it?* Hell yeah, she was, because deep down it truly bothered her. Men, in general, bothered her, yet she missed one of those men terribly. As hard as she tried to erase him from her memory, it just wasn't possible. *When will I ever be over Gideon?*

Mackenzie was lost in thought when she heard a knock on the door. She turned to see who was there. "Gideon." *Speak of the devil.*

"I figured since you haven't been returning my calls, I would come to you." Gideon held up a paper cup. "Plus, I brought a bribe."

Mackenzie smiled at his thoughtfulness. *Now, let's see if it's the one I love.* Gideon strolled in and handed her the coffee. She took a slow sip. *Damn, he still remembers.*

Gideon grabbed one of the small chairs and brought it next to her desk. He looked ridiculous as he sat on it. The man was far too large for the seat. She couldn't help but think how adorable he looked.

"So, why are you avoiding me?" Gideon asked as he sipped on his own coffee.

Mackenzie studied Gideon, who seemed relaxed and comfortable. They had been that way together once. Mackenzie found it odd that she wasn't nervous around him and she was half-tempted to spill her guts — confess all her secrets and tell Gideon how much she missed him.

"I'm not avoiding you," she lied.

"Yes, you are," he countered, not breaking eye contact.

"I've been busy." Mackenzie fed him another lie. Well, she had been...kind of.

Gideon laughed. "You're a terrible liar. You know that?"

"Where's the baby?"

"Oh, you noticed? Come on. Don't change the subject, Mac," Gideon said. "She's at Mom's."

"How is your mom doing?" Mackenzie had seen her only a few times over the last two years. There had been brief near encounters when Mackenzie had seen her at the grocery store then darted down another aisle like a coward.

"She's good. It's funny. The other day she mentioned you," Gideon said with a laugh. "Mom always liked you."

Could've fooled me. Mackenzie cradled her cup in both hands, enjoying the slight caffeine buzz as it surged through her, and replied, "She's a lovely lady."

Gideon released a heavy sigh. "Can we talk yet?"

"Gid, I don't know if I can."

"What's stopping you?"

"You."

"Me?"

"Yes. I can't seem to get over you. I've tried to move on," she admitted. Mackenzie's throat went dry and her eyes began to sting with the threat of tears. She took a deep breath and told herself to settle down.

"Babe, there's a reason why you can't. I have the same exact problem. I haven't been able to get over you either."

"So what's the reason then?"

"We belong together."

Mackenzie let out an awkwardly loud laugh that she just couldn't keep inside.

"I'm serious, Mac. I fucked up bad. We both know that." Gideon looked at her with an intense stare.

At least he owns it now.

Gideon rose from his seat. His eyes never left hers. Mackenzie froze in her chair as he stood in front of her. Then Gideon crouched down and wrapped his arms around her legs. As he squatted there, Gideon said, "Mac, I will always love you. And I will spend the rest of my life trying to prove it to you."

He rested his head on her lap as she let the words sink in. Mackenzie wove her fingers through his dark-blond hair. It was still military short and just a little longer on the top than she'd remembered. Her heart squeezed. She'd always love this man, and it wasn't a good thing. Just being here with him like this was almost crushing. Mackenzie couldn't give him another chance, could she? Mackenzie wished she could travel back in time and right all the wrongs with everything she now knew. She suspected Gideon would do the same if given the chance. *What if, just maybe, we could try again?* Mackenzie knew she wouldn't survive another breakup. *God, I love him so much.* The vulnerable tenderness he displayed in this quiet moment gave her hope. It felt right on so many levels, but was it? She couldn't ignore the emotional scars that would always be there. A battle raged inside her. Mackenzie was aware that Gideon possessed the power to hurt her. As she raked her fingers through his hair and cradled him in her lap, Mackenzie's heart broke all over again.

God, I hate him.

* * * *

"Uh, no, you are not canceling," Tiffany said.

"I can't do this whole dinner thing."

"And just why not?" Tiffany didn't sound very happy with her since tonight was the night she was supposed to meet Ian.

"Mac, I'm going to kill you," Tiffany said after Mackenzie grew quiet.

Gideon is right. I'm not a very good liar. She was also terrified to tell Tiffany the reason why she couldn't meet Ian. Mackenzie needed time to think after her unexpected visit with him the other day. He'd wanted them to have dinner that weekend and she'd agreed. She was opening her heart back up a little.

"You know what? No."

"No?" Mackenzie echoed her.

"No, you are not getting out of this date. I don't give two flying fucks if this has anything to do with Gideon or you just being chicken-shit. You're meeting Ian and we're going to have a wonderful time."

"Tiffany, I can't. Please understand." Mackenzie hoped that Tiffany would just drop it.

"I'm sorry. Did you not just hear me?" she fired back.

Mackenzie groaned. "I'm a grown-ass woman, you know."

"Who obviously has no clue what she's about to miss out on. You're having dinner with us, so be ready by eight. We're all riding together," Tiffany said. "Quit being difficult. Dress to impress. Love ya." And she hung up.

Mackenzie had no choice and screamed that it was a school night into the phone. *Why do I even bother?* Mackenzie knew that she'd have to go on this stupid date. A sneaky thought crossed her mind. *What if I like Ian? What if Tiffany is right?* It had been easy enough to cancel drinks with Marcus earlier in the week. He happened to be on call unexpectedly. '*The life of a man who saves lives.*' Marcus had explained it that way as he'd tried to reschedule.

The other more pressing problem was that Mackenzie had been texting back and forth with Gideon. She felt like a stupid schoolgirl crushing on some boy. They'd sent each other silly jokes and pictures. It felt so much like old times. The texts had graduated to talking on the phone, which had led to many late-night conversations. She'd forgotten just how easy it was to talk to him. He'd always been a great listener. But the truth of the matter was that she wasn't dating Gideon. They weren't a couple. Heck, they weren't even really friends yet. *Why does it feel so wrong to go to meet Ian? Like I'm cheating on Gideon?* Her future with Gideon was so up in the air. Mackenzie wasn't even a hundred percent sold that she wanted one with him again.

This sucks. Mackenzie stretched out on her couch. The thought of a power nap was inviting. Just ten minutes. It seemed that as soon as she'd drifted off, Mackenzie heard a loud knock. She opened her eyes to find that her house was almost dark. *Shit.*

"Mac, open up." Then more loud thumping followed.

Mackenzie made a quick dash to open the door and found Tiffany and Colin standing there.

"Why aren't you dressed?" Tiffany's pretty face became masked with horror. Colin remained still for a moment then turned heel back to the large black SUV that was parked in the driveway. *Smart man.*

"I'm sorry. I must've fallen asleep. This is why I shouldn't go out on a school night," Mackenzie complained as Tiffany dragged her toward her bedroom.

"For fuck's sake, Mac, we're already running a little late." Tiffany began to rifle through her closet. "Here, just throw this on. We can deal with your makeup in the car."

"I'm sorry," Mackenzie offered, but Tiffany wasn't having any of it.

"I don't know why you're acting like this again. Last week you were totally good with meeting guys. What happened?" Tiffany asked.

Mackenzie avoided Tiffany's eyes and started to undress. Tiffany sat on her bed and waited for an answer.

"Gideon. That's what has happened," Tiffany filled in for her with an annoyed tone. "I'm not stupid, Mac."

"I never said you were," Mackenzie replied.

"Why are you still even thinking about him?"

"I don't know. He stopped by my class on Monday," Mackenzie admitted.

"I knew that's why you were trying to cancel. Mackenzie, let me level with you, okay?"

Mackenzie pulled up the short aqua dress. "Can you zip me?" The pale color set off her summer tan beautifully. Tiffany popped off the bed and quickly zipped up the dress. "Thanks."

"Here's the thing. Gideon had his chance. He can't just come back and think things will pick up where they left off. Maybe you don't remember how badly he hurt you. Well, as one of your best friends, I'm here to remind you." Tiffany pulled Mackenzie in for a hug. "You deserve better than that, Mac."

Mackenzie nodded. She was touched by this sensitive side of Tiffany. She came from a genuine place of concern. Tiffany and Molly had endured the break-up, too. They'd eaten lots of ice cream and used plenty of tissues from countless snotty bouts of ugly crying, along with plenty of alcohol to try to forget Gideon. They had nursed Mackenzie back to life, revived her from the dead of heartbreak. Then, when her sister had died, they'd cycled through her grief with her. They had been there, not Gideon. He should have been the one to hold her, to reassure her that God wasn't a monster who had stolen her sister. It was her friends who'd held her hand, not the man who was supposed to be her rock — her everything.

"Wear the silver heels." Tiffany grabbed them from the top shelf of the closet. Mackenzie quickly shoved her feet into them. Now she towered over Tiffany. "Okay, we need to go now," Tiffany ordered as she ushered Mackenzie out of the room.

The ride to the supposedly swanky upscale restaurant was a quiet one. Tiffany and Mackenzie kept their voices low as Colin pretended to be hard at work on his phone. The large SUV was more than roomy and the camel-colored leather seats were incredibly soft and comfortable. She felt spoiled in this luxurious vehicle.

"This is going to be great, and you look fantastic," Tiffany complimented. Colin looked up and smiled.

"She's right. You do look lovely, Mackenzie."

"Thanks." Mackenzie fussed with her hair, combing it with her fingers.

"It looks fine. Stop fidgeting," Tiffany said as she reapplied a burgundy lipstick. She wore a black dress with metal beading and precise slashes on the sides. It shimmered in the light and had that edgy rock n' roll style Tiffany was well known for. The black-studded ankle boots made the outfit.

"Cute shoes," Mackenzie commented as she tried to distract herself.

"Right? How hot are these?"

"Very," Colin added as he leaned over and kissed Tiffany on the cheek. He looked over at Mackenzie. "Try not to worry. You'll like Ian."

"I have no doubt that I will. It's just that—" Mackenzie started as Tiffany interrupted her.

"She's got her head all mixed up."

"How so?" Colin asked.

"Gideon," Tiffany said and Colin's face dropped.

"That guy, huh? Yes, Tiffany told me he's come back. Some nerve," Colin said but avoided Mackenzie's eyes.

"He's not that bad. I promise. Colin, you'd probably get along rather well with him."

Tiffany laughed. "Uh, no. Colin wouldn't like Gideon one bit. He doesn't think too kindly of cowards. Do you, babe?" Tiffany snuggled closer to Colin and dug her nails into his thigh. He kissed the top of her head.

Mackenzie sighed. "Coward is a little harsh, Tiff."

"We're almost there, lovelies. Let's not taint the night with soiled memories," Colin redirected the conversation. *Bless his heart.*

"You're absolutely right, babe. I want tonight to be all about Mac meeting Ian, hopefully making a new love connection and not dwelling on ancient history," Tiffany purred.

Mackenzie stared out of the darkly tinted window. Seattle was alive at this time of night. The red taillights blinked as they crawled along. Luckily, it was a dry night. The car suddenly drifted to the right and pulled up to a curb. Mackenzie could see a line of people who stood against a battleship-gray concrete wall. The building itself was drab and looked very industrial, nothing like she'd imagined. Mackenzie had expected a bright, trendy place with lots of fanfare. It was understated, muted and maybe even a little creepy in this district of downtown Seattle.

"We're here," Tiffany announced as she gathered a small Chanel clutch. Mackenzie locked her eyes with Tiffany's as she asked about the clutch with a look that only a bestie could use and be understood. "Fake," Tiffany answered. They both giggled. *Good to know some things never change.*

Colin assisted the girls out after the driver opened the door. Colin offered each of his arms to Tiffany and Mackenzie and led the way to the large door. Eyes glued on them as they were allowed to enter the building without having to get into line. *Colin probably feels like a stud walking in with two gorgeous ladies on his arm.* Mackenzie had to admit it did feel pretty cool to be given such special treatment and they weren't even inside yet.

Then Mackenzie learned a valuable lesson. Never judge a book by its cover. *Damn, this place is stunning.* A soft light spilled on the brick walls, casting a shadowy blue color everywhere. The restaurant, though still industrial, had a romantic flare. It was intimate, with candles at each table, but more importantly, it was packed. Mackenzie didn't notice any empty tables as they were led through the dining room then up a flight of stairs. It gave way to a secluded eating area with a view of the dining room below. The balcony was equally, if not more, romantic. The place was gorgeous and it smelled divine. *Why haven't I heard of this place before? Because you live under a rock and are a complete homebody, Mac.*

Colin appeared to be searching for someone. "Where's Ian?" he asked the hostess.

"He had to take care of something in the kitchen but asked for you all to get settled in. He's already arranged dinner for the evening." The hostess stood by the large table as Colin pulled out a chair for Tiffany then Mackenzie. *Who says chivalry is dead?* The hostess smiled and said, "I'll be right back with the wine."

"Tell me this isn't fabulous, Mac," Tiffany said as they both surveyed the room.

"Wait until you try his food," Colin added. "I wonder what he's made for us tonight."

"I'm sure anything will be wonderful by the looks of this place." Mackenzie was in awe of the space and loved the view.

"That's delightful to hear you say, love," a voice with a very Colin-sounding accent said behind her. Mackenzie turned around and saw who had to be Ian.

Double damn. Hot as fuck didn't even begin to describe this man. *Play it cool, girl.* Mackenzie rose from her seat and extended her hand. "I'm Mackenzie. Your restaurant is beautiful and I'm sure the food is nothing short of stellar."

"Lovely to meet you, Mackenzie. I'm Ian, as I'm sure you've figured out by now," he introduced himself and laughed. Ian held her hand longer than necessary and neither seemed to want to let go. "Thank you kindly for the compliment, but I think it just may pale in comparison to you, dear. Having you in here may not be so good for business," he flirted.

Butterflies took flight in her belly. Ian stood significantly taller than her, which was quite a feat due to her own height and the fact she'd worn three-inch heels. His tousled dark-blonde hair had that, *"I don't care, I just woke up this sexy"* style and made her want to touch it. The rumpled *"Let's stay in bed all day"* look really worked for him and turned her on. She found herself snapping mental pictures of Ian. The lady spank bank always needed new material. He gave her tons of inspiration that she might need for when she got home if the pulsating zing in her pussy was any indicator.

He sported a darker goatee on his squared chin and a straight nose that was slightly too large but added character on his definably masculine and handsome face. His eyes were the most breathtaking olive green shade she'd ever seen. She could tell that Ian was made of lean muscle and had the body of an athlete, even under his pale pink dress shirt and dark gray pants. Mackenzie's gaze wandered to his arms. His shirt was partially rolled up, exposing tattoos that decorated his forearms. One of the tattoos grabbed her attention. They were shadowy pine trees that seemed to grow from his wrist. It was a unique design and intrigued her. The man was yummy, which she found kind of fitting. He was a chef, after all.

"Sorry to keep you waiting, mate," Ian apologized to Colin and hugged him.

As Mackenzie listened to his voice, she found herself growing all giddy and acting almost as bad as Tiffany, who seemed to be in heaven with the men's accents. Tiffany had always been obsessed with a sexy Irish brogue, as most women were, but Mackenzie never really thought she'd fall so hard for one. It wasn't just his voice. It was Ian's entire aura. He just had a ridiculous but cool presence about him.

They shared a bottle of wine and the conversation flowed. Ian was more than charming. He was intelligent and funny. He was also a pleasure to look at. Mackenzie felt like she was bordering on obsessed stalker as she watched him. She had lots of material for later, because she was going to need it. Mackenzie hoped the batteries in her vibrator were still good. She especially enjoyed looking at his arms and had to keep herself from touching him. Ian would graze her skin with a fingertip, flash her a sexy grin every so often and even the occasional wink. There was no question that she was insanely attracted to him. The man was scrumptious and he knew it. She was relieved when the food finally arrived. She was starved, but not for the fun arrangement that now sat in front of her.

Tiffany had been right. This guy was a culinary rock star. The food was beyond delicious and unlike anything she'd ever tasted. Everything was perfectly cooked with flavors complementing each other in an artistic way. The presentation was more than spectacular and the explosion of flavor in her mouth was unbelievable. Not only was Ian hot and had a personality to match, but he could cook, too. *Okay, so maybe Tiffany has hit a grand slam with this one.*

Hours passed, they consumed more wine and Mackenzie found that she didn't want the evening to end. Ian asked if he could see her again. *Is that even a question?* Mackenzie gave him her number without a second thought. It killed her to think it was almost time to go home. For the first time in a very long while, she didn't even care that it was wickedly late on a school night. This had been worth it. When Ian walked her to their car, he kissed her goodbye on her cheek. He then moved to her neck and left a feathery trail of kisses there. Mackenzie felt her knees grow weak and somehow managed to stumble to the car. She was punch drunk in lust with Ian.

Lord, help me.

Chapter Six

She panted and thought her heart was going to come through her chest. *Damn, that was good.*

Self-love — it was a fact of life for any woman or man, one that any healthy creeping-into-middle-age woman with a ravenous sexual appetite should be handling…literally. Mackenzie was coming down from the high of her orgasm. She was still turned on and might need to go for round two. Her brain had been filled with conjured-up images of Ian from earlier. The key was a good imagination. She'd only met the man a few hours ago and already had gotten herself off at the very thought of him. Mackenzie wasn't about one-night stands but she'd almost make an exception for him. The naughty things she'd like to do to him all while he spoke in that sexy as sin accent of his… She'd kill to see what Ian looked like naked. *Are there more hidden tats? How big is his cock?* Not that Mackenzie was a size queen or anything — she'd just been lucky enough to have partners who were well endowed.

All those thoughts got her revved up again and caused a deep ache. She played with her nipple, tugging it and pretending that it was Ian biting her. She moved her other hand to between her thighs that were still damp from earlier. As she flicked her still-tender and swollen clit, she was shocked at how wet she was again. She traced her silky folds and released a whimper. *God, I need to be fucked and not with some stupid toy.*

For the first time in her life, she considered making a booty call just to get some relief. It was one thing to get her own rocks off but to have someone steering her toward orgasm was an entirely different story. Though Mackenzie could admit she'd become quite good at pleasuring herself over the last two years, she wanted a man. Desperate times called for desperate measures, and well, a girl had to do what girl had to do, like teasing her clit, which was exactly what Mackenzie was doing. The sensitive little bud was her golden ticket to coming. She needed to work it just right and she'd climax soon. As she moaned, Mackenzie imagined Ian eating her out, his tongue lapping up her juices and sucking on her precious little clit. *Almost there.*

Mackenzie flipped over and got on all fours, her hand buried between her legs. She'd love for him to take her from behind and with all the trimmings — hair pulling, deep fucking and maybe a little spanking for good measure. Her body locked up as several spasms of another powerful orgasm surged through her. Her hand was soaked. It was good but could be much better. *Damn, I need to get laid.*

Mackenzie flipped onto her back and released a heavy sigh. *Will I always be alone?* The euphoria had worn off and guilt replaced it. *Gideon.* It wasn't as though Mackenzie hadn't thought of him when she masturbated. That man still turned her on, even when she'd hated his guts. But Ian? He'd sparked something wild and very naughty inside her and Mackenzie's wet bedspread could prove it.

* * * *

Coffee, proof that magic was real. What other way was there to explain the amazing powers that came from coffee beans? There wasn't. It was all magic. Mackenzie had just started a pot of her potion when she heard a knock on the door. She glanced down and realized she looked like hell. Purple fuzzy socks, blue polka-dotted pajama shorts and a yellow tank top. Mackenzie looked more like Rainbow Brite from her childhood than a woman inching closer to forty every day.

Well, they'll just have to take me as is. She had slept like utter shit. Despite fingering herself to oblivion, Mackenzie had spent most of the night hornier than hell. She'd felt like a dog in heat. Mackenzie's hand had been on her phone at one point. She'd come pretty damn close to calling Gideon. Because, in her hearts of hearts, that was who she really wanted. Sure, Ian was gorgeous and would probably be an incredible lover, but he wasn't Gideon, the man she'd been truly crooning over since they'd had split up. He was the guy she needed inside her, fucking away the last two years. Mackenzie had been so beyond exhausted that she'd called in sick to work, something she rarely did.

Another knock sounded at the door. "I'll be right there," she called out and hurried from the kitchen.

She swung the door open to find Gideon standing there.

"Damn, I'd almost forgotten how cute you were in the morning," Gideon said.

Seriously? Cute is the last thing I am. She looked like a hot mess and knew it. Mackenzie tried to hide behind the door.

"There's no point, I already got an eye full, sweetheart. Plus, I've seen all of you before." He winked.

Yes, he has. The memory found its way to her sex, causing a wetness in her panties. *Shit.* She was still a little horny.

"I thought we were having dinner, not breakfast," Mackenzie managed to say as she attempted to smother the growing fire inside.

"I couldn't wait to see you. So, we brought breakfast." Gideon's hand gripped a baby carrier and the other held a white paper sack. "Why aren't you at work?" he asked with concern.

"You should've called," Mackenzie scolded him as she allowed him to enter and closed the door.

"And miss out on seeing you looking all adorable like that? No way." Gideon brought the carrier into the living room and sat it on the couch.

"Is she awake?" Mackenzie peeked under the soft pink blanket. A gorgeous baby was sleeping peacefully. "She's so precious, Gid."

"Yeah, I think I'll keep her," he answered as he carried the baby to the living room.

"You weren't going to?" Mackenzie asked in horror.

"I'm kidding. You haven't had your coffee yet, and by the smell of it, looks like I'm just in time. But seriously, you okay?"

Is that a trick question? "I just took a personal day. How'd you know that I'd be home?"

"Stalker confession. I drove by a little bit ago and saw your car. I figured maybe it was an in-service day or something, so I took a chance." After setting the carrier in the living room Gideon walked toward her kitchen. He knew her home like the back of his hand. He'd spent so much time there yet had never moved in. Gideon was fairly old-fashioned, which had come as a shock considering all the terrifically naughty things they had done, but he believed that they should wait to live together until they were married. *And look how that turned out.* Mackenzie tried to dismiss the ugly thought.

Gideon pulled two mugs, one being her favorite one. A jumbo-sized, cheery yellow and pink cup. "Where's my mug?"

He really needs to ask? "Probably still at Goodwill," she said.

"Very funny." Gideon started to pour their coffee. "What kind of creamer do you have?" he asked as he opened the fridge. "Wow, this is insane, Mac."

"What?"

"Coffee creamers. Why do you have so many?"

"Umm, I like variety." *Shit. A Freudian slip.*

Gideon gave her an annoyed look as he pulled out a coconut creamer and added it to their coffee. "I brought scones."

"Really? You're so sweet," Mackenzie gushed as she accepted her mug from him.

"I know they're your favorite." Gideon kissed her forehead.

As Mackenzie stood there in her kitchen, it felt as though time had rewound itself like an old VHS tape. The overwhelming sense of déjà vu took her by surprise. *How many times have we done this?* Gideon used to always bring scones and she'd have coffee ready for them. Then they'd spend the day together, sometimes the entire day in bed. Other times they went on mini adventures or hung out at Pike's Place Public Market. She missed those days and would almost give anything to relive them. They'd been happy, full of hope and plans. *What in the fuck happened?*

"Come on, pretty lady," Gideon said from the dining room.

"She going to be okay in the other room?"

"Yep, I fed and changed her right before we got here and car rides knock her out," Gideon explained. "Sit. Let's eat. This huckleberry scone has got your name on it."

"I love these." Mackenzie's mouth watered as she eyed it.

"I know." Gideon smiled at her as he sipped his coffee.

Mackenzie sat down next to him and pinched off a piece of the buttery scone. It almost melted in her mouth. "Oh, my goodness, this is so yummy."

"But not nearly as yummy as you," Gideon whispered and moved closer to her. He snared her with his arm, securing Mackenzie to him. He found the sweet spot on her neck. He hadn't forgotten anything — the way she liked her coffee, scones from her favorite bakery or how to turn her on. "God, I've missed you," he said in a low voice as he continued to nuzzle her neck. He delicately rested his fingers on her nape, applying just the right amount of pressure and contact. "You know, I've been looking forward to this all week."

"Me, too, even though I thought we were just having dinner."

"Oh, we can have that, too," Gideon teased as he released her and leaned back in his chair. "I've really enjoyed talking to you on the phone, but this is much better."

"Yeah, it's funny. You're like the only guy I can stay up and talk to about everything and nothing until crazy hours in the morning. I've been living off chocolate-covered espresso beans all week because of you. Sleep deprivation is not cute. You see these hideous black circles under my eyes?" Mackenzie blinked at him and giggled.

"You poor thing. And it's good to know that I'm the only guy," he commented playfully with a serious undertone.

"Oh, just the only guy I'm losing sleep because of. I didn't say you were the *only guy* in my life," she shot back with a little extra sass.

Gideon laughed. "You're right. I shouldn't assume that you're single."

"Exactly. I'll have you know I'm quite a catch. These bags under my eyes are super sexy," Mackenzie teased as she flicked a crumb at him. "Guys can't resist."

"Trust me. No one knows that better than me," he added. "I remember when Moll and Tiff were both single and hated that you were with me."

"Well, rest assured that you're still hated," Mackenzie stated sweetly.

"What?"

Mackenzie raised her eyebrows at him and threw Gideon a knowing look. "Can you blame them, Gid?"

"You have a point. So, how are those troublemakers?" Gideon and her friends had never fully gotten along. He'd always complained that she spent too much time with them and vice versa. It had been as though she were the rope in a tug-of-war match, being pulled in two opposing directions. In some strange way, since Gideon had broken things off, she'd often wondered if her girls had thought of it as a victory. They'd gotten Mackenzie all to themselves. They had won.

Time to bring him up to speed and best to start with the one who hated him the least. "Well, Molly is married and expecting her first baby."

"No way. That's great. Wow," Gideon said. He seemed surprised. "And does she still do the photography thing?"

Mackenzie nodded. "She still has that fabulous studio, too. Molly's kind of a big deal now."

"No doubt. She was always talented. Good for her."

"She met Owen nearly a year ago and it's the funniest story."

"I'm all ears," Gideon said as he took a leisurely sip of coffee, looking quite comfortable in her house.

Mackenzie told of the entire hilarious encounter from when Owen had nailed her with a fish at Pike's Place to the Hawaiian wedding. Their awesome little love story still made Mackenzie feel all warm and fuzzy. Gideon laughed and seemed genuinely happy for Molly.

"And Tiff? I'm guessing she finally found her prince charming?" Gideon asked as he got up and refilled his mug. "You want some more, babe?" He paused to go check on his daughter, who was still sleeping soundly.

"Sure," she answered, choosing to ignore that he called her 'babe'. *Old habits die hard.* "Yes, Tiffany had her happily ever after...kind of."

"Uh-oh, that doesn't sound good," Gideon commented after he brought both of their mugs back to the table. "Do tell. I want to know all the gossip," he added in a high-pitched feminine voice. Mackenzie giggled at him. Gideon had always been so silly.

"Well, it's the craziest story and it's still sort of not completely done, I suppose."

"How so? Is she married?" Gideon blew on his coffee and jerked back after he'd tried to take a sip. "Damn, that's hot."

"Poor baby." Mackenzie felt brazen and leaned over and kissed him. He grabbed her head and sealed their mouths together. Mackenzie pulled back and felt dazed. "Wasn't I telling a story?"

"Yeah, but this is more fun. Wouldn't you agree?" Gideon countered with a sexy grin and a lusty sparkle in his sapphire eyes.

The air seemed to crackle between them and she could feel her body grow warm and tense. *Damn him.* Mackenzie stumbled over her words at first as she tried to catch her breath and calm her shit down. She then told him how Tiffany and Colin had met and didn't leave out any details of their crazy Vegas wedding. She made sure to include the fat Elvis who had married them. However, she felt it was important to not mention Jason. "Anyway, they're having their real wedding in Ireland."

"But they're married."

"Yeah, but it wasn't Tiffany's dream wedding, and Colin is all about making sure she has everything that her heart desires, which also includes having us girls at her wedding. Bless his heart. He's such a great guy."

"Because he spoils her?" Gideon asked as he finished another buttery scone.

"No, not because of that. He's really a nice person. Last night on the way to dinner, I was telling him that he'd probably like you." Mackenzie slipped up.

"You should've invited me," Gideon teased. "Well, I'd love to meet both of these guys."

Mackenzie knew Tiffany would never go for it—maybe Molly, but even that was a long shot. "So, what are you doing for work now that you're a civilian?" Mackenzie steered the conversation back to him because she was curious.

"Well, you're probably going to laugh, but I plan to teach."

"Why would I laugh? That's awesome. Did you finish getting your degree?"

"I did. I have some state certifications I need to pass, but then I'll be teaching art." Gideon seemed quite proud and his cheeks were tinged pink. He used to paint and sculpt. Mackenzie had often teased him that she always wanted to re-enact that scene in the movie *Ghost*, with the pottery wheel and all that wet clay. It had never happened.

"That's so great, Gid." Mackenzie was playing with fire when she got up from her seat to hug him. She wasn't sure what had come over her but Mackenzie needed to feed the hungry beast that was running wild inside her.

He instantly put his hands on her hips and ran them down the outside of her thighs. Mackenzie rested her hands on his shoulders as she braced herself. He slid one hand under the fabric of her shorts. The warmth of his touch did more than just tempt her. She knew this could get out of hand, but considering her pent-up sexual desire and need, she threw caution to the wind. It was as though Gideon was waiting on her signal, the green light for him to proceed. Her answer was simple enough—a kiss. She connected their lips, savoring the feel of his against her own.

He needed no further encouragement and he cupped her mound. Gideon worked one finger gingerly over the thin fabric of her panties as he traced the folds of her sex. He gripped her ass, molding to her cheek as he deepened the kiss. There was no question that he wanted her as much as she wanted him in that very moment. Chemistry had never been an issue for them. They'd always had a firecracker-hot sex life. This kiss proved things were still explosive and dangerous.

Gideon paused and looked at her like she was a goddess. "I need you, Mac, but I won't take what you aren't ready to give me back."

Mackenzie held the sides of his handsome face and kissed him again.

Between the hungry kisses, he moved his fingers inside her pussy and, standing there like a fool, Mackenzie didn't know which way was up and what was down. *Fuck, this is hot and exactly what I need.*

Gideon lifted her tank top to expose her braless breast. Her nipples already stood at attention and begged to be sucked. He kindly obliged without disturbing the strokes he pleasured her sex with. Mackenzie needed more than just his fingers. She knew what hard and long prize awaited her. Mackenzie reached down to claim it during the whirlwind of kissing and finger fucking. *This can't be real. I have to be dreaming. This feels too good to be happening.*

Mackenzie moved like a gymnast and straddled Gideon's lap. He pulled his hand from her soaked panties. As he gazed up at her, she watched Gideon put his fingers in his mouth.

"You still taste delicious," Gideon growled. He grabbed her hips and lifted her up onto the dining room table. She sat there as he worked her shorts down her legs, leaving her panties on. Gideon threw her shorts aside and placed his hand on her belly, pushing her back onto the table. He ran his hand down her tummy and back to her sopping-wet, panty-covered mound. Mackenzie stared up at the ceiling, already missing the feel of his lips on hers, but she knew what was coming next. Mackenzie heard him sit. Gideon traveled his fingers up her thighs and she waited with anticipation. She knew his face was hovering just inches from her pussy. She pushed her pelvis up toward him.

"I know what you need. Patience, baby," he ordered.

That was just like Gideon, to command the pace and show restraint. He knew exactly how to torture her. She wanted to feel his tongue on her hot clit *now*. Instead, Gideon blew out a steady flow of air. It came through the thin fabric. It only turned her on more. Her insides clenched and contracted as she tried to control her body's response. Gideon took his time as he spread her legs apart. Mackenzie wanted nothing more than to wrap them around his head and squeeze him to death. He was driving her crazy with all this teasing, starving her of pleasure and release. She didn't deserve this. Why was she even allowing him access to her without his having earned it? Her brain was a jumbled mess of thoughts. Lust-infused and hornier than hell, she wasn't making much sense in her own mind.

Then she felt it. It was like greeting an old friend. He first kissed her clit through the fabric. She wanted to pull his face closer but he had somehow pinned her arms. He was now doing everything with his tongue. He licked, sucked and probed all from the outside of her panties. She was so turned on and needed more.

He removed one hand from her arm, parted her legs farther and rested her calves on his shoulders. He stroked the muscle of her legs and moaned. "I've always loved your legs," he said in a breathy tone filled with longing.

Gideon slid her panties to the side after one more teasing flick of his tongue. Then he did what he always did best — ate her pussy like he was a man starving and in need of nourishment. He hummed into her pussy as he fucked her simultaneously with his tongue and fingers. Mackenzie arched as her body caught fire. Heat soared in her veins as he tugged on her clit, causing her to cry out.

Gideon paused as her body quivered from being under attack with a mind-blowing orgasm. "Does that feel good, baby?"

"Yes," she purred.

"I need to fuck you," Gideon said as he bit down hard on her inner thigh.

She wanted him to claim her, to show her how much he'd missed her. Mackenzie needed this. She could hear the chair move again and when she looked at Gideon, she saw him naked. His tan chest was still toned into lean muscle, his stomach tight with ripples formed from dedicated sit-ups. But she wanted to see the main attraction. He gripped it in his palm and Mackenzie saw her prize. Gideon's hard cock had a pearlized bead of pre-cum on the velvety tip. She'd kill to taste him. Mackenzie had almost forgotten the girth and length of his dick and was eager to feel him inside her — where he belonged. Then, Mackenzie became emotional. It was as though a switch had been flipped. She boiled with anger and resentment. Love and hate burned through her. Two years of heartache and misery surfaced.

"Baby, are you okay?" Gideon asked in a whisper. The passionate moment turned tender and sweet. That wasn't what Mackenzie wanted or needed.

"You should never have left me," Mackenzie said in a voice she didn't recognize.

"I'm here now." Gideon leaned over to kiss her stomach. "I'm not going anywhere."

Could she trust that his statement was true or was he only saying that because he wanted to fuck her? Her brain and heart rallied up every angry memory it had sheltered. She felt her heart splinter as all the pain became unleashed from its prison. Mackenzie almost couldn't stand to look at him because she saw her past, present and future. She wanted him to make her forget everything. Tears slid down her face.

"Mac, baby," Gideon cooed as he positioned himself at her entrance. He hesitated, likely not wanting to enter without permission.

"Don't be such a pussy, Gideon. Fuck me... Like really fuck me," Mackenzie demanded. She wanted to fuck away all the hurt that had been buried and chase all her pain away.

His eyes darkened with a reignited fiery lust, and in one fluid motion, Gideon spun her around on the table, gathered her blonde hair in his fist and drove into her hard. *Finally.* Her body felt a fullness she'd longed for. Mackenzie gripped the table's edge and braced herself for Gideon's powerful thrusts.

This wasn't gentle, tender lovemaking. To Mackenzie, it was animalistic and primal. She had a desire that needed to be quenched and needed to forget everything that had happened two years ago. For her —

and she suspected for Gideon too—it was about righting wrongs and starting over. It was raw emotion in expression at its finest.

This was what she wanted—no, needed—from him. Mackenzie *needed* Gideon to prove that he craved and missed *them* as much as she did, that she wasn't alone in all of this and that he had hurt just the same.

Chapter Seven

A piercing wail from the living room shattered the quiet that surrounded Mackenzie and Gideon as they remained sweaty, limp and exhausted. She could feel Gideon's heart beating hard inside his chest as he rested on her back.

"Daddy duty calls," he said. Gideon pulled out of her and covered himself with his shirt as he went to check on his daughter.

Mackenzie caught an eye full of his cute bare ass as he hurried to her living room. She gathered her clothing as she followed him. Mackenzie watched as Gideon retrieved the crying baby from the carrier. He handled her as though she were made of glass. A happy smile never left his face as he tended to her needs. *We could've had this. This should have been us.*

"I'm going to go shower," Mackenzie announced. She needed some space to process what had just transpired between them.

When she hid in her bathroom, Mackenzie's brain came alive with worry. *What did I just do?* She climbed into her shower and allowed the hot water to beat against her back as she kicked herself for what had to have been the hottest quickie ever. *Oh, for fuck's sake.*

After she'd stewed on it for a while, she got into the shower. Mackenzie wasn't sure how to handle it as she lathered up with a sweet floral body wash. She'd made a colossal mistake, that much she did know. The last week with Gideon had been nice. They were slowly working on forging a new relationship. *But what about meeting Ian?* That man had gotten her all hot and bothered but Gideon had reaped the rewards.

Mackenzie was lost in her thoughts as she heard Gideon say, "Room for two?" He already knew the answer to that and his gorgeously naked body joined her.

She feasted her eyes on every cut piece of lean muscle. His abs and sculpted arms were by far her favorite feature. Well, that and his already-growing cock. Mackenzie tried to move back closer to the tiled wall. She wanted to put as much space between them as possible but Gideon wasn't having it.

"Baby's fed and changed. It didn't take much to get her back to sleep." Gideon smiled as he reached past her for a large bottle of shampoo. "That was incredible," he commented as the water rained down on him. Gideon helped himself to her body wash and rubbed her still-soapy loofa on his skin.

He had no problem making himself at home and it pissed Mackenzie off.

"What's wrong?" he asked.

"Everything," Mackenzie answered as she tried to shield her body. There was no point in trying to lie and pretend that she could hide in the shower. He'd seen a whole lot of her only a few moments ago.

"I wouldn't say that was the case ten minutes ago, babe," Gideon countered with closed eyes as he worked the shampoo into a lather in his dark blond hair.

"About that—" Mackenzie started.

"It was amazing." Gideon rinsed and stared at her. "I could go for seconds. How about you?"

"Gid, we really should talk," Mackenzie said as Gideon moved closer. She could see the beads of water clinging to his lightly tan skin. It took all her willpower not to lick him.

Gideon pressed her up against the tiles and kissed her neck. He squeezed her breasts and his hard cock rubbed against her stomach. Mackenzie couldn't deny that her body's immediate reaction was to climb him like a tree and relive their lusty dining room encounter.

"Baby, I've missed you so much," he whispered in her ear.

Their bodies were wet and erotically slick with soap. He took her nipple into his mouth and tugged gently with his teeth. Mackenzie cried out when Gideon found shelter for his fingers inside her. She straddled his hand and anchored her arms around his neck. Water cascaded on them both. The soft glow from the bathroom light created a romantic scene that was truly Hollywood-worthy. Mackenzie's body tightened as Gideon worked to get her off, climbing his fingers deeper inside her while his thumb pressed her sensitive bud. Her brain wanted to halt this but her throbbing pussy had other ideas. It clamped down as a hard jolt of light pierced her. The orgasm surged through her entire body. She was no match for Gideon's magic fingers. That man knew his way around her. It was as though he'd never left.

"I love when you come," Gideon growled into her ear. He brought his hand up to her neck then pulled her mouth to his. She wanted to feel him inside her again. She was in way over her head as she fell deeper into a past she didn't live in anymore. There had been many hot quickies in the shower. How many times had he gotten her off over the years they'd been together? How many times had she pleasured him here? Mackenzie's chest tightened as emotion swept through her. A strange blend of panic and lust went off inside her like a bomb. She felt starved for air...starved for Gideon.

* * * *

The sweet smell of babies never got old. Mackenzie inhaled the scent of the precious girl she held in her arms. Gideon was making them a simple lunch of grilled cheese sandwiches while she snuggled the smiling infant. Mackenzie catalogued every detail of the beautiful baby girl and fell deeper in love with her as each second passed. There was a time when that was all Mackenzie had wanted — to be a mother, to raise lots of babies with Gideon.

Mackenzie heard her cell phone buzz on the coffee table. Whoever it was could wait. It wasn't every day that one got to cradle such a darling and she intended to cherish every second.

Gideon brought two plates into the room, wearing a happy expression on his handsome face.

"How are my girls doing?" Gideon asked as he sat next to Mackenzie on the couch. He leaned over to kiss his daughter on her forehead. "I just love her so much, Mac."

"It would be hard not to," Mackenzie replied. "She's such a doll."

Together they stared at the baby and ignored their lunch.

"I always wondered what our babies would've looked like," Gideon said in a quiet voice.

"Me, too." Mackenzie felt her throat tighten.

"When Azita is a little older, we should try." Gideon wiggled eyebrows. "She'll need a brother or sister."

Mackenzie bit her tongue from responding. Her heart skipped a beat as she remembered they hadn't used a condom. She pushed the worry aside and asked, "What does her name mean? It's beautiful."

"It was the name of an ancient Persian princess. Her parents had named her before the attack that killed them." Gideon's eyes stayed trained on the baby. Mackenzie watched as he appeared to fight through a battle of emotions.

She knew that war was awful, but no one really knew just how terrible it was unless they'd seen it first-hand. Mackenzie had survived a few tours with Gideon. Each time he'd come back, it had taken a little while for him to adjust, for him to shove those feelings deep inside and pretend everything was roses until he'd left again. It shattered her heart each time, knowing he had to face that nightmare. She could see it in his eyes every now and then. He was still suffering.

"Well, the name suits her very well. And with all the pretty pink clothes you dress her in, she looks very much like a little princess." Mackenzie smiled as the baby drifted off to sleep.

"That's mostly my mother's doing. Here, I can take her." Gideon gathered her slowly from Mackenzie's arms. Instantly she missed the warmth and weight of the tiny girl. He rested the baby on the opposite couch, barricaded safely from falling with some pillows. "Now, we can eat."

Mackenzie bit off the corner of the grilled cheese sandwich she held. She felt like they should talk about everything that had happened.

"What's on your mind? You're too quiet," Gideon said as he chewed on his own sandwich.

Mackenzie swallowed then said, "Where do I begin?"

Gideon waved his deeply golden toasted sandwich. "By telling me how good this grilled cheese is," he teased. "Seriously, what's up?"

"I don't know," Mackenzie answered as she placed her sandwich back on the plate. She'd suddenly lost her appetite. "I guess I'm still trying to process everything that happened today."

"Babe, that was mind-blowing. You're so fuckin' hot," Gideon whispered as he moved closer and went for her neck. Mackenzie pulled back and rested her hands flat against his hard chest.

"I'm not sure we should've done this yet."

"Why?" Gideon leaned back with a hurt and confused expression on his face. "And it's a little late to take it back now." He laughed, though she could hear his nerves.

"I have no clue where we stand," Mackenzie said.

"I told you what I want and that's you, Mac." She believed him, but as much as Mackenzie loved hearing those words, they somehow weren't sinking in. A mental barrier kept her from accepting it — the wall she'd spent two years building.

"I just feel like we haven't really addressed why we broke up in the first place. If I'm to be totally honest, picking up where we left off just doesn't sit well with me," Mackenzie admitted. Various emotions washed across his face. She had to be strong and needed to be truthful.

"I'm a little confused, Mac. We've been talking almost every night and I thought you wanted this, that we were *good* with being together again."

"We are and we aren't, if that makes any sense at all." *Not a whole lot does.* Mackenzie felt like a see-saw. One minute she was high, completely thrilled that Gideon was back in her life. The next she was low, troubled by and reminded of the hurt he'd caused her. Nothing was even-keeled. Mackenzie could love him one minute and hate him the next. She'd desire Gideon within seconds of seeing him, then be repulsed at herself for being so quick to welcome him back in. The way Mackenzie saw it, there was just no winning.

"No, it doesn't. I've already apologized and laid all my cards out on the table," he explained in an irritated tone. "I just don't get where this is coming from. Why didn't you say something earlier?"

"Gid, I do care about you. That has never stopped. I just need to know where we stand and get a clear idea of what to expect this time."

"A clear idea?" Gideon raised his eyebrows and rubbed his bare chin. She could feel tension grow heavy between them. He had never been one who liked to talk about their relationship. God forbid the man opened up.

"How did things turn out last time?" Mackenzie unintendedly snapped. Residual anger and bitterness fueled her brain and words.

Gideon threw his hands up in the air. "That was two fucking years ago, Mac. Let it go, for Christ's sake."

How can I just let it go? She felt sick. Her belly became a queasy ball of nerves. Mackenzie knew that within minutes they'd end up fighting. They always had. *Nothing has changed.*

"You always bring up shit and want to discuss it to death," Gideon accused. "It doesn't matter how many times I apologize. I can say I'm sorry until I'm blue in the face and you'll never let it go. We both know I fucked up. I hurt you. Don't think for a damn second I didn't hate myself for leaving you. I don't live in the past like you do, Mac."

"Gid, I'm just being honest. I'm just a little gun-shy about us." *That's an understatement.* Mackenzie hated that she had to defend herself. "Trust me. I want to move on. I really do."

"But you just can't, can you? You haven't changed one bit." Gideon rose from the couch and looked away. "You're right. We shouldn't have done this. You weren't ready."

"And you were?" Mackenzie jumped up and matched his strong stance. "You thought we could pretend we're some happy little family? That we didn't need to discuss what happened? I don't give a crap if it was two years ago. You show up here unannounced and ask me to play mommy to your daughter. How do you think that makes me feel?" she spat.

"If anything, it should tell you that I still love you and need your help, that I wanted you in her life." Gideon reached down and picked up the sleeping baby, putting her into the carrier.

In what felt like mere seconds, he was gone. Mackenzie stood alone in her living room wondering just what in the hell had happened. The realization was that Gideon had left her…again.

* * * *

"Can you hand me the tape?" Tiffany asked in a muffled voice. She held a decoration in between her lips and was balancing on a small ladder.

Mackenzie gave her the tape dispenser. "It looks really good."

Tomorrow they were hosting Molly's baby shower after weeks of planning and shopping. Mackenzie wished her heart was more in it. Yesterday, after Gideon had stormed out of her home, Mackenzie had sulked for the remainder of the day.

"What's going on with you?" Tiffany asked as she climbed down and grabbed a roll of buttercup-yellow paper streamers from Mackenzie's hand.

They were decorating Mackenzie's house for the baby shower and had been working on it since before lunch time. The theme consisted of everything associated with babies. Bottles, bibs and diapers barely scratched the surface of the very cheery-looking shower. Sunny yellows and soft minty greens along with robin-egg blues and rose-petal pinks worked beautifully to create something special. Mackenzie was proud of what they'd come up with. Not knowing the gender had concerned them both when they'd started shopping, but in the end, all the colors had come together to celebrate one thing—a baby. They didn't care if the baby was a boy or a girl. They already loved that tiny human and couldn't wait for him or her to be born.

"Have you talked to Ian?" Tiffany asked. "I know he mentioned to Colin that he'd really like to get to know you better. I hope you're going to give him a shot."

Mackenzie nodded. "I've just been a little busy."

"Work being a bummer?" Tiffany frowned. "And I know I've been stressing out about Molly's baby shower. I just want it to be perfect for her."

"It will be," Mackenzie reassured Tiffany.

"I feel like I sort of screwed up her wedding and I kinda owe her."

"Yeah, that was sort of mini shit storm, wasn't it? But everything worked out."

Tiffany smiled. "And it will for you, too. Maybe you and Ian should get drinks with us. Like, a couple's night out," Tiffany offered.

"We're not a couple."

"You could be. Ian is gorgeous and you'd be stupid not to consider dating him," Tiffany teased, but there was a serious undertone in her statement. "He's perfect for you. You two complement each other well. He's fun and edgy. You're boring and normal." Tiffany giggled as she hung another paper decoration.

"Wow, thanks." Mackenzie rolled her eyes at Tiffany. "I'm not super boring, am I?"

"Well" — Tiffany bit down on the bottom of her lip — "you're not nearly as exciting as Ian, but that's what makes this so perfect. You are total wife material and could help him settle down."

"I suppose," Mackenzie answered as they migrated to her kitchen in search of food and drinks.

"Molly and Owen are perfect for one another. Molly balances Owen and vice versa. I'm good for Colin and he's my sensible other-half," Tiffany explained as she peered into the cupboards. "You only have healthy shit in here. Where's all the crappy junk food?"

"At your house," Mackenzie countered.

"Yeah, right. Colin is a health nut like you. I may exercise all the time but chocolate and carbs are my dietary staple."

"Funny, I thought coffee and vodka were."

"Vodka is made from potatoes. Potatoes are a veggie, so I'm good." Tiffany closed the cupboard door and shuffled over to the dining room table. Mackenzie sliced a few pears and mangos along with some cheese and crackers for them to snack on. She joined Tiffany at the table with the food and two wine glasses.

"See? I've got your back. Carbs and fruit. You're welcome." Mackenzie smiled as she held up what she carried.

Tiffany giggled as she poured the wine. "I think we kick ass at decorating, you know?"

"We do. It looks amazing."

"Have you talked to Moll today?"

Mackenzie shook her head. "She left me a message yesterday and I meant to call her back."

"Have you heard from Gideon?" Tiffany nibbled on a slice of pear.

"Do we need to discuss him?"

"Oh, trouble in paradise?" Tiffany raised her perfectly tweezed eyebrows. "I don't know what makes you think things can work with him. He's the past. Ian is your future."

"You're so sure about that, huh?"

"If not Ian, someone amazing is going to snatch you up. I just hope it's Ian. Colin thinks the world of him." Tiffany reached for a piece of the bright mango and eyed Mackenzie suspiciously. "Spill it."

"What?" Mackenzie was confused as she chewed on the deliciously sweet pear.

Tiffany waited as she stared at Mackenzie. "Something's up. You aren't acting normal."

"I have no idea what you're talking about," Mackenzie lied. Her voice was too high pitched, a dead giveaway that something was indeed up. "You just called me boring and normal like two seconds ago."

Tiffany huffed. "I've been your friend for a very long time. You're pretty much my sister. So, when I say that you're not acting *normal*, I'm not talking out of my ass. Just say it."

Mackenzie wasn't sure if she should. She wanted to tell someone what had happened between her and Gideon. It would be helpful to get a take on what to do next, but sadly, she knew how Tiffany would react. She was the last person Mackenzie should tell. Yet Mackenzie felt like she was going to burst if she didn't talk about her and Gideon. She needed advice, to hatch a game plan and to vent. *Why is everything so darned complicated now? It wasn't always this way, right? Shouldn't I be able to go to my friends without having to worry about defending my actions?*

"If you aren't into Ian, I totally understand," Tiffany began. "Or if this is because of..."

"What?" Mackenzie asked. She had no clue what Tiffany was suggesting.

"You know, about the baby you lost. I can't even imagine how hard that must be. You should've come to us, Mac. You didn't deserve to go through that alone." Tiffany reached across the table and squeezed Mackenzie's hand.

"I wasn't alone. Gideon was there."

"Was he? How soon after the miscarriage did he leave?" Tiffany asked with vitriol in her voice.

Mackenzie hadn't really thought about that. She'd lost their baby only a little over a week before they were expected to get married. They'd been shell-shocked and distraught—or maybe that had just been her. Perhaps she was making excuses, but Mackenzie had not been in the right frame of mind at the time to get married. They could've postponed it, but Gideon had decided their next course and it hadn't included being with her. The suddenness and shock of it hadn't truly hit Mackenzie until Tiffany had asked that question.

How long did Gideon stick around? Why am I so quick to let him back into my life?

"Mac, you just need to remember he isn't your knight in shining armor," Tiffany said as she sipped her wine. "You need someone who will be there, no matter what kind of shit life throws your way. When life hands you lemons, you need the right guy to make the lemonade."

Mackenzie laughed. Leave it to Tiffany to bestow some great words of wisdom on her. Mackenzie was the reasonable, reliable and boring one.

"You slept with him, didn't you?" Tiffany asked.

Shit. How in the hell did Tiffany figure that out? She couldn't even deny it. A fact was a fact. Mackenzie had slept with Gideon. Well, there had been no bed, no sleeping, just some of the best fucking she'd ever had.

"There's only one good thing about this." Tiffany smiled.

"And what's that?" Mackenzie asked.

"The drought is over, baby." Tiffany raised her hand and gave Mackenzie a high five.

Chapter Eight

Molly had tears in her eyes as she held up another tiny outfit that was speckled with an adorable fish pattern. "How cute is this?"

Everyone agreed. There was no doubt this little baby was going to be one well-dressed kid. Mackenzie and Tiffany looked over at each other and smiled. They'd pulled it off. This had been one spectacular event. There had been silly games, gifts, delicious food, lots of laughs and plenty of stories about labor and delivery. Molly looked wide-eyed and overwhelmed most of the time by all the information and tales the other mothers fed her.

"Look at this one," Molly said as she raised another cute onesie for them all to see.

A few more gifts were opened then the party started to die down.

Mackenzie and Tiffany handed out thank-you favors as each woman said goodbye. After the party guests had left and it was just the three of them, they plopped onto Mackenzie's couch.

"Wow, that was nuts." Molly let out a big breath and rubbed her belly. "I can't thank you guys enough. The shower was amazing."

"You deserve it, and just keep that in mind when it's our turn," Tiffany teased.

"Is there something you aren't telling us?" Molly asked with a hopeful expression.

"Oh, trust me. You guys will be the first to know when there's a bun in my oven," Tiffany replied. "If Colin had his way, we'd be popping babies out left and right. The man is insane."

Mackenzie laughed, but inside all the baby talk bummed her out. In addition to that, she was exhausted from the full day and eager to climb into bed. She hoped an exaggerated yawn would give Tiffany and Molly the hint.

"Molly, I will load everything into my car and drop it off at your place," Tiffany said. "Mac, we can get together tomorrow to clean up. I don't know about you but I'm beat."

"Me, too. I really appreciate you guys going to all this trouble. I better head home." Molly scooted awkwardly off the couch. "Do you guys think I'm going to get much bigger?" Molly asked after she managed to get to her feet.

"You've got like another month, Moll. Right?" Tiffany answered.

Molly huffed. "I'm so big as it is now. I feel like a whale."

"You are not a whale. You're a beautiful pregnant woman," Mackenzie offered from her side of the couch.

"Easy for you two to say. Neither one of you is shaped like a house." Molly pouted. "I suppose I'm just anxious to have this baby."

"Even after all those stories today? You're brave is all I have to say," Tiffany said.

Molly shook her head. "I don't know about that. I think it's more that I can't wait to experience being a mom and seeing Owen as a daddy," she gushed.

Mackenzie smiled. "You two are going to make great parents, Moll."

"I sure hope so. You two amazing friends of mine are going to be the best aunts ever." Mackenzie and Tiffany rose from the couch and hugged Molly. "Seriously, you guys are the best."

As Mackenzie walked Molly to the door, she paused as asked, "So, have you and Marcus gone out yet?"

Mackenzie frowned. "He's a very busy man, that doctor buddy of yours."

Tiffany piped in, "We had her meet Ian, though."

Molly looked surprised. "Really? How'd that go?"

"He's pretty nice, but we've only just met," Mackenzie answered.

"Oh, yeah, by the way, Mac's drought is over," Tiffany added as she leaned against the wall, looking all too pleased with herself.

"What? When?" Molly started to waddle back toward the living room. "How do I not know about this? Details now, Mac, and leave nothing out," Molly demanded.

"There's not really a whole lot to say." Mackenzie tucked her leg under her as she got comfortable again on the couch.

"She's lying. Go on, Mac. Tell her," Tiffany urged as she squeezed in between them.

"Out with it," Molly ordered with a huge smile. Then her expression changed. "Gideon?"

Tiffany nodded before Mackenzie could respond. "Can you believe it, Moll?"

Molly scowled at Mackenzie. "Why? I mean, I thought we were focusing our efforts on someone new. Are you and Gideon back together now?"

"Nope," Tiffany answered. "They basically banged and got into a fight. Go figure. Right, Moll?" Tiffany threw Mackenzie an annoyed look. "I told her not to mess around with him. She needs to give Ian a shot."

"What about Marcus?" Molly asked.

"Marcus isn't Mackenzie's type," Tiffany supplied. Mackenzie's mouth remained open, ready to speak.

"And this Ian guy is?" Molly countered. "Why is this the first I've even heard about him?" She looked over to Mackenzie. "Why is he so great?"

Tiffany smiled broadly. "He owns Blu."

Molly blinked. "That really hot new restaurant?"

"The one and only. He's also Irish."

"Damn, he may just be better than Marcus," Molly said. "What do you think of him, Mac?"

"He's nice enough."

"That's it?" Tiffany and Molly both asked in unison.

"I don't know," Mackenzie said.

"How in the heck did you end up screwing around with Gid?" Molly asked, her pretty face twisted with confusion.

"It just kinda happened," Mackenzie answered.

"Uh, no, it doesn't." Molly shook her head. "Are you going to try and make things work with him?"

Mackenzie sighed. "I tried talking to him and we sort of got into a fight."

"Because she was honest with how she felt. He's such a fucking idiot," Tiffany spat. "Mac deserves an explanation as to why he left."

Molly nodded. "I agree. I mean, it's fairly obvious that part of it was because of you two losing the baby. But he should've been there for you."

Her friends were right. Mackenzie was now even more pissed off that Gideon didn't want to discuss what had happened two years ago. She did deserve more than an apology.

"You guys are right," Mackenzie piped up. "Molly, I think I'll give Marcus a call."

Tiffany glared at her playfully. "What about Ian?"

"I'm going to call him, too," Mackenzie answered with a smile. "I'm going to date and be merry."

"Hell yeah, that's our girl," Tiffany said as she patted Mackenzie's thigh. "And if neither of those dudes fit the bill, there are more out there and we will hunt them down."

"I have no doubt." Mackenzie rolled her eyes.

Molly was quiet for a moment and looked as though she were deep in thought. "What about Gideon?"

"What about him?" Tiffany said in a harsh tone.

"Well, I highly doubt that's over. Right, Mac?" Molly searched Mackenzie's eyes. "Sure, you had a fight, but he'll be back. Then what?" Molly's voice hummed with genuine concern.

"I don't know, Moll." Mackenzie bit down on her lip. "I still care about him. I think I always will."

"We know," Tiffany said with annoyance. "I think you need to seriously stop living in the past and think about your future."

Didn't Gid tell me the same thing? She was sort of beginning to get tired of being told what to do and how to live.

"I do agree Gideon can't just waltz back into your life, Mac, especially without discussing everything." Molly reached for Mackenzie. "He owes you that, at the very least. And Tiffany's right. Maybe you need to quit living in the past."

"I am not trying to live in the past," Mackenzie defended herself. "You know, you guys didn't always hate him."

Tiffany and Molly both frowned at her.

"Yeah, only after he broke your heart," Tiffany supplied. "But if I'm to be perfectly honest, I'm not sure I ever fully liked him."

"There was a time when I didn't mind Gideon, but as much as I hate to admit it, Tiff's right...again. After he hurt you the way he did, I sort of lost all respect for him," Molly added. "He doesn't deserve to be with you."

"But I *loved* him. You didn't have to," Mackenzie said.

"We know, but you're still in love with him," Molly replied. "That's the problem."

Mackenzie exhaled. It was easy for them to tell her to move on, to get over Gideon. "How do you just stop loving someone?"

Tiffany looked over at Molly. Neither answered.

"I admit it. I do still love Gideon. I don't think I ever stopped. So, please tell me. How do I make my heart not care about him?" Mackenzie hadn't realized the potency of her question. It didn't matter how many guys she dated, Gideon would always reside somewhere in her heart. She'd always love him.

* * * *

Mackenzie walked around with a large black trash bag and tossed away various pieces of garbage left over from the baby shower. Tiffany and Molly had offered to come back and help, but Mackenzie needed the distraction. Cleaning was her go-to therapy. It ranked right up there with retail therapy when she was down in the dumps and needed to feel better. Her house now sparkled and just about every single piece of trash from the party had been picked up.

She had just grabbed another piece when her doorbell buzzed. Mackenzie placed the bag on the ground and headed toward her living room. She had no idea who could be visiting her. She prayed it wasn't Gideon.

Mackenzie opened the door and found Ian standing there looking every bit as handsome as she remembered from the other night. It was a huge surprise.

"Ian, hi," Mackenzie greeted him. His dark-blond hair was perfectly tousled and he was dressed casually in jeans and a Seattle Mariner baseball tee.

"I know this is very forward of me. I happened to be in the neighborhood and wanted to pay you a visit," he said with a sheepish smile. "These are for you." He handed her a bright bouquet filled with autumn colors of burnt orange, red and yellow.

"Thank you. These are gorgeous." Mackenzie inhaled their scent. "Come on in." Ian followed her inside.

"Lovely home, Mackenzie," Ian commented as he stood and surveyed her living room. "Lots of character and charm."

"I love this house, but I think you're the one with all the charm," Mackenzie flirted as she went to put the flowers in a vase. "Please make yourself comfortable," she called out.

Mackenzie wanted to kick herself. She wasn't any good at flirting and found that she was in way over her head with a guy like Ian. He was of a different caliber and the playing field wasn't exactly even.

"Fancy ordering a pizza?"

Mackenzie scolded herself for not having more self-confidence. She wasn't the hottest thing on the block, but she wasn't too bad either. She calmed her nerves and returned to the living room where Ian had made himself quite comfortable on her couch. Mackenzie teased, "A chef wanting pizza?"

"Everyone — even chefs — love pizza." Ian winked.

"You have a point there." Mackenzie motioned for them to sit. "So, exactly how did you end up in my neighborhood?"

"I'm not a very good liar, am I?" Ian laughed. Mackenzie loved the sound of his voice. Now she totally understood why Tiffany went crazy over accents. They were hot, especially Irish brogues. The way common words just rolled off an Irishman's tongue was magical, to say the least.

"Colin?"

"You guessed right, love. He was a good mate and told me where to find you."

"I've been meaning to call," Mackenzie lied.

"We're obviously both terrible liars," he pointed out. "I asked Colin to furnish me with your address. I hope you don't think I'm some sort of nutter."

"No, it's normal for a guy who've I only just met to show up unannounced at my doorstep. Nothing strange about that at all."

"Valid point. I really enjoyed meeting you the other night." Ian scooched closer to her and Mackenzie froze. A zing shot straight through her. The man projected a sexy aura that both captivated and frightened her. Ian's hand found the back of her neck and guided her to him. Before Mackenzie could react, Ian's mouth was on hers.

After Ian released her, Mackenzie's body hummed. There was no doubt that she was attracted to him but it all seemed so rushed. Her mind had a difficult time keeping up.

Ian stared back at her and said, "I hope you don't mind, but I've been wanting to do that since I said goodbye to you."

Mackenzie traced her lips. She was stunned by the kiss and a sudden onset of nervousness filled her. "You still want that pizza?" she asked.

* * * *

The bell rang and all her students stood semi-neatly near the door. It had been a long day. Luckily, the weather had held up and the kids had been able to go out for recess. Mackenzie was worn out and just as eager as they were to go home. School had only started last month but she found herself already looking forward to the holiday break.

Her cell phone chimed as she shut the door to her classroom.

"Hello?" she answered, as she began to place the tiny chairs onto the tables.

"You know what today is?" Molly asked excitedly on the other end.

Mackenzie racked her brain, but she had no idea. "No, what?"

"It's the official start of fall."

"I don't think it is," Mackenzie countered. "It's not even the end of October."

"Uh, I just saw a sign for pumpkin spice lattes. It's autumn now." Molly laughed. "Wanna grab one with me?"

"Oh, I got ya. It's like when eggnog lattes or peppermint mochas are the official kick-off to the holiday season. When will your awful UGG boots be making an appearance?"

"They already have," Molly replied. "I'm wearing them right now."

Mackenzie laughed. "Sure. I'll be done here in a few minutes. Where are you at?"

Molly answered, "I'm at my studio finishing up on some edits. I called Tiff, too. Why don't you grab three of those lovely pumpkin lattes and get your butt over here?"

"Sounds like a plan. See ya in a little bit." Mackenzie ended the call and shoved her phone back in her pocket. She finished with cleaning up her room and headed out. The thought of a pumpkin spice latte sounded fabulous and so did a little girl time with her besties.

The drive over didn't take long as the traffic was light. The true miracle happened when there was no line at the coffee shop. She was in and out in a flash and scooting down the street toward her destination—her besties.

Armed with a sack of freshly baked cookies and balancing a cardboard drink carrier with three pumpkin spice lattes complete with whipped cream and a generous sprinkle of cinnamon on the tops, Mackenzie waited for Molly to open the door.

"Yay, you brought goodies," Molly cheered when she saw the paper sack. "Tiff is on her way now."

The studio was dimly lit. The indigo sky could be seen through the enormous floor-to-ceiling windows. Mackenzie had always loved the space. It gave an ample view of the gorgeous city of Seattle below. They'd shared so many good times here—late night Chinese food runs, dancing to their favorite eighties childhood songs and finding out that Molly was pregnant. The studio held a lot of memories.

Molly waddled over to the large table where many meals and gossip had been shared. "So, how was work?" she asked as Mackenzie handed her one of the lattes. Molly quickly put it to her lips and released a long sigh. "This is so good. I've been looking forward to it all day."

Mackenzie took a sip and agreed. The blend of flavors with the creaminess of the latte was absolutely delicious. "Work was okay."

"You got anything special planned for Halloween with the kiddos?"

Mackenzie and Molly sat across from one another. "I'm thinking of doing this tissue paper pumpkin design I saw on Pinterest. I try to change up the crafts every holiday. Fingers crossed my students will like the project."

"Oh, they will. So, what are we doing for Halloween? It falls on a Friday and I was thinking we're long overdue for a *Friendship Friday*. Might be fun to pass out candy at your house."

Mackenzie nodded. "Let's see what Tiff thinks, but I'm game."

"Speak of the devil." Molly smiled and looked past Mackenzie.

"Hey, girls," Tiffany announced as she approached with a large, flat cardboard box. "The door was unlocked. I brought a pizza."

"You're a godsend." Molly peeked into the box. "And it's my favorite—pineapple with jalapenos." Molly hugged Tiffany.

"You're welcome." Tiffany draped her purse on the back of one of the chairs. "Mac, you brought pumpkin lattes and are those cookies?" Tiffany peered into the bag. "You're amazing," she said after removing a chocolate chip cookie from the sack.

"Tiff, Mac and I were just discussing Halloween. You got any plans?" Molly asked as she helped herself to a slice of pizza.

"I doubt we've got anything going on. Why? What are you two thinking?"

"*Friendship Friday* and passing out candy at Mac's place." Molly held her pizza and chewed on the cheesy slice.

Tiffany reached for her latte and took a sip. "I'm down for sure. I could use some girl time."

"Fridays used to be my favorite. That's the one drawback of married life," Molly admitted.

"We all get so busy now, but I agree," Tiffany said. "We need to make time for it and each other."

"Moll's about to be a mom, so I doubt we'll really be able to commit to *Friendship Fridays* on a regular basis. We should try to have it at least once a month, though," Mackenzie suggested.

"True," Tiffany agreed then switched gears in the conversation. "Have you by chance heard from Ian?" She darted her eyes away.

"Hmm, I wonder how you knew about that?" Mackenzie teased.

Tiffany looked at her. "Okay, fine. Ian asked Colin where you lived."

"What if this Ian guy is a weirdo?" Molly interjected. "Mac, remember when you warned me about Owen?"

"Molly, the jury's still out on Owen. Rest assured, Ian is not," Tiffany joked. "He's rather lovely, isn't he, Mac?" Tiffany winked.

Mackenzie replayed her little impromptu visit from Ian the previous night. *That man knows how to kiss. That's for sure.* She traced her still slightly bruised lips.

"Well, I take it you worked on trying to forget Gideon?" Tiffany asked as she raised her latte. "Amen."

"I didn't do anything with Ian," she said.

"I need to meet this Ian," Molly said with a scowl. "Is Marcus out of the running now?"

Mackenzie shook her head. "I wouldn't say that. He's just such a busy man. I don't really think he even has the time to date right now."

"Why did Marcus even bother messaging you then?" Tiffany asked. "Ian is serious about getting to know Mac. He's super interested. You should've heard him talking to Colin."

"Oh gosh, what did he say?" Mackenzie felt her cheeks grow warm.

"Besides how gorgeous he thinks you are?" Tiffany gave her sly smile. "He's totally into you."

"There's just one problem with him," Mackenzie started.

"Seriously, Mac?" Tiffany complained. "You're always looking for something."

"Let her speak," Molly said. "I'd like to know."

"He's quite charming, but Ian sort of moves a little faster than I'd like," Mackenzie admitted.

"You're such a prude. I swear," Tiffany said as she rolled her eyes. "You guys aren't getting any younger."

"Yeah, but I think Mac would like to get to know him a little more, right?" Molly looked over at Mackenzie, who nodded.

"There's definitely chemistry and that man can kiss."

"So, what's the problem?" Tiffany asked.

"He's not really taking the time to get to know me, if that makes sense. We hardly talked last night."

"That's only because Ian sees what he likes and isn't afraid to go after it. That's how these successful business guys are. Look at Colin. He knew a good thing when he saw it," Tiffany joked as she batted her mascara-thick lashes at them.

"Owen was sort of the same way. He knew instantly that he wanted to be with me. I was the one having trouble with it all. He was very patient with me, bless his heart," Molly added with a happy smile. "I love that man and have no idea how he deals with being with me."

"He's a good one. That's for sure," Mackenzie replied. Owen had been more than patient with Molly. The man was nearly a saint for putting up with her friend's antics.

"Which is why you should see Marcus again. Owen picked him out, remember?" Molly urged. "That has to count for something."

"Marcus is all wrong for Mac," Tiffany argued. "We've already hashed that out."

"I'm just saying she should at least play the field a little and not settle on Ian," Molly suggested.

The two carried on as if Mackenzie wasn't sitting right there. *Hello?*

"I'd hate to see her miss out on a catch like Ian," Tiffany explained as she sipped her latte. "She needs someone who isn't afraid to chase her."

"He sounds more like a hungry wolf than a prospective husband," Molly countered.

Mackenzie watched Tiffany and Molly battle it out over her potential suitors while she ate a slice of pizza. Molly continued to defend Marcus and even added that she had a few other men she wanted Mackenzie to meet. Tiffany pushed for Ian and claimed that he was the *one*. *Seriously?* If nothing else, this little argument was entertaining.

Dinner and a show.

Chapter Nine

Mackenzie was fully absorbed in a bestselling romance book. The sexy and inviting cover was one of Molly's, and it was turning out to be a fantastic read. Her cell buzzed and she sent it an evil glare. The scene that Mackenzie was enjoying was rather hot and she didn't appreciate the interruption.

"Hello?" she answered and closed the book.

"Mac, it's Marcus."

"Hi, Marcus. How are you?" Mackenzie was a little surprised to hear from him. *Why does he insist on calling me Mac?* It wasn't as though he knew her. They weren't even friends.

"I've been on-call all week and have been meaning to reach out," he explained. "I was wondering if you'd be interested in dinner tomorrow?"

"Sure," Mackenzie answered. She owed it to Molly and Owen to try to go out with Marcus one more time. She hadn't felt any butterflies when she'd met him or any tingles hearing his voice now. *'Give him a chance.'* Mackenzie could almost hear Molly in her head.

"Wonderful. I was thinking we could try that hip, new place — Blu. One of the ER docs here was just telling me it's amazing. Have you been there yet?"

"Yes," Mackenzie managed. "I went not too long ago with some friends." Mackenzie decided it was best not to mention lip-locking with Ian. Maybe she should suggest an alternative restaurant.

"Is it any good?" Marcus asked, trying to make small talk.

This was her opportunity. "It was incredible," she answered with honesty and blew it. *Damn.*

"Fantastic. I'll make our reservation now."

"Great." Mackenzie hoped and prayed Ian wouldn't be there tomorrow. It was mid-week. Maybe he'd have the night off.

After they hung up, her phone rang again. *Looks like this book is going to have to wait.* Mackenzie set the paperback aside.

"Hello?"

"Hey, you," Molly's perky voice said.

"What's up, Moll?"

"Oh, nothing."

"So, by any chance did you have a hand in Marcus calling me just now?"

"Maybe. You can't really blame me, can you?" Molly asked.

"He just asked us to meet for dinner tomorrow."

"Nice. Where at?"

Mackenzie let out an obnoxious laugh. "Take a guess."

"I have no idea. The Space Needle?"

"Blu."

"Oh shit. Like, Ian's Blu?" Molly asked.

"Yep," Mackenzie confirmed. "What if Ian's there?"

"Who cares? It's not like he's your boyfriend. You're a sexy single lady and allowed to date, Mac," Molly explained.

"I just got done making out with Ian on my couch the other night. How does it look dining with Marcus at Ian's restaurant?" Mackenzie countered. The whole dating thing was proving to be a whole lot harder than she'd imagined.

"Good point. Well, damn. This sort of backfired, didn't it?"

"Just a little."

Molly released a heavy sigh. "You know, maybe it won't be so bad. It's only dinner."

"It's a date, Molly."

"It's only food, not a marriage proposal," Molly reminded her. "If you see Ian, simply introduce him to Marcus. Just act casual and friendly. Please, for the love of God, don't make a scene."

Mackenzie huffed. "Make a scene? Are you serious? I'm the last one who would make any kind of scene."

"You tend to get weird when you're uncomfortable. Just play it cool."

"Maybe I should just cancel," Mackenzie suggested.

"No, you should go. If you're not feeling Marcus after this date, then I'll let it go."

Mackenzie chuckled. "In that case, I'll go for sure."

* * * *

Does he have to keep looking at his phone? What is so bloody important? Mackenzie sipped her third lemon drop Grey Goose Martini. She stared across the table at a very distracted Marcus. The guy was handsome enough but had no social manners whatsoever. Mackenzie's cell phone was tucked away in her purse, ready for her to do this whole date thing. Instead, she was dying of boredom, Marcus hadn't looked up from his phone since she had finished her last Martini. His plate was in front of him, untouched and cold now. Mackenzie pushed the remaining bits of her meal around. At least the food and drinks had been excellent. That had been the only shining point of the evening.

The date had started off well enough. She'd met Marcus at Blu and she'd been a complete ball of nerves when she'd first arrived. Mackenzie had fretted all day that she might run into Ian and things would be super uncomfortable. She'd decided to play it cool as Molly had instructed. Marcus wasn't her boyfriend and she wasn't doing anything wrong by having dinner and drinks with him. Luckily there had been no sign of Ian when they'd entered the restaurant. *Thank God for small favors.*

Marcus and Mackenzie had shared a cocktail at the bar and seemed to get along. Though if Mackenzie were completely honest with herself, the conversation did feel a little forced. There wasn't much chemistry either. Marcus was a really good-looking man. He was dressed well and carried himself with confidence. There just wasn't any type of connection. He didn't make her feel all tingly inside like either Gideon or Ian. At least she could tell Molly she'd tried.

She looked at him as she finished her drink. Mackenzie had tolerated more than enough of his rudeness and was beyond ready to go home. It was long past time to say something.

"Marcus, I have to ask what is so important on that darn phone that you can't pull yourself away?"

Marcus' gaze shifted away and focused on her. "I'm so sorry. There's this patient I'm monitoring," he tried to explain but something seemed off, as though he were lying to her.

Mackenzie nodded. "Maybe you should go then," she suggested and saw Ian walking toward their table. *Shit.*

Wearing a dark-blue chef's jacket and sexy crooked smile, he greeted her. "Mackenzie, I didn't realize you were here." The way the sound of her name rolled off his tongue made her toes curl and her tummy grow nervous. That hot as hell accent of his was going to be the death of her. Ian seemed delighted to see her then turned his gaze toward Marcus, whose attention was back on his phone. "You've brought a friend."

"Yes," she answered. "This is Marcus."

Marcus mumbled something then looked up at Ian. His face twisted in confusion and he said, "Can I order something else? I wasn't exactly feeling this fish. Thanks." He returned to his phone.

Mackenzie was beyond embarrassed and made a mental note to kill Molly. "Marcus, this is Ian, the owner of Blu," she stated. Mackenzie felt as though she were scolding one of her kindergarteners, reminding him to use his manners.

Marcus nodded. "You have a beautiful restaurant. I'd still like to order something else. That fish just wasn't spectacular." Marcus glared hard at Ian, who simply smiled and seemed unaffected by the blatant rudeness.

Ian rested one hand on the back of her chair. "No problem, mate. I'll have your waitress come by and take your order." Ian looked to her and winked. Ian bent down and his lips grazed her earlobe as he whispered, "I'll call you later, love."

Mackenzie saw it then. These two males knew what was up. This was the start of a pissing contest and she wanted no part of it. *Damn men and their stupid egos.* Mackenzie watched as Marcus paused and placed his phone on the table. A picture of a very pretty woman stared back at her. *Patient, huh?* Mackenzie might be a lot of things but stupid wasn't one of them. *Why waste another minute of my time and endure more of this torture?* She rose from the table and said goodnight as politely as humanly possible. Her teeth were still clenched as she walked away from the dining area and toward the entrance of Blu. She was grateful she'd met him there and could drive herself home.

"Leaving already?" Ian stopped her as she neared the door. Mackenzie watched a mixture of concern and delight move in his eyes. "What are you doing with that bloke anyway, Mackenzie?"

Mackenzie bit down on her lip. *What am I really doing?* Ian grabbed her elbow and led her away from the door. She had no idea where he was taking her.

"He didn't even have the decency to walk you to your car," Ian growled under his breath.

"I appreciate your concern for my well-being, but I'm a big girl, Ian," Mackenzie defended herself.

"Sweetheart, I have no doubt you could take care of yourself. That's not how any decent man should treat a lady, especially one as lovely as you." Ian paused and turned her to face him. The hallway held a dim blue color from all the lights in the dining area. Ian stroked her cheek with his thumb as he looked down at her mouth with obvious hunger.

Just kiss me already. Mackenzie couldn't explain the magnetic attraction she had with this man. It almost rivaled how Gideon made her feel. She feared one thing. As fast as it burned and raged, would it fade just as quickly? But slow burning didn't mean shit either. Take her and Gideon, for example. That love had burned long and slow but had been nearly devastated in the blink of an eye. *Fuck it.* Mackenzie was tired of playing everything safe and by the book. *Where has all that gotten me?* Nowhere. It had left her alone and *single.*

Mackenzie didn't have to reach too high to make her lips meet his. The look of pleasant surprise on Ian's face caused a happy thrill inside her as she reminded herself to close her eyes when kissing him. He pressed her against the wall. There was no denying the instant spark that flickered between them. Intense feelings of hunger started to boil inside her.

Ian ran his hand down her body as he took possession of her mouth and pushed the kiss deeper. *God, I need this.* The strength behind his kiss didn't give her any mixed signals. This wasn't a man distracted by a damn cell phone or one who was unwilling to give her the answers she needed. Ian knew what he wanted and he made no apologies as he showed it. He traveled his hand up her thigh and parted her legs with his body. Ian traced the outline of her mound through her drenched panties. Mackenzie bit his bottom lip and tugged it. It was all the invitation he needed. Ian slipped a finger inside her, then another. Her body's immediate response to his touch went into a wild frenzy as she straddled his hand. For a split second, Mackenzie worried someone might cross their path and witness them all tangled up in each other. It wasn't like her at all to act like some wanton woman with no willpower or shame.

Ian used his other hand to play with her breasts and he teased her nipple until it stood at attention. He rolled his thumb over the sensitive bud. Mackenzie would kill for him to take her nipple into his mouth. He grinned at her as he worked his fingers faster inside. Mackenzie's brain grew fuzzy as she felt her body rock with his hand while he worked at getting her off. An orgasm was on the horizon. It was building up and intensifying. Ian moved his thumb over her clit and pressed down on her throbbing button. Mackenzie's legs turned to water and she found she could barely stand as a hard wave crashed inside her. The wall was her saving grace as it supported her.

Ian wore a satisfied expression and whispered in her ear, "I'm a much better dinner date, love."

* * * *

Friday. Not only was it Halloween, but Mackenzie and her besties were also about to celebrate a long overdue and much needed *Friendship Friday*. She was antsy to share everything that had happened only a few days prior. She was still reeling from her very sexy encounter with Ian and couldn't wait to hear the girls weigh in on it.

Mackenzie had stocked up on candy for trick or treaters and even decorated her front porch with more than a few pumpkins and cotton cobwebs. The golden light of the afternoon sun made everything look perfectly festive and she was quite proud of her efforts. She'd also managed to incorporate the elements of spooky ghosts and witches with adorable fall pieces, like leaves, hay bales and even a rather handsome scarecrow. *Thank you again, Pinterest.*

As she stood there surrounded by the bright orange jack-o-lanterns, Mackenzie inhaled the moist scents of fall. The air carried with it a blend of spice and sweetness. The leaves were clinging to the trees in their last hoorah in a variety of burnt tones of red, gold and orange. It wouldn't be long before they littered the sidewalks and worse, her yard. Mackenzie loved this time of the year and found herself a little more excited about the upcoming holidays than she'd been in a very long time. She could thank Ian for that. The other night, as hot as hell as it had been, marked the beginning of something new, at least as far as Mackenzie was concerned. She wanted to date Ian. It was as simple as that. Okay, she wanted to do a lot more, but admitting that she wanted to see him was a step in the right direction. She even planned on thanking Tiffany. Her friend had been right. She needed to stop living in the past. There was no going back or trying to fix what had gone wrong between her and Gideon. Mackenzie deserved a shot at something real, something like both Tiffany and Molly had.

Mackenzie smiled as she saw Tiffany's shiny SUV pull up to the curb. She watched as Tiffany and Molly got out and made their way along her brick path.

"Hey, guys," Mackenzie called out.

They both greeted her with happy smiles as they came onto her porch.

"It looks awesome, all spooky and cute," Tiffany exclaimed as she touched one of the glowing pumpkins that had a wide and lopsided grin. "I really miss carving pumpkins."

"Hey, in a few years, you will be helping me carve jack-o-lanterns with my little pumpkin," Molly said as she rubbed her enormous belly.

"Moll, if Charlie Brown asks, you swallowed the Great Pumpkin," Tiffany teased. "But what an adorable one he or she will be."

"I've got candy for when the kiddos start showing up, which will be any minute." Mackenzie led the way inside. "I got us a few pizzas."

Molly groaned, "I'm still recovering from that last pizza."

"Crap, I forgot about the heartburn," Mackenzie replied.

"I brought a movie and a little something for us." Tiffany held up a bottle. "Being preggers sucks, doesn't it, Molly?"

"I hate you guys," Molly groaned. "I really miss adult beverages."

"I have cider for you, Moll," Mackenzie offered.

"It's not the same as that," she motioned to the bottle Tiffany had placed on the counter.

"Stop your whining, mama. That baby is going to be here like in a month or so." Tiffany patted Molly's stomach.

"Gosh, around turkey day, right?" Mackenzie asked. "Moll, you'd better have your precious little one either before or after Thanksgiving. I don't want to go to all that trouble cooking if you're going to be busy popping out your own turkey."

"Good grief." Molly rolled her eyes. "Speaking of turkey day, are we having it here like we always do?"

Mackenzie shrugged. "I don't see why not, unless either of you want to take the reins this year?"

"Not me. I can't cook a thing," Tiffany said. "I look forward to Mac's Thanksgiving dinner every year."

"Even though you're always forced to peel potatoes?" Mackenzie asked with a smile.

"It's a price worth paying for those amazing pumpkin and pecan pies," Tiffany replied.

"Dang, I want pie now—and turkey," Molly commented as they migrated to the living room.

Before Mackenzie could sit down, the doorbell rang. She raced to the door and was greeted by nearly a dozen children all dressed in costumes. After filling their plastic pumpkins and sacks with some treats, Mackenzie returned to the living room.

"I have a feeling we're going to get a lot of kiddos tonight. The weather is amazing."

"Last year it rained and we got like, what? Maybe ten kids all night?" Tiffany asked as she combed her fingers through her long, dark hair and twirled it into a messy bun.

That was what Mackenzie loved about *Friendship Friday*. It was when they could be truly comfortable with no makeup and in just their jammies. Of course, it was fun to get all dressed up and go out, but sometimes staying in and laughing the night away in fuzzy slippers and messy buns was the best thing ever.

Molly looked uncomfortable, despite the black stretchy pants she wore and silly tee with purple bats on it. *The joys of pregnancy*. Mackenzie would love to experience it, not just the teensy sneak peek she'd gotten. Molly didn't realize how lucky she was and Mackenzie envied her in many ways. Granted, she was also thrilled for her bestie, who truly deserved to be happy and was going to make a wonderful mother.

Mackenzie just wished it were her who looked as though she'd swallowed a pumpkin whole.

The doorbell chimed again and Mackenzie went back there. Tiffany was behind her and giggled at all the adorable children.

"How flipping cute are they?" she asked after they'd closed the door.

"You should've seen the kids in my class today. Some of the costumes were super creative and not like anything we wore as kids," Mackenzie explained. "One little girl was dressed up as a 'Crazy Cat Lady'. She had stuffed cats pinned to her little terry cloth robe and wore rollers in her hair. It was beyond adorable and super funny."

"That's hilarious," Tiffany said as she poured herself some of the wine she'd brought. "Moll, you want a slice of pizza?" she called out.

"Yes, please," Molly answered.

"This is nice, isn't it?" Mackenzie asked. It felt great having her friends together again, just the three of them. *God, I've missed this.*

"We need to make more of an effort to try and do this often," Tiffany said as she put pizza on three plates. Mackenzie loaded the plates on her arms as Tiffany grabbed the wine.

"I wanted to thank you," Mackenzie said as they walked back to the living room.

"Why?" Tiffany smiled but looked confused.

"For introducing me to Ian," Mackenzie said. She could feel herself blush.

Tiffany raised her eyebrows. "Really? Get your ass in the living room. We want all the deets."

Mackenzie laughed as they got situated on the couch and floor. She handed Molly her plate and cider, which she frowned at. Tiffany joined Molly on the couch. Mackenzie crossed her legs and sat on the floor directly across from Tiffany and Molly.

"Mac has a story she'd like to share with us," Tiffany announced.

Molly focused her attention on the pizza and Mackenzie. "Go on. I'm listening."

Mackenzie took in a large breath and prepared to share her story about the other night at Blu when her doorbell rang. *Damn.*

"Just put an 'out of candy' sign on the door," Tiffany yelled as Mackenzie finished passing out more.

"Oh, stop. It's once a year," she said as she returned. "Where was I?" Mackenzie took her place back on the floor.

"Just spill it before another horde of kids ruins story time," Molly joked.

Mackenzie giggled. "So, I went out with Marcus the other night."

Molly nodded and Tiffany rolled her eyes.

"Seriously? Gosh, why?" Tiffany asked.

"He asked me out and I wanted to give him one more shot," she answered.

"That's sort of my doing," Molly admitted.

"Stop trying to set her up with him," Tiffany ordered with a smile. "Ian's the one she needs to date."

"I'm getting there, jeesh." Mackenzie laughed. "So, Marcus and I are like never happening again, just FYI. He was on his phone the entire time."

"That's rude as hell," Tiffany said as she sipped her wine.

"Maybe it was for work, but even so it's rude," Molly agreed.

"He did claim it was one of his patients but I saw the profile pic of some very hot redhead when he had his phone on the table," Mackenzie explained. "Here's the other thing. There was like no spark or connection with him. I really wanted to like him, Moll."

"I know," Molly replied as she wiped her mouth. "What an ass, though. Who talks to another chick while on a date?"

"Who cares? We're done with him now. So, tell us about Ian," Tiffany urged with anticipation in her espresso-bean-colored eyes.

Mackenzie went on to explain to them about how Marcus was rude to Ian and how well Ian had handled it…then how he'd handled her.

"Holy hotness, are you kidding me?" Molly fanned herself.

"I told ya. I knew Ian was the right pick," Tiffany added with a wink. "That's like super-hot, Mac."

"I'm excited to see where this goes. Here's to dating and hopefully finding the right guy." Mackenzie raised her glass and they all clinked them together.

"I hate to rain on your lovely parade, but have you heard from Gid?" Molly asked.

Tiffany threw her an annoyed look. "Why do you always do this? Why are you bringing *him* up?"

Molly shrugged. "I don't know. Mac, did he ever text or call you after that fight?"

Mackenzie nodded. "He's texted a few times," she admitted. "I've sort of ignored him."

"Good for you," Tiffany complimented her with a happy smile.

"I've been busy with stuff, too, so it was kinda easy to not reply."

The doorbell buzzed and all three hurried to answer it. Mackenzie pulled the door back and there stood Gideon.

"Speak of the devil," Tiffany spat.

"You were talking about me?" Gideon asked with a sexy tease in his voice. A happy light filled his eyes.

"What are you doing here, Gid?" Mackenzie asked as she peered down at Gideon's daughter. She was tucked into her carrier, sleeping peacefully and dressed as a kitty.

Mackenzie's smile disappeared when Gideon said, "I see you both had the same costume idea." She readjusted the cat ears on the top of her head. Mackenzie had decided to dress up, just a little in the spirit of the holiday. She'd worn some whiskers at work but had washed all that off before her friends had arrived for *Friendship Friday*.

"She's adorable," Molly cooed from behind Mackenzie.

"Thanks, Molly," Gideon replied. "I hear congrats are in order."

Mackenzie turned her attention to Molly, who beamed with delight. "Bring her inside so we can get a better look," Molly insisted.

Mackenzie led the way back inside the house and into the dining room. Tiffany acted cold toward Gideon after he'd set the carrier on the dining table. Gideon worked on unbuckling the baby and lifted her from the carrier. Mackenzie felt her heart squeeze as she watched Gideon tenderly kiss the baby's head.

"Want to hold her?" Gideon offered to Molly.

"I can use the practice for sure," Molly joked as Gideon handed the baby off to her. "Oh, my God, she smells amazing." Molly smiled as she held Azita like an old pro.

"See, Moll? You're going to be such a good mom," Mackenzie assured her. Tiffany remained quiet and kept her focus on Gideon.

"Tiffany, you need to hold this precious little girl," Molly said. "You're going to want one after you do."

Tiffany shook her head. "I'm good, thanks." Tiffany looked at Mackenzie, clearly begging her to get rid of Gideon.

Mackenzie could feel the awkward tension brewing between Tiffany and Gideon. Molly was in pure baby bliss and oblivious to it all.

Gideon moved to closer to Mackenzie and whispered, "Can we talk?"

"Now?" Mackenzie felt Tiffany's eyes on her. This wasn't the first time she'd been caught in the middle of Gideon and Tiffany. Molly was quick to forgive and seemed distracted by Gideon's daughter.

"Tiffany, let's take her in the living room," Molly suggested. So, she wasn't nearly as oblivious as Mackenzie had thought. Tiffany huffed as she glared at Gideon and followed Molly.

Gideon laughed. "She still hates me."

"You can't really blame her."

"I know," he said. "Mac, we need to talk."

"Well, I'm not sure if now is really the best time." Mackenzie felt her stomach twist in uneasy knots. Only moments ago, she had been sharing with her besties how into Ian she was and now here was Gideon. As much as she tried to step away from her past, it kept pulling her back into it. It was like a net that she was caught up in and couldn't quite escape from.

"I've been trying to find a way to tell you how sorry I am," Gideon said in a low voice. "I acted like a complete asshole last week."

"You kinda did," Mackenzie agreed.

"But do you see my side at all?" Gideon grabbed her arms and searched her eyes. "I know you want to know why things ended with us. I just hate revisiting the past."

"But we have a lot of unresolved issues there." Mackenzie met his stare.

"You're completely right. The thing with the past is that there's no going back there. We can't change it."

There was no denying the man had a point. It didn't change how Mackenzie felt. She liked resolution — more like needed it.

Gideon hugged her. "I understand if you don't want to be with me again, but can we at least be friends? I need you in my life, Mac." The words broke her heart.

Couldn't we be friends? Could I date Ian and be Gideon's buddy? Who in the hell am I trying to kid? There was no such thing as men and women being *just friends*.

Chapter Ten

"Friends? He wants to be *friends*? You've got to be kidding me," Tiffany said with annoyance. "Please tell me you told him to shove it up his ass."

Mackenzie released a heavy sigh. Gideon had only left about ten minutes before. There had been no more trick or treaters demanding candy and Molly looked beyond exhausted as she yawned. *Friendship Friday* was coming to an end a whole lot earlier than Mackenzie had planned.

"His daughter is precious and he seems like a really good dad," Molly added then she covered her mouth as another yawn escaped her.

"He is." Mackenzie couldn't deny that. Gideon was a good father and he would've been an amazing dad to their baby. It was the whole fiancé part he'd fallen short on.

Tiffany rolled her eyes. "So what if he's a fucking a saint for adopting that baby? He's still an asshole. Let's not forget that, ladies."

"Tiff, don't worry, I'm still going to date Ian. Gideon just wants to be friends now," Mackenzie explained.

"For how long? Men can't just be our friends, Mac — unless they're gay. Then you can totally be besties with a dude, otherwise it's just not possible," Tiffany countered. "Last time I checked, Gideon wasn't gay."

Deep down, Mackenzie knew Tiffany was right. *Wasn't I just telling myself that only moments ago? That it isn't possible for men and women to just be friends?*

"I think it's sweet that he wants you in his life," Molly added with drooping eyes. "He still loves you, Mac. I could totally see it tonight."

"You better not start rooting for him, Molly. I'll kill you," Tiffany threatened her with a wavering stare.

"Don't worry about Gideon. I'm interested in Ian. I absolutely want to pursue that and see where it goes."

"Good. Just please keep your distance from Gideon. I don't entirely trust that he only wants to be your friend. In case you've already forgotten, he just fucked you silly last week," Tiffany pointed out.

Molly erupted into laughter. "That's right. Mac. That's one helluva a friendship if I've ever heard of one."

Mackenzie felt herself blush at the memory of their very hot encounter. "Would you two please stop?"

"See? Men and women can't be buddies. It always comes down to sex," Tiffany explained as though she were an expert on the subject.

"Do tell us, wise one," Mackenzie teased.

"I know what I'm talking about," Tiffany defended herself.

"I have no doubt that you do. I'm just saying that Gideon and I could be friends."

"In a perfect world, maybe. We'll play this your way and when shit spirals out of control, don't be surprised when I'm saying, 'I told ya so', okay?"

Molly laughed. "Isn't it usually Mac who is always telling you, 'I told ya so'? How did your roles get switched?"

"Right?" Mackenzie laughed. "I was the one giving out all the sound advice and looking after you crazy chicks like a good mother hen. What in the hell happened?"

"Well, it's our turn. We owe you," Tiffany said as her voice began sounding watery with emotion. "You've always been there for me and Molly and suffered through all those ridiculous guys we dated. You were more than supportive when I went through everything with Colin. I just want to protect you and make sure you find someone who makes you happy."

Mackenzie rose from the floor and pulled Tiffany to her. She hugged her then Molly joined in on the hug. These were her girls.

"No matter what happens, who we date or marry, no matter how many kids we all have, let's not forget this. You guys are more than just my friends. You're my sisters. Damn, I love you, bitches." Mackenzie felt the tears flow down her cheeks.

"Don't even think about wiping your snot on me," Tiffany teased.

* * * *

Her students were sluggish today and recovering from candy-induced comas from the weekend. Mackenzie wondered if giving the kiddos a shot of espresso would be frowned upon. She felt fantastic and full of pep and she wished they shared her enthusiasm. Mackenzie did her best to encourage the children to get through their lessons and found herself smiling the entire time. Even the rainy November day couldn't diminish the happiness she felt.

After Friday, Mackenzie had spent Saturday sending naughty and very dirty messages back and forth with Ian. The little romance, whether it was just a fling or the beginning of something much bigger, was fun. She felt like a new woman — young and sexy. Ian was witty and so different from any of the other men she'd dated. He pushed her to be playful and not to take life too seriously. They had made plans for dinner that week and she was counting down the days until she got to see him.

The final bell rang and she wished her students goodbye. She hummed as she finished picking up the classroom and readying to leave. Mackenzie was wiping down her whiteboard of the day's lessons when she heard a knock. She turned to see who was there and saw Gideon. He raised two paper cups containing what was more than likely her favorite coffee.

"Late afternoon latte?" Gideon walked to her and smiled.

"That's so sweet of you, thanks," Mackenzie said as she accepted one of the cups and motioned for him to sit.

"What are friends for?" Gideon replied with wink.

He is really running with this whole friend thing, isn't he? Oh well, at least our friendship includes coffee.

"My students could've used coffee today."

"Mac, they're five years old. A little young for coffee, don't ya think?" he joked with a raised eyebrow.

Mackenzie laughed. "Valid point. They were all recovering from a Halloween hangover."

"Kids aren't built the same as when we were kids. We'd trick or treat all night—no mom driving us around in a heated SUV, just our own feet hiking to all the neighborhoods, rain or snow—it didn't matter. We were on a mission for that candy. Then we'd go home and rummage through our loot and eat almost all of it that very same night. Who cared about the tummy ache? It was worth it."

"My sister and I would organize our candy from the night. We'd spend hours trading candy back and forth. She'd always sneak my candy corn, thinking I'd never notice, and I always let her get away with it, too. It was her favorite, after all, and what are big sisters for?" Mackenzie smiled at the memory. She had a lot of good ones with her sister.

"I bet you miss her," Gideon interrupted her trip down memory lane.

Mackenzie nodded. "I sure do."

"How are you doing with all of it?"

"All of what?" Mackenzie asked, confused by his question.

"You know, her death and all," Gideon reworded his question. She saw genuine and deep concern in his eyes.

She exhaled. "It's hard. I still think about her all the time, but it's getting a little easier to talk about her now. I miss her like crazy, but I'm better than I was a few months ago. Hell, I'm better than I was a few weeks ago."

"That's all we can do, just take it day by day." Gideon sipped his coffee. Mackenzie mimicked his action. The pumpkin spiced latte was delicious and hit the spot.

The sweet and creamy flavors of fall danced in her mouth and warmed her belly.

"Thanks for the latte. You didn't need to, you know," Mackenzie said.

"I wanted to." Gideon winked at her. "Who else would I rather sit and have coffee with?"

Mackenzie smiled but looked away from Gideon's deep stare. "Where's that precious little girl of yours?"

"With my mom," he answered. "I figured it'd give us a chance to talk."

"I just saw you on Friday. And thanks for that unexpected visit, by the way," Mackenzie said as she smirked in his direction. "You should've brought lattes for the girls."

"So that's how I win over Tiff?"

"I don't think there's any winning her over." Mackenzie laughed. "She was a little less than thrilled about your visit."

"I didn't realize you guys still did *Friendship Fridays*. It's pretty cool that you guys kept that tradition going."

"It's becoming fewer and further between. They've got a lot going on now with their own lives," Mackenzie said.

"You got any plans after this?" Gideon asked as he studied her.

Mackenzie looked up at the ceiling as though the answer were floating up there somewhere. *He is going to ask me to dinner, isn't he? The latte was a ploy, a caffeinated trap, and I fell for it.* She didn't want Tiffany to be right. Mackenzie wanted to prove that she and Gideon could be *friends*.

"Uh, I'm not sure," she managed when no decent excuse found its way into her brain.

"Wanna grab some food?"

"I don't know if that's such a great idea, Gid," she answered. Mackenzie didn't want to come off as scared but she worried these new friendship lines might get a tad blurry if she didn't draw them.

"Opposed to having dinner with a friend?" he teased.

Mackenzie threw him a knowing look. "Gid, are you serious about just being friends?"

"Why wouldn't I be? If that's all I can have, I'll take it."

"I think friendship is really all I'm prepared to give you." Mackenzie was surprised as the words left her mouth. She watched as disappointment washed over Gideon's handsome face.

He raised his coffee and said, "To friendship." Mackenzie couldn't help but think Gideon wouldn't just settle for that.

They drove in separate cars toward the waterfront and somehow found parking near one another. *How is it is so crowded on a Monday evening?* Mackenzie tightened her charcoal-gray sweater around her as the wind chilled her. A light mist fell from the sky as fog rolled in off the Puget Sound. Gideon met Mackenzie at her car.

"Clam chowder sound good?" he asked as zipped up his navy-blue Seattle Seahawk hooded sweatshirt. Gideon grabbed Mackenzie's hand and led her across the busy street to the waterfront walk.

"Still love those Seahawks, huh?" Mackenzie questioned.

"Was there ever a doubt? Twelfth-man proud, baby," Gideon teased back. "Remember going to those games? You would get so mad."

"That's because instead of playing, some stupid flag was being thrown every five seconds. It was ridiculous." Mackenzie smiled up at Gideon. They had watched a lot of those Sunday football games in bed. Halftime had been her favorite part.

The raw sea scent mingled with the smell of freshly baked bread that was used as bowls for the legendary chowder. That was one of Mackenzie's favorite things about living in the Puget Sound and coastal living in general—fresh seafood and incredible atmosphere. She and Gideon had spent much of their time here and it felt comfortably familiar. People chatted and enjoyed their delicious meal. It was a very popular place and one where Mackenzie had been coming since she had been a child.

"This is one of my favorite places. Remember coming here all the time in the fall?" Gideon asked as they found a seat.

"Because it's so damn good, especially when it was cold and gross outside."

"It was always a toss-up—here or our Chinese place," Gideon said with a happy smile.

"I think I like this place better," Mackenzie countered. There weren't any negative memories here, unlike the Chinese restaurant.

"Two bread bowls?" Gideon asked her. "You want any hushpuppies?" He stared at the menu.

"Sure. I'd like a beer, too."

"That sounds really good. I'm thinking about a Rainer—you?"

"How about an Oly?" Mackenzie countered.

"Gotta love a cold Olympia beer, but a Rainer is calling my name."

"I know you've always loved Rainer best, though," Mackenzie patted his hand. The instant her hand touched his, she pulled it back. It was like playing with fire. Gideon frowned at her regret.

They ordered their clam chowder and beers. Mackenzie expected things to feel awkward but it was the exact opposite. He had her laughing until her sides ached and she begged for him to stop. *Maybe this whole friend thing can work out after all.* They'd been through some shit together and that was truly the basis of any real friendship. It wasn't all that crazy to imagine them being friends.

Their food arrived and conversation continued to flow as it always had between them. They strolled down memory lane and it wasn't nearly as painful as Mackenzie would've thought. They shared even more memories of their childhoods. Mackenzie opened up more about her sister and it felt good reliving those stories. They reminded her just why she loved her sister so much.

"Funny running into you two here." Mackenzie heard a voice say and looked up to see Molly and Owen standing at their table.

Mackenzie watched Gideon's eyes light up at the sight of her friend.

"Hey, Moll. Here, sit," Gideon offered as he quickly got up. "You must be Owen. Nice to meet you, man." He extended his hand to Owen, who shook it and glanced over at Mackenzie.

Molly smiled at Mackenzie as she sat down. "Sorry to bug you two."

"She was craving some Ivan's and, well, I can't deny my pregnant wifey," Owen added proudly as he slipped in next to Molly and gave her peck on the cheek.

"I had some edits I was working on and the thought of clam chowder sounded really good." Molly motioned toward Mackenzie's bread bowl. "I'd kill for that Rainer."

Owen laughed. "Soon enough, babe."

"Why don't you guys join us?" Gideon suggested as he scooted next to Mackenzie.

"We'd hate to impose," Owen said.

"I wouldn't," Molly countered.

"Good." Gideon waved down their waitress and ordered for Molly and Owen. "Owen, a Rainer?" Gideon asked.

"I'll take an Olympia if you don't mind," Owen answered as he winked at Mackenzie.

"Fine, side with her. But we all heard Molly say she'd kill for a Rainer," Gideon joked and placed the order with the waitress. He gave Owen and Molly his full attention but reached for Mackenzie's hand under the table. He gave it a gentle squeeze.

Damn, this all feels so right and wonderful.

"Owen, I got to meet Gideon's baby daughter, Azita," Molly announced. Owen's stormy gray eyes grew perplexed. "He stopped by Mackenzie's house on Friday. She was the sweetest little thing ever. It makes me so excited to meet our baby." Molly rested her head on Owen's shoulder.

"We're very excited about becoming parents. I can't wait to become a dad. How about you, Gideon? How do you like being one?" Owen asked.

"Well, for starters, she's one of the best things that has ever happened to me." Gideon expressed his love for his daughter and went on to explain just how he had adopted her.

Owen gave him a smile that told Mackenzie that a friendship was in the offing.

Gideon and Owen continued to chat about everything under the sun. From what Mackenzie heard, they had many things in common. Mackenzie nursed her beer as Molly sipped on her water and ate her chowder.

She motioned toward the guys as they laughed and talked like long lost friends, completely oblivious to either Molly or her, though Gideon still held Mackenzie's hand under the table.

After dinner and a few more beers were finished, they prepared to head out. They exited the restaurant and were greeted by heavy fog.

Molly hugged Mackenzie and whispered, "This was really nice. Don't tell Tiff, but I'm rooting for Gideon."

Mackenzie laughed. "It'll be our little secret." They said goodnight and began to walk in different directions.

Gideon grabbed her hand again and asked, "What little secret?"

"Oh, it was nothing, just girl talk."

"You can tell me. I'm your friend, remember?" Gideon teased. "Isn't that what friends do? Like…share secrets?" They had reached Mackenzie's car. Mackenzie fished her keys out and Gideon stopped her as she began to open her door.

"I had a lot of fun tonight, Gideon. Thanks for dinner. Sorry about Molly and Owen," she rambled. Despite the cold dampness of the fog that clung to her hair and cheeks, she felt warm.

"It was awesome meeting Owen. I really like him. Molly's great, too, and it's so wonderful that she's going to be a mom soon."

"We're super excited about the baby. She's due at the end of the month."

The yellow parking lights were nearly hidden by the fog and behind Gideon as he looked down at Mackenzie. He raised his hand, moved a strand of hair from her cheek and tucked it behind her ear.

"When's the last time I told you how beautiful you are, Mac?" Gideon asked.

She blushed. Damn, Mackenzie wanted him to kiss her. *But friends don't kiss, right?* But he didn't. Instead, Gideon opened her door and helped her inside. "Goodnight, Mac." He closed the door and stood there as she started her car.

Mackenzie pulled out of her parking space feeling a mixture of relief and confusion. She'd been so sure that Gideon was going to kiss her and when he hadn't, it had rattled her a little. Maybe he was okay with them being *just friends*. Maybe it was *her* who wasn't okay with it?

* * * *

Mackenzie had just slipped into her sexy-as-sin black stilettos when her doorbell chimed, causing her to jump a little. She was a nervous wreck but excited to see Ian. She combed her fingers through her freshly trimmed blonde bob and went to answer the door.

There he stood, even hotter than she'd remembered. His hair was styled to look every inch the seductive bad boy they both knew he was, and the wicked grin only confirmed it. Ian wore a dark-gray dress shirt that brought out the lavender flecks in his eyes and played off his slightly tan skin.

"You look stunning, Mackenzie," he said. The man's voice did funny things to her lady bits. No wonder Tiffany was such a happy girl now. Colin's voice wasn't much different from Ian's, except for the delivery and the fact that it came from someone Mackenzie was attracted to. When Ian spoke, it was like he was teasing Mackenzie, tempting her to follow him down a naughty path that she very much wanted to travel down.

"You look great, too," she managed. "Let me grab my purse."

"In such a rush?" he asked. "Not interested in inviting a fella inside?"

Mackenzie laughed. "Ian, if I invite you inside, we may never make it out for dinner," she admitted.

He moved close and snared her with his arms before she had a chance to get away. "And that'd be such a pity, wouldn't it?" Ian kissed her neck, causing her to moan. "Maybe we'll come back for dessert."

Ian held her wrap for her and helped her get comfortably seated in his sports car. Mackenzie was anticipating the night and the ending that Ian had hinted at. She felt a small flutter inside as he pulled the powerful car away from the car and into the traffic.

Ian drove fast along the freeway in his midnight-blue Porsche. Everything about the man was fast, and in all honesty, it both frightened Mackenzie and turned her on. Ian reached over and rested his hand on her thigh. He always seemed to be touching her, making sure she felt the electricity that burned between them.

"I've arranged for us to eat at a mate's restaurant. He cooks with nitrogen. It's all very cool. He's well-known for this molecular dining experience."

Mackenzie was a little confused. "Really? And it's safe?"

"Yes, completely," he reassured with a laugh. "If anything, it's more of a fad — something of a show to bring attention."

"I see. Well, it sounds like fun," Mackenzie said as they zipped along.

They arrived at Ian's friend's restaurant. It was a building made entirely of glass. Nearly all the walls were constructed of long windows and gave a fishbowl view of all the happenings going on inside, except there was one problem. There was not a single person inside. The place was completely empty.

"Is he closed tonight?"

"For everyone else," Ian answered and winked. He held the large glass door open for Mackenzie.

They were greeted by a handsome man with dark, stylishly messy hair and thick black-rimmed glasses. He was the very essence of a hipster. "Ian, you guys made it," he said as approached them.

"Curtis, this is Mackenzie," Ian introduced her proudly, not taking his eyes off her for a second.

"Lovely to meet you," Curtis said as he shook Mackenzie's hand. "I hope you're ready for a totally bizarre and wild dining experience."

"Mate, you don't have to sell it," Ian joked. "I've already taken the liberty of warning her."

Curtis laughed. "Well, in that case, let's get you guys seated and grab some drinks."

Dinner was indeed weird, to say the least. Every single thing they were served looked like it came from a laboratory, with billowing frozen smoke wafting from it. Mackenzie was hesitant to eat anything, but Ian insisted it was all perfectly safe. It turned out that he was right, and while it wasn't as tasty as the food at Blu, she was okay with it. Mackenzie watched as cars drove past the building. Street lights pooled in the wet streets. Even with all the glass, the space felt intimate and warm. The restaurant was quite incredible and unlike any place Mackenzie had ever dined.

I have to bring the girls here.

"Thank you so much for bringing me here. This place is pretty fantastic," Mackenzie said as they finished another cocktail.

"I knew you'd enjoy it. It's different than Blu. It's rather experimental and edgy."

Mackenzie nodded. "But Blu is sexy and elegant," she pointed out.

"Thank you," Ian replied. "I'm glad you see it that way. I find food incredibly sexy."

Somehow just his mention of the word made Mackenzie blush.

"Just like you." Ian leaned across the table. He pinched her chin and tilted her lips to his. "I've wanted to do that all night."

"You shouldn't have waited so long," Mackenzie teased as she licked her lips where he'd been only a moment ago.

"I don't think I'd be able to behave myself as well as I had at Blu last week," Ian countered and gave her sexy grin.

"Ian, that was so naughty. What if one of your staff would've seen us?"

"I certainly didn't hear you complaining. Besides, if they had, what could they say? It's *my* restaurant. If I feel the need to finger a hot blonde in a dark hallway, then so be it," Ian joked.

"Valid point," Mackenzie agreed as she swallowed her icy cocktail in hopes it would cool the heat that was burning through her. The images and sensations he made her feel swarmed her.

"You ready for dessert?" Ian asked. "I'm ravenous for something blonde and sweet tonight," he added seductively.

Mackenzie couldn't seem to find her voice. Her body was wound up so tightly with desire and need. She wanted nothing more than to have Ian take her home. Ian excused himself and went in search of Curtis. He returned with a satisfied expression on his face and led Mackenzie through the empty dining room.

They were nearing the restaurant's exit when Mackenzie's cell phone rang. She slid her finger along the smooth glass screen to ignore it without even looking at who was calling. Ian winked at her and asked the valet to bring his car. "We can't have anyone getting in the way of spoiling our dessert, now can we?"

Her phone disagreed and rang again. It almost seemed more insistent and Mackenzie peeked down to find Tiffany calling. Something in her gut told her to answer it, but the look on Ian's face caused her to ignore it once again. He gave her kiss on the cheek as he held the car door for her to get in. He ran around, got into the driver's seat and turned to her with a grin.

"Good girl." Ian patted her thigh then his hand began to move higher up. "Oh, baby, the things I want to do to you," he purred before he returned his hand to the wheel to pull away from the restaurant into traffic. He seemed to be in a hurry to get them back home for dessert.

Then her phone went off again, persistent and demanding to be answered. It was Tiffany calling back.

"I'd better get this," Mackenzie apologized. Ian looked less than thrilled at the disturbing intruder.

"Hello?" Mackenzie answered.

"Hey, Mac, where are you?" Tiffany sounded a little panicked.

"I'm on a date with Ian," Mackenzie answered, feeling Ian's eyes burning into her. "Everything okay?"

"I'm so sorry to bug you but Molly's in the hospital."

"Wait, what? Why? Is she okay, Tiff?" Mackenzie began to worry. All the lust that was inside her had evaporated.

"It might be early labor. They aren't sure. Molly and Owen called me a little while ago and I'm on my way to the hospital now," Tiffany explained. "I was going to pick you up but you kept sending me to voicemail hell."

"I'm on my way back to my house now." Mackenzie looked out of the window and saw Ian steering them toward her neighborhood. "Go ahead and come get me."

Mackenzie hung up and peered over at Ian. "What's going on with your friend?" he asked.

"Our friend Molly is possibly in labor."

"Good for her," he said. "And just why is Colin's wife coming to pick you up?"

"Tiffany and I need to be there for Molly," Mackenzie explained. "She needs us."

"But babies take a long time getting here. I don't think there's a tremendous rush, do you?"

Mackenzie stared at him. "Ian, this is her first baby. She's undoubtedly terrified and in a great deal of pain. We're her friends and need to be there for her."

The disappointment couldn't be dismissed. "It just seems a pity we'll have to cut our evening short."

"I'm sorry you feel that way," Mackenzie said as they arrived at her home. *Doesn't he understand that this is important?*

Ian parked the Porsche and looked over at her. "Mackenzie, I really like you and I'm sorry for being insensitive. You're completely right. You should be there."

Her heart softened as he apologized.

Ian moved closer and pulled her to him. "I'm incredibly attracted to you and just didn't want the evening to end." He kissed her. It was hard and forceful, as though he needed to get his point across. In the tiny car, he'd managed to sweep her into his arms and caused her to go breathless as he ravaged her mouth. Ian released her. "Let's get you inside so you can hurry and see that baby be born."

Mackenzie leaned over and kissed Ian on the cheek. "I promise to make this up to you."

"I'm holding you to that." Ian winked and got out of his side of the car. He hurried to her side and opened the door. Ian walked her to her door and kissed Mackenzie again. This time it was less rushed, more thought out and sweet. Ian explored her mouth. Then he pulled back and stared at her.

"Thank you again, Ian," Mackenzie said as Tiffany's SUV pulled into her driveway and Tiffany hopped out. She raced toward them.

"Come on, Mac. We gotta go. Hey, Ian," Tiffany said after she bounded up the stairs and onto the porch. "I'm sorry to ruin your date. You can blame Molly." Tiffany smiled as she ushered Mackenzie inside.

Ian left and gave Mackenzie a final wave goodbye before he sped off. She felt her heart dip a little when he was out of sight.

"Get changed, you sexy thang. We gotta go," Tiffany ordered. "So, tell me, how was dinner?"

Mackenzie started to shed her clothing and grabbed jeans and a sweater to wear. "It was amazing. Remind me to kill Moll. Why does this baby need to come now, of all times?"

"You guys were totally headed back here to bone, weren't you?" Tiffany asked as she picked up Mackenzie's discarded clothes off the ground.

"Must you be so crude? We were going to have dessert." Mackenzie winked as she slipped on some comfortable running shoes.

"Is that what the kids are calling *it* these days?" Tiffany teased as they headed out the door. "Gosh, I hope Moll is okay," she said in a far grimmer tone.

"She will be," Mackenzie promised and hoped she was right.

Mackenzie didn't like hospitals one bit and prayed that Molly and her baby were doing well. It was only the start of November. *Isn't the baby due after Thanksgiving?* Her stomach went queasy. Mackenzie wasn't sure if it was all the nitrogen-infused food she'd eaten or the worry that something was terribly wrong.

Chapter Eleven

The scent was the same as she'd remembered — that pungent antiseptic cleaner. The floors the same glossy beige, just a different level in the enormous hospital. *God, I hate being back in this place.*

Tiffany squeezed her hand. "You okay?"

Mackenzie nodded as they reached the nurses' station. Tiffany asked which room Molly was in and the nurse told them to wait in the small waiting room off to the side.

Stainless steel coffee pots beckoned Mackenzie. "You want any?" she asked after helping herself to the overly hot coffee.

"Sure," Tiffany answered. "Hope Molly is okay."

Mackenzie brought Tiffany her coffee and joined her in the less-than-comfortable chair. "Gosh, you'd think they'd make these seats a little comfier."

"I know, right? It's a waiting room, after all." Tiffany sipped her coffee. "And putting some decent coffee in here wouldn't kill them either."

Mackenzie forced down the contents of her small paper cup and grimaced. Tiffany was right. It was awful. Being cooped up in this small room brought back too many terrible memories of the day her sister had been killed. She'd sat in a similar seat deciding the fate of her sister's organs. Tiffany and Molly had been there with her and Mackenzie wondered if they really knew how much that had meant to her.

A nurse in pale pink scrubs entered the room with a large smile on her face. "I can take you back to see her now."

Tiffany and Mackenzie leaped from their chairs and tossed the wretched coffee in a waste basket as they followed the nurse. They came to a giant double door and the nurse swiped her badge for them to enter. All the sounds of machines beeping bothered Mackenzie a great deal. She prayed harder than she had in a very long time. *Please let Molly and the baby be okay.*

The nurse pulled back a teal linen curtain and there was Molly, looking small in the wide bed. Owen had concern etched on his face and greeted them with a stiff smile.

"Hey, Moll," Mackenzie said as she went to Molly's side. Tiffany went to the other. Together they acted as a wall of protection, holding Molly's hand and offering comfort.

Mackenzie looked over to Owen, who had moved to the foot of the bed, granting them access to their friend. "Owen, so what's going on?"

He ran his hand through his dark hair. "She complained about not feeling well earlier today and just seemed off, you know? She fainted after dinner." Owen looked terrified as he retold the story.

"I'm fine," Molly muttered and grimaced as pain washed over her face. She did look pale and little sickly.

"If you were, you wouldn't be here," Tiffany countered as she rubbed Molly's hand.

"Is she in labor?" Mackenzie asked Owen.

"They think she might be. Her cervix is starting to dilate. The cause for her fainting is still being checked out." Owen smiled at Molly, and Mackenzie witnessed the transfer of love he had for her. She wanted someone to look at her like that.

"I'm not sure I'm ready to have the baby," Molly whined as she tried to roll over in obvious pain.

"I'm not sure you have much choice, sweetie," Mackenzie replied as she peered over at Tiffany.

"Moll, we're here for you. You got this," Tiffany tried to reassure her.

Molly suddenly cried out and both Tiffany and Mackenzie jumped at the sound she'd made. A nurse drew back the curtain and asked Molly how she was feeling. *Seriously? There is no way that no one in a mile radius didn't hear Molly's scream.* The nurse checked Molly and smiled. "You've dilated a little more. They're getting you a room on the Labor and Delivery floor."

"So, she's having the baby?" Tiffany asked.

The nurse nodded. "She's definitely in labor. I'm still waiting on her labs to see why she fainted this evening." The nurse removed her gloves and washed her hands in the stationary sink. She added another clear bag of fluid to the medicine pole and checked Molly's IV. "I'll let you know when we have her room ready."

"Thank you," Owen replied.

"Moll, you hear that? You're going to have your baby," Tiffany squealed. "We're finally going to meet that little bugger."

Molly groaned and appeared more uncomfortable. Mackenzie went into full-on soldier mode. It was something she'd learned from Gideon a long time ago. When shit got tough—because it always did at some point—she'd need to go into soldier mode. It meant pulling strength from deep inside her gut and pretending she wasn't the least bit scared. The key was being calm, even if she was faking it to make everyone around believe that things were in control and going to be just fine. Mackenzie was downright terrified for Molly. Childbirth wasn't exactly a walk in the park and the cause of her fainting spell was still unknown. Mackenzie had never seen Molly look so miserable.

"Tiffany, hand me that pillow," Mackenzie ordered. She positioned it behind Molly's back and relief was obvious on Molly's face. "Owen, did you bring her bag?"

"Yeah, we've had it packed since last week... You know, just in case." Owen grabbed the duffle bag and offered it to Mackenzie.

She began going through the pockets until she came across Molly's favorite lotion. It was a delicate lilac-scented cream that Molly wore all the time. Mackenzie squeezed a small bit into her palm and motioned for Tiffany to take some as well. Mackenzie began to massage the lotion onto Molly's hands and up her arms. A relaxed sigh escaped Molly's lips and her eyelids closed. Tiffany smiled over at Mackenzie as she massaged Molly's other side. Owen seemed helpless and needed to be given a task.

"Owen, here, put some on her legs and feet," Mackenzie suggested as she waved the container of lotion at him. He nodded and got right to work. Molly had grown quiet and was now resting.

The nurse from earlier entered again and informed them that they would be moving Molly to her room upstairs.

Mackenzie patted Owen's arm. "You ready to become a dad?"

"I don't think I have much choice," he replied, but there was the hint of a smile on his lips.

"You guys are going to be amazing parents. I know it's going to be difficult seeing Moll in so much pain, but we just need to get through this." Mackenzie hugged him.

"I'm so glad she has you two as friends. You both mean the world to Molly. Thank you for being here," Owen said as two uniformed men came in to move Molly.

"We're your friends, too. We're here for both of you. If you need anything, just ask us, okay?" Mackenzie offered as they left the room.

Tiffany came to Mackenzie's side and whispered, "He's scared shitless, poor guy."

"Can you blame him? He's never seen her in this kind of pain. Hell, we haven't seen her like this before."

"But this is so exciting, isn't it?" Tiffany's dark eyes sparkled with joy. "We're going to be aunties, Mac."

"You're right. This is pretty amazing," Mackenzie admitted, despite the worry she felt.

"Also, good job taking control in there," Tiffany said as they entered an elevator. "That was totally the old Mackenzie back in action," she teased after pressing the button to go up.

"It's going to be a long night. Let's hope this floor has better coffee," Mackenzie joked as they arrived at the next floor.

Mackenzie and Tiffany were allowed to see Molly once the nurses got her settled and all hooked up to another fetal monitor. Molly had color back in her cheeks and seemed a little more perky.

"Hey, guys," she greeted them as they entered the room. "Turns out I was severely dehydrated. I have been working on the baby's room the last few days and —"

"And pushed herself way too hard," Owen finished for Molly. "And now our little guy wants to see it."

"His?" Mackenzie asked. "Oh, my gosh, did you guys find out?"

Molly rolled her eyes. "No, we didn't. Owen is certain we're having a boy."

Tiffany shook her head. "I think you're having a girl."

"I guess we'll all find out soon enough." Mackenzie laughed. She was so relieved that Molly was feeling better but knew this was the calm before the real storm.

The hours began to pass and they tried to keep Molly from dying of boredom now that the contractions had slowed. Tiffany and Mackenzie went in search of some much-needed caffeine and to give Molly and Owen a little time alone. This was their special moment, after all.

"How long does this usually take? With how much pain she was in earlier, I thought for sure the baby would've been here by now," Tiffany said as they roamed the quiet hospital.

"It's a very long and sometimes slow process," Mackenzie explained. "I think the dehydration somehow had an effect on those contractions. She is dilating, though, so, at least there's that."

"I texted Colin. He's bringing us food." Tiffany stared down at her phone. "I can't even imagine going through childbirth. I am totally asking for a C-section."

"Tiff, having a baby vaginally is really the best option—a lot fewer complications and quicker recovery."

"And have my little fuzzy taco destroyed? I don't think so," Tiffany balked.

Leave it to Tiffany to worry about the state of her vagina. "Good grief. I'm sure Colin will still love your fuzzy taco," Mackenzie teased.

"No, I want him to continue to love it and he won't if the darn thing is all stretched out and weird."

Mackenzie couldn't help but laugh. "Let's just get through Molly's birthing experience and maybe you'll feel differently."

"Do we have to see her push the baby out?" Tiffany's eyes went wide. "Do we even *want* to see that?"

"It might be a little scary, but I sort of want to."

Tiffany shrugged. "I'm good with not seeing it." They turned down another deserted hall. "Let's talk about what happened tonight."

"With Moll?" Mackenzie asked as they walked down the dimly lit wing. The hospital had lowered the harsh lighting to a more tolerable brightness.

"No, you. More specifically, you and Ian."

Mackenzie felt herself smile. "I like him."

"I know that. I want to know more the reasons why. Obviously, you two are super attracted to one another."

"True. I totally get your obsession with Colin's accent now."

Tiffany squealed, "Right? Oh, my God, isn't it the biggest turn on?"

"It's pretty dang hot coming from Ian, just the way he says my name."

"Mac, it gets even hotter in the bedroom. Trust me." Tiffany stopped to look out of the large window. Mackenzie stared out too and saw rain had started to fall again. The windows were splattered and cars splashed in the puddles below. "Do you think things will get serious between you and Ian?"

"I hope so. He's different than any guy I've ever dated."

"Dare I ask if you've spoken to the enemy lately?" Tiffany joked, her gaze remaining on the stormy night outside.

Mackenzie inhaled sharply. "I have. Tiff, we're just friends. That's it."

"We'll see how long that lasts."

"I know you hate Gideon—" Mackenzie started.

Tiffany cut her off. "It's not that I hate him. I *hate* what he did to you. I just don't trust him. It's that simple."

Well, on the plus side, at least Tiffany no longer hates Gideon. They might not ever become besties, but this is progress.

"We better get back and check on Moll," Mackenzie suggested. "We've got to tell that baby it's show time. I'm dying to meet this little guy or gal."

Tiffany giggled. "Colin will be here soon with food. I'm starving."

"Me too."

"Didn't you eat dinner?" Tiffany asked with concern.

"Yeah, but it was this weird stuff."

"Oh, you went to Ian's friend's restaurant. He does that liquid nitrogen cooking or something, right?"

"Yep. It tastes fine but I was a little scared to eat it," Mackenzie admitted as they began the walk back to Molly's room. She noticed another pregnant woman, bent over and bracing herself against the wall. She appeared to be in excruciating pain. Mackenzie offered the man—who looked stressed out—a tight-lipped smile.

"See? Scheduled C-section. That's all I'm sayin'," Tiffany whispered as they walked past and Mackenzie had to admit Tiff had a valid point.

Not much had changed since Mackenzie and Tiffany had gone on their stroll. Owen was resting in a chair next to the bed. Molly smiled when she saw them enter.

"Please tell me you found food," Molly whispered, looking over at Owen and clearly trying not to wake him.

"Colin is bringing some," Tiffany answered.

"Bless his heart." Molly peeked over at Owen. "You'd think he was in labor."

"He tired himself out with how worried he was about you. You gave us all a major scare," Mackenzie said in a hushed voice.

"Yeah, I still don't know how it happened. I felt like crap all day and should've taken it easy."

"But you were in full-on nesting mode. We get it." Mackenzie said as Tiffany leaned in closer to Molly.

"I'm so scared, you guys," Molly admitted. "I was in a lot of pain earlier."

"That was just the sneak peek, the movie trailer of what is to come," Tiffany said. "When I'm preggers, I'm asking for a C-section."

"And like that shit won't hurt?" Molly countered. "Thanks for the vote of confidence, by the way," Molly said as she glared at Tiffany.

"Tiffany's worried about the status of her vagina," Mackenzie added with a silly smirk.

"It goes back to normal, Tiff. Our bodies are made to have babies," Molly explained as though she were a seasoned pro at the motherhood business.

"Talk to me after the delivery." Tiffany winked.

"So, do you want us here for the actual birth?" Mackenzie felt it was necessary to ask. She wasn't so sure she'd want her besties watching her lady bits get wrecked.

Molly hesitated. "I'm not sure I'll really care once I'm pushing. It's totally up to you guys. Just no filming it, okay? I don't want my lady parts on social media."

"Oh, just think of the views it would get. Might really give your career an extra edge that would set you apart from the other photogs," Mackenzie teased.

They all laughed. Molly sighed. "My back was killing me earlier and honestly, I was about to beg for an epidural and I'm not even close to delivery."

Mackenzie and Tiffany both cringed. "You are made of strong stuff, Moll. You got this, no matter what," Mackenzie reassured her.

"Let's hope you're right. I've been feeling tiny contractions again and I know the big ones are going to kill me."

"You'll survive." Mackenzie patted Molly's blanket-covered leg. "You wanna take a walk and see if we can speed things up?"

"Yeah, we saw another mommy-to-be doing laps," Tiffany said. Mackenzie was relieved that Tiffany had left out the painful details of the poor lady hugging the wall.

"Sure. I'm starting to go a little stir crazy. When's Colin going to be here?" Molly asked as they helped her out of the bed.

"In a little while. We might as well kill some time." Tiffany fixed Molly's hospital gown. "This is seriously a fashion crime all on its own."

"I should change, shouldn't I?" Molly asked.

"After the baby is born. Right now, let's just work on getting him or her out," Mackenzie suggested.

They left the room and entered the empty hallway.

"Owen really thinks you're having a boy, huh?" Tiffany asked as they cruised down the hall toward the large windows they had looked out of earlier.

"I think it's more wishful thinking. I'm honestly happy with either."

"Just as long as the baby is healthy, right?" Mackenzie added. "But let's face it. We all want a certain gender, don't we?"

Molly gave them a sheepish smile. "Okay, I'll admit it. I want it to be a girl. I don't know why. I just do."

"Couldn't agree more," Tiffany replied. "Dresses, bows, dolls…" she started to name things off.

"Don't forget shoes." Mackenzie laughed. "She's going to be spoiled rotten by her aunties."

"Even if the baby is a boy… Spoiling is happening, regardless. But just imagine all the pink, you guys," Tiffany cooed. "And she can even join us on Fridays."

"*Friendship Fridays 2.0,*" Mackenzie teased as they made another lap around the floor. Molly had grown quiet and she knew what that meant.

They watched as Molly paused to lean against a wall. "Shit, I think this walking is working a little too good."

"Let's get her back to her room. We don't want to have the baby in the hall," Tiffany teased.

They managed to get Molly into bed and Owen hadn't moved since they'd left. The nurse entered and checked Molly. The walking had helped. She was more dilated. Colin knocked on the door. He carried a cardboard drink carrier and few paper sacks. He also had a backpack slung over his shoulder.

"What? No baby yet?" he joked as he greeted Molly. "How you feelin', love?"

Molly winced and tried to smile through her discomfort.

"I don't think she can answer you right now, babe." Tiffany kissed Colin on his cheek and tried to peek into the sacks he'd brought.

"He brought the most important thing," Mackenzie reached for one of the coffees. "Thanks, Colin."

"My pleasure. I hear you were out with my mate when Molly decided it was time to have this baby," he said as put the sacks on a small table and left the backpack on the floor.

"I thought you were dating that Gideon guy," Owen said. He rubbed his eyes and was now awake, probably due to all the commotion.

"No, she's seeing Colin's friend, Ian," Tiffany explained.

"What about the other night?" Owen seemed confused and Mackenzie felt her stomach drop.

"He's just my friend. We used to date."

"Mac, you had dinner with Gideon and them and you didn't tell me?" Tiffany asked.

"It was a spur of the moment thing after work on Monday and we sort of ran into Owen and Molly."

"Just sort of ran into them? Why were you out with Gideon in the first place?" Tiffany asked.

"Ladies, let's not do this here, shall we?" Colin said. Tiffany huffed and helped herself to a coffee.

"I just think it's ridiculous to even consider seeing Ian if you're going to be hanging out with Gideon, too," Tiffany said under her breath.

Mackenzie chose to not engage in any more discussion of her dating life, at least not until Molly popped the baby out.

The room was growing a tad crowded and Molly was becoming more agitated and cranky as each contraction took hold. Mackenzie and Tiffany worked on massaging her back and fed her words of encouragement. Colin took Owen out of the room for a breather and the three women were alone. It had grown intense. Molly was really in pain and the nurses had explained that she was almost fully dilated and it wouldn't be too much longer before they would try and have her push.

"Guys, I think I pissed myself," Molly exclaimed.

Mackenzie looked down and saw a lot of clear fluid tinged with blood. "I think your water just broke, Moll."

"This is really happening, isn't it?" The fear in Molly's mocha-colored eyes broke Mackenzie's heart.

"We got this. You're going to do great. It'll be over before you know it," she promised. Molly cried out again. Tiffany had disappeared then returned with a nurse.

"Let's see if your water broke, dear." The nurse checked the bedding under Molly and smiled. "We need to get Daddy and get ready to practice pushing."

"Practice pushing?" Molly complained. "Why do I need to practice?" The nurse was about to explain when

Molly gripped the woman's arm and cried out. "I think I need to push *now*!"

"I'm going to find Owen." Tiffany hurried out of the room.

"It's going to be okay, Molly," Mackenzie said but could only imagine how her bestie felt.

"I feel like I'm being split in two, Mac," Molly hissed through clenched teeth.

Owen suddenly appeared and bent down and kissed Molly's sweat-soaked forehead. He whispered something that Mackenzie couldn't quite catch. A flurry of activity swallowed them all as everything started to happen. It was officially 'go time' and Mackenzie found herself in the thick of it. Tiffany snuck out after wishing them all good luck. Mackenzie held and supported Molly's leg as she pushed with all her might. Owen held Molly's other leg and smiled down at her. Molly growled through the pain and panted after each contraction. The doctor gave her simple instructions and praise for how well she was doing.

"Our baby is almost here, babe," Owen encouraged Molly when she wanted to give up from exhaustion. She pushed again and Mackenzie watched as they became parents and welcomed a baby with the loudest pair of lungs Mackenzie had ever heard. She was fierce, this chubby and very healthy baby girl.

The doctor placed the screaming newborn on Molly's chest and Mackenzie felt tears stream down her own cheeks. She hadn't seen anything more beautiful than what she was witnessing in that very moment.

"She's so precious, Moll," Mackenzie said through her tears. It had been an incredible experience, spiritual and something Mackenzie wasn't soon going to forget.

Mackenzie brought Tiffany in to introduce her and they fell in love with the swaddled bundle. They took turns holding the baby and singing Molly's praises of how strong and brave she had been.

Mackenzie was worn out when she decided to leave Molly and her little family. "I'll be back later. You guys try and rest." She gave them one more look before closing the door. They were both staring at their new daughter, enthralled with the precious little being. She left the hospital feeling very different from when she'd entered. Her perspective had changed. She knew one thing for certain. Mackenzie wanted what Molly had. She wanted her own little family and to be a mother...again.

* * * *

Mackenzie arrived back at the hospital after getting some much-needed rest. It had been difficult to fall asleep at first. Her body had still been reeling from the excitement of the birth. She had eventually succumbed to pure exhaustion and had slept like a log. That afternoon, she felt refreshed and joyful. Mackenzie came to the hospital bearing gifts of flowers and a few extra goodies to spoil the baby with. Tiffany had called and said she was also on her way.

She found there was more pep in her step as she made her way to Molly's room. Mackenzie knocked on the door, being careful not to wake the baby. She peeked in and found Molly sitting up in bed cradling the newborn.

"Hey, Mac," Molly said.

"How are you feeling?"

"Pretty darn good," Molly replied, keeping her eyes trained on her daughter.

"You look fabulous for only having given birth a few hours ago. You ready for another one?" Mackenzie teased.

"Uh, not quite." Molly laughed and the baby let out a tiny cry.

"Oh no, don't wake that precious little darling," Mackenzie scolded. "How in love are you with her?"

"Head over heels. I didn't know it was possible to love someone so much," Molly answered as she stroked her baby's cheek.

"Hey, what about me?" Owen joked as he entered the room.

"I love you, too," Molly said. "You gave her to me, after all."

"It was a team effort," Owen replied as he kissed Molly and their baby.

"Hey, Owen, I didn't see you when I got here. How are you holding up?" Mackenzie asked, feeling very much like a third wheel.

"Couldn't be happier." Owen beamed pure love and joy from his gray eyes.

"Did you guys get any sleep?" Mackenzie asked as Molly handed her the baby to hold. Mackenzie relished the feel of the tiny girl in her arms.

"A little," Molly admitted with a yawn.

"You keeping your parents up?" Mackenzie cooed to the sleepy baby.

"I think we were too excited to sleep. She's such a good girl," Owen complimented his daughter. The pride in his voice warmed her heart.

"So, you ended up with a little girl," Mackenzie said. "How awesome is that?"

Owen laughed. "I still plan on teaching her how to throw one helluva curve ball. Besides, this just means we get to try for a boy." Owen kissed Molly on top of her head.

"Slow your roll, mister. It's going to be a while," Molly joked with a smirk.

There was a knock on the door and Tiffany and Colin entered. Colin carried a bouquet of pink roses and cheerful balloons.

"Those are lovely," Molly said.

"Those were Colin's idea, but I brought cookies and coffee." Tiffany lifted the cardboard tray and waved a white paper sack.

"Sorry, Colin, but that's way better," Molly teased as she accepted a coffee from Tiffany.

Tiffany handed Mackenzie a cup and she handed over the infant. "How did she get even cuter?"

"Doesn't it make you want one of our own?" Colin asked as he peered down at the baby in Tiffany's arms.

"Eventually. Let me enjoy this little girl for a minute, okay?" Tiffany laughed.

They were enjoying their coffees and cookies and discussing future babies when there was another knock at the door. Mackenzie dusted off the chocolate chip crumbs from her and went to answer it. Gideon smiled. He was holding flowers, three balloons and a bright pink gift bag.

"What are you doing here?" Mackenzie asked. Gideon leaned down and kissed her on the cheek as he moved past.

"The proud papa texted me," Gideon answered. It was rather sweet of Gideon to show up with gifts, and it was a reminder of just how thoughtful he could be.

"Rumor has it a beautiful little girl was born," Gideon announced.

"Hey, man, you didn't need to go to all this trouble," Owen said as Gideon hugged him as though they were best friends. Gideon went to Molly's side and kissed her on the top of the head. "I hear you did an amazing job and I wanted to bring you a little something."

"Oh, Gid, you didn't need to do that." Molly smiled at him as she accepted his gifts. The small gift bag contained a teddy bear and a few adorable outfits, all pink and very girly. "These are so stinking cute." Molly held up the outfits for Mackenzie and Tiffany to view.

"I know you guys wanted to keep the gender a surprise and figured you probably didn't have a whole lot of pink for her," he rambled.

"It's very sweet of you, Gid. Thank you." Molly reached up and kissed his cheek.

Mackenzie felt Tiffany's eyes on her and was surprised to see a faint smile on her face. Colin grabbed the newborn and handed her to Gideon. "I'm Colin, by the way." He shook Gideon's hand.

"Great to meet you. Mackenzie's told me nothing but awesome things about you. I've really been wanting to meet you for a while now."

Colin seemed pleased hearing that and invited Gideon out for a celebratory pint with Owen. Mackenzie and Tiffany spent the next hour cuddling the baby and Mackenzie could see Molly looked wiped out.

"Why don't we let mama and baby rest for a while," suggested Mackenzie as she placed the infant in her plastic tub-looking crib.

"Mac, can I talk to you outside?" Tiffany asked.

"Sure," Mackenzie answered as she gathered her purse. Once they were outside the room she asked, "What's up?"

Tiffany chewed on her bottom lip. "I guess I owe you an apology."

Mackenzie was surprised. "For what?"

"How I acted about hearing that you went out with Gideon and Molly and Owen."

"It honestly wasn't a big deal. It was just clam chowder and beers."

"I know, but I sort of acted like a bitch. It was really sweet of Gideon to come here today."

"It was, wasn't it?" Mackenzie smiled at the tender thought. "He's really a sweet guy."

"I see that. I just felt like I needed to say I was sorry. That doesn't mean I want you to date him, but I guess it's okay if you and Gideon are friends. But *just friends.*" Tiffany hugged Mackenzie.

"Thanks, Tiff. I swear that I'm going to try and see where things go with Ian. I really like him," Mackenzie said.

"Good. Maybe you should call him," she suggested.

"Maybe I already did."

Chapter Twelve

Mackenzie was running around like a chicken with her head cut off getting ready for her date. *Where are those damn boots?* She was on the tips of her toes and scouring the top shelf of her closet for her favorite brown riding boots. Ian was going to be there any minute. She spied the leather strap in the dark corner and jumped in an effort to reach it. One thing Mackenzie loved about the fall weather was wearing boots, jeans and oversized sweaters. She owned an enormous collection, thanks to the gloomy and wet Seattle weather. Today's sweater was a cream cable knit paired with dark-wash skinny jeans. Mackenzie yanked the other boot from the shelf and quickly zipped them up her calves.

Another dab of lip gloss and Mackenzie was ready for Ian to arrive. She had no idea where they were going for their date other than he'd instructed her to dress warmly. A knock sounded at her door and Mackenzie sprang into action. She grabbed her purse and answered the door.

Ian smiled the moment she pulled the door back. "Lovely as ever," he said as he kissed her cheek.

He wore jeans and a forest green sweater that brought out various colors in his eyes that she hadn't noticed before—tiny flecks of amber and olive green. He grabbed her hand and led her to a bright red Jeep. Ian helped her in and hurried to the driver's side. Mackenzie was excited for whatever adventure awaited them. The day was early and the sun attempted to pierce the gray clouds.

Once they were on the road, Mackenzie asked, "So, what's the game plan for today?"

"How do you fancy a ride on a boat?"

Mackenzie laughed. "Oh dear, where are you taking us?"

"How do you feel about whales?"

"Whale watching. Gosh, I haven't been in ages. They still offer tours this late in the season?"

"They do, and I have chartered a boat for us to go out. I'm hoping the weather gets a little nicer," Ian said as he drove.

"I think the last time I went was a few years ago and I was substituting for a teacher and tagged along for the field trip. Have you ever been?"

Ian shook his head. "No. I've never seen an orca up close either. In West Cork, not too far from where I'm from, there's whale watching."

"And you never went?" Mackenzie asked.

"No, my mum was terrified of the sea and wanted no part of it. She didn't want her children out on the water, either." Ian let out a deep, sexy laugh.

"Can't say that I blame her. Do you come from a large family?" Mackenzie asked. They hadn't really shared much about their lives and had only navigated their new relationship solely on attraction. She was curious to learn about him.

"A fairly large family, I suppose. I have two brothers and a sister. They all live in Ireland," he went on to explain. "My sister is married with a family of her own. My brothers both work together. They own a small bakery. Neither are married yet."

"And are you all close?"

"I'd like to think so. My brothers and I are all close in age. I'm the middle one of us lads. Our sister is the oldest and always nagged us to death, bless her. She and my mum had their hands full."

"How about your father?"

"He passed away suddenly when I was quite young. My mum never remarried."

Mackenzie watched as the sad memory settled into his eyes. She reached over and gave his biceps a gentle squeeze.

He smiled at her and said, "It's been a very long time and it still bothers me some."

"I'm so sorry. I know the feeling," Mackenzie replied as she looked out the window. "We lost our parents several years ago and my sister passed a few months back."

"Oh, you poor dear," he said.

"It's hard. I miss my parents, but losing my sister was a whole lot tougher." Mackenzie's throat tightened.

"I can't even begin to imagine that kind of loss." Ian turned toward in the direction where the boats for the tour were docked.

There was no one else around as they walked hand in hand toward a large boat.

"Oh, I may have failed to mention that I rented the cruise just for us today," Ian said with a sly smile.

"The entire boat, Ian?" Mackenzie couldn't imagine how ridiculously expensive that must have been. Having a rich boyfriend would take some getting used to.

"I wanted to share this experience with you and you alone."

A young man greeted them and welcomed them aboard. The boat was a tad larger than Owen's and had been designed to accommodate people to view wildlife and the gorgeous surroundings of the Sound. Mackenzie inhaled the briny air and snuggled closer to Ian as he wrapped his arms around her. It felt really good and she could see them as a couple. She was a perfect fit against his chest.

The rest of the day was spent trying to spot whales and learn more about one another. Mackenzie discovered a lot about Ian. His passion for cooking had come from his father, not his mother, who could barely put a proper meal together. Luckily, his sister had inherited a love for cooking as well and none of them had starved. She also learned that his family was not entirely happy about his decision to move to America.

Ian explained that he'd lived in many countries and that was his other passion — travel. He loved finding new places to explore, seeing and trying things he'd never done. Ian didn't want to see the world through a book. He wanted that hands-on, tangible experience. Mackenzie felt so plain and ordinary compared to Ian, who was full of life and vigor. Mackenzie hadn't really traveled anywhere too far and she was content with quiet nights at home. Ian seemed quite the opposite. When he wasn't working on establishing Blu as an incredible restaurant, he was out enjoying the nightlife — clubs, bars and scenes that Mackenzie would much rather steer clear of. Little bits of doubt started to form in her mind.

Is Ian all talk? Does he ever want to settle down? Are we on completely different paths?

It wasn't that Mackenzie didn't enjoy her time with Ian, the stolen kisses as they were misted by the salty ocean water or the wicked attraction she felt every time he looked at her or said her name. There was just a slight nagging sensation that seemed to pester her, warning her not to expect too much from him.

But I can change him, right? Help him see that having a family and being boring can be nice?

They finally did get to see a few orcas, which Ian seemed thrilled about and the smile never left his handsome face. All in all, the day had been great. Ian was the perfect gentleman and Mackenzie found herself really falling for him. She pushed away her worries about the future and decided she needed to keep positive thoughts about any kinds of plans with him.

They were nearly at her home. Mackenzie was exhausted and stifled a yawn.

"You're all tuckered out," Ian said as they pulled up to her house.

She smiled at him. "I had a really great time today."

"Me too," he answered. "It doesn't have to end." Ian wiggled his eyebrows at her.

Mackenzie wished she had the energy to invite him inside and get to know him more…on a physical level. "Interested in brunch tomorrow?" she offered.

Ian seemed to be going through his mental calendar. "Will there be dessert?"

"There might be, if you play your cards right," she teased and let herself out of the Jeep. Ian laughed as Mackenzie turned and walked up to her door. She looked back and found that Ian was sitting there and watching to make sure she got inside okay. Mackenzie gave him a wave and let herself in.

She yawned again and raced to get out of her boots. The day on the boat had worn her out more than she'd realized. She'd be turning in early tonight.

Mackenzie had showered and was now in warm pajamas, contemplating if she should have cocoa or hot cider when her cell phone chirped. She found her phone on the kitchen counter and peered down at the screen. *Gideon*.

"Hello?" she answered.

"Hey, Mac," Gideon said.

"What are you up to?" Mackenzie spotted a cinnamon stick and was almost convinced to go with the cider. "Cocoa or cider?"

"It's November, definitely the cider."

"Really?"

"Yeah, cocoa is more of a December thing anyway." Gideon said, weighing in on the matter of hot beverages.

"I thought eggnog was."

"True, but everyone knows fall is when you drink hot cider. Cocoa is more for those chilly winter nights. And why am I not being invited over for either of those drinks right now?" Gideon caused Mackenzie to laugh. He was such a goofball.

"Because it's late and yours truly is about to go to bed."

"I'm happy to join you," he teased.

"I bet you would, but remember... Friends don't do that."

"Yes, they do. It's called friends with benefits," Gideon countered.

"Oh please. In your dreams, pal," Mackenzie shot back with a smile in her voice. She heard the distinct cry of a baby and Gideon explained that he had to go. He wished her a good night. It dawned on her how comfortable they'd grown together. They truly were friends.

* * * *

Mackenzie was cutting up a cantaloupe when Ian called and canceled brunch. She stared at all the fruit she had already diced and arranged on a lovely platter. She'd organized bright strawberries, plump grapes and perfectly sliced oranges. Mackenzie was bummed, to say the least. Ian had offered to stop by after the so-called Blu emergency had been handled and make her dinner. For some reason, Mackenzie just wasn't in the mood and told him she had plans. *Maybe I should check in on Molly?* She was going to be released from the hospital today, but Mackenzie wanted to give her a little time to get settled.

She was tempted to put all the fruit in some containers and go back to bed. It was another gloomy day—the rain was coming down in hard sheets and there was no sign of it stopping anytime soon. Mackenzie peeked out her kitchen window and released a heavy sigh. *Maybe I should start decorating for Thanksgiving?* She'd already cleared her porch of all the spooky Halloween items but had left the haybales and that cute scarecrow. The inside of her home could use a dash of fall and decorating always cheered her up. She always made a big production of how she set up her dining table for the get-together. *Might as well make use of today.*

She had ventured out to the garage in search of some holiday boxes she had stashed away. Mackenzie was juggling an awkward box when she felt her phone buzz in her jeans pocket.

"Hello?" she answered without looking at the screen.

"You home?" It was Gideon. Since becoming *'friends'*, they seemed to always be talking—a phone call here, a text there.

"Yeah, I was just looking for some Thanksgiving stuff in the garage. What's up?"

"I just happen to be in the neighborhood and wanted to swing by. Need any help with those boxes?" he offered.

"Oh, it's fine. I can manage." Mackenzie pulled another one to the ground as she cradled the phone in the crook of her neck.

"So, you're decorating for Thanksgiving?"

"Sure am." Mackenzie peeked into another box.

"And where is my invite?" Gideon teased with a serious undertone.

"You'll be spending it with your mom and daughter, won't you?" She paused after locating a box she'd been searching for. Mackenzie scanned the tower of cardboard boxes.

"You looking for that paper turkey your sister made when she was a kid? You used to always put that out," Gideon recalled. It was the tackiest thing ever but Mackenzie didn't have the heart to throw it out.

"I think I know which box it's in," Mackenzie said with a laugh. "I can't believe you remember that thing."

"Mac, you always made all the holidays special, even if that included that goofy-looking turkey."

"They holidays are meant to be special," Mackenzie said as she located the box containing the old paper turkey. Some of the construction paper was faded and a few of the feathers had come unglued. Mackenzie felt her throat tighten. This would be the first holiday season without her sister.

"You found it, didn't you?" Gideon asked with concern.

"I did," she managed to say through the onslaught of tears.

"I just pulled up." Gideon disconnected the line.

Mackenzie stood there and stared at the turkey she held in her hands. It was almost weightless and didn't match the heaviness she felt in her heart. It was the kind of thing a kid brings home from school for their parents. It had been that year when their father had gotten sick. That stupid turkey symbolized a period of time when their lives had begun to change. When their childhood changed... Mackenzie swatted the tears away and felt familiar arms wrap around her.

Gideon kissed the side of her head as she melted into him. "I miss her so much, Gid." Mackenzie cried into his chest as he held her close to him.

"I know you do, baby," he responded. She didn't want him to let her go. *Damn, we are a perfect fit.* Gideon was quite a bit taller than her. He always made her feel protected anytime he'd held her in his arms and against his muscular chest. His hard body against her soft frame felt as though they were molded together. Ian flashed across her mind and she recalled how nice it was to be held by him, too, but not nearly as perfect as this.

Gideon gently pushed her away but continued to hold her arms and look down at her. "Mackenzie, damn, I wish I would've been here for you when you lost her. I should have been," he growled through clenched teeth. "I never should have left you."

"Gideon, you had no way of knowing," Mackenzie countered as she wiped away more tears. "It was so sudden."

"I don't think we can ever prepare ourselves for that kind of shit. It doesn't matter if it's a slow process or a quick one. It sucks."

"You're right, but I will get through it. The holidays are always hard, especially the first ones."

Gideon pulled her close again. "You don't have to go through it alone."

"I have Molly and Tiffany."

"And not me, right?" Gideon said.

"You know what I mean," Mackenzie replied as she pulled away. "Let's not do this, okay?"

"I'm just saying that I know I let you down and I want to make it up to you."

Mackenzie saw hurt swim in his eyes and her heart softened. "Gid, you're here now, aren't you?"

There was something so utterly sexy about the way he looked at her. Gideon used his thumb to wipe a tear from her cheek. It felt rough against her skin. He winked and said, "What are friends for?"

* * * *

The late afternoon sun was almost blinding with how bright it shone. Mackenzie welcomed the warmth it brought with it. It was a beautiful fall day, picture perfect in every way imaginable. Her students loved the sunshine and didn't want to return from recess. Mackenzie couldn't blame them. They'd all had enough of the awful rain that had plagued the city for the last few weeks. She decided to take their after-lunch lesson outside. She thought she'd pretty much won the best-teacher-ever award when she broke that news.

After Mackenzie wrapped up things at work, she decided to pay Molly and that precious new baby a visit. Equipped with coffee and pumpkin bread, Mackenzie knocked on Molly's door.

Molly answered with dark circles under her eyes and her wavy dark hair in a loose pile on top of her head. "You brought coffee. You realize how much I love you, right?"

"I also brought some pumpkin bread I baked last night." Mackenzie followed Molly inside. The sun's rays washed the large living room with beautiful, golden light.

"I love you even more."

Mackenzie joined Molly on the couch. A bassinet was next to it and Molly put her finger to her lips. "I just got her to sleep," she whispered.

"So, how are you feeling?"

"Exhausted. Fucking exhausted," Molly answered as sipped her coffee. "Owen is gone super early in the morning then he's wiped out when he returns. He's been trying to help at night. This little one seems to have her nights and days mixed up."

"You look fabulous," she lied.

"I haven't showered because she won't let me and I look like hell warmed over. Thanks, anyway."

"What are friends for?" Mackenzie smiled and recalled Gideon saying that same exact thing to her last weekend.

"What's new with you?" Molly asked as she peered over into the bassinet.

"Nothing much. Went whale watching with Ian and Gideon stopped by on Sunday."

"Let's start with Ian," Molly instructed in a whisper. "What's happening there?"

Mackenzie sighed. "Well, it's funny. I like being with him. He's very witty and charming."

"And hot as hell."

"There's that, too," Mackenzie agreed.

"And things are progressing with him?"

"We haven't gotten together as much as I'd like. Our work schedules are a little different from one another, as you can imagine. I invited him to brunch on Sunday and he had to cancel due to something at Blu."

"That's a shame," Molly said, but Mackenzie sensed that her friend didn't mean it. "And how's Gid these days?"

"You just saw him last week," Mackenzie teased.

"True, but you've seen him since then, haven't you?" Molly raised her eyebrows.

Mackenzie laughed. "I did. Nothing happened. We're friends now."

Molly covered her mouth to stifle a yawn. "Oh, come off of it. There's no way that's going to last."

"It needs to," Mackenzie said.

"Does it? I think you two can fix whatever went wrong between you. He's different now. I can see it. Gideon's softer and just completely changed. I like this new and improved Gid," Molly commented as she took another sip. "Owen really likes him, too."

"You guys haven't even met Ian yet," Mackenzie said as she patted Molly's leg.

"I don't need to. I see how you and Gideon are together."

"Moll, we had our chance. I want to see where things go with Ian."

"You're totally wasting your time," Molly said with an eye roll.

"I think the sleep deprivation has gotten to you," Mackenzie deflected. She really didn't feel like having to defend her choice. "You better nap when she does." Mackenzie motioned toward the sleeping baby.

Molly yawned again. "I think you're right. Thanks for the coffee."

Mackenzie rose off the couch and kissed Molly on the cheek. "Try to shower."

"Tell her that."

As Mackenzie let herself out, she ran into Owen, who was just arriving home.

"Hey, Mac," Owen said. "Leaving already? Sure you don't want to stay for dinner?" He lifted up a wrapped package, probably containing some of his fresh catch of the day.

"I just stopped by to check on them and brought Moll a coffee. There's some pumpkin bread in there," Mackenzie informed him.

"Once Molly starts feeling better, I'd like to have you and Gideon over for dinner. He and I got to talking about halibut," Owen explained.

"Sounds great. You get some rest and remind Molly to sleep when the baby sleeps."

"Molly is such a great mom but is a worry wart. She's constantly checking to make sure the baby is breathing." Owen let out a throaty laugh. "You drive safe and I'll let you know about dinner."

"Thanks." Mackenzie got into her car and watched as Owen grabbed a bouquet of flowers from the passenger side of his truck. *Who says romance is dead?*

* * * *

Several days zoomed by and Mackenzie realized that Thanksgiving was less than a week away. She needed to get her shopping done and had been working on the detailed grocery list. Mackenzie sat in her kitchen. The house was eerily quiet. She'd spoken with Ian but knew that Blu was insanely busy on Friday. He'd felt terrible about not seeing her for nearly a week and had invited her to his place the next evening. Mackenzie was looking forward to it but had to kill time until then. She tapped her pen against the notepad as she tried to think of what else to add to the list. Her doorbell buzzed and she reluctantly got up from her chair.

There stood Gideon, a large pizza box in one hand and a baby carrier in the other. Mackenzie had to admit that it was a pretty impressive juggling act.

"Let me help you," Mackenzie said as she grabbed the box from him. "This smells really good." She led the way inside.

"I even brought beer. It's in the car, though. I'll have to go back out. You mind holding her?" Gideon asked as he lifted Azita from her car seat.

"Do I mind? I don't mind getting to hold this precious girl," Mackenzie cooed to the beautiful brown-eyed baby who rewarded Mackenzie with a slight smile. "Oh, Azita, you sweet little thing."

"She just started to really smile and does it all the time now." Gideon darted outside and returned in record time with two six-packs of beer. One was Olympia and the other his favorite, Rainer.

Mackenzie cradled Azita close to her and followed Gideon into her kitchen where he began to pull plates from the cabinet. She didn't even bother asking if he knew where anything was. The man had spent enough time here to know this place as well as his own house.

"So, you're probably wondering why I'm here," Gideon said as he carried two plates to her dining table. "Want me to take her so you can eat?"

"I'm good." Mackenzie enjoyed the feel of the baby in her arms. The whole scene seemed so domestic and everything that she wanted. The problem was, this wasn't her baby or her man, even if he did bring pizza and beer.

"You sure?" Gideon asked again as he pulled a chair out for her to sit.

"We're fine, aren't we?" Mackenzie cooed again to the precious little being staring up at her in wonder. "So, you were telling me why you're here," she said after sitting down. Gideon sat next to her.

"Remember the last time we sat here?" Gideon wiggled his eyebrows at her.

How can I forget? Every single time I sit at my table I think of the intense fucking. Maybe I should buy a new dining set.

Mackenzie chose to ignore his comment and managed to grab her pizza slice. Gideon shook his head. "I won't ever forget it." He popped the tab on a beer and took a long drink. "I figured since it was Friday and Molly just had the baby, you guys probably weren't having your girly Friday night thing you all do."

"*Friendship Friday*," Mackenzie said. "They are becoming fewer these days. Everyone is so busy."

"Like you?" Gideon teased as he tapped her shopping list that was still on the table.

"I'll have you know, mister, I was organizing Thanksgiving dinner. It takes a great deal of thought and preparation."

"You mean beyond throwing a bird in the oven?" Gideon joked as he leaned back in his chair. "You still make those pies?"

Mackenzie giggled. "Tiffany was just asking me about those. Yes, I do."

"Then it's settled. I'll be here for turkey day."

"Gid, you should spend it with your mom. I know it would mean the world to her."

Gideon took another sip. "She's planning a vacation back east to visit some family there. The pretty little lady and I will be left to our devices, won't we, sweetheart?" Gideon bent over and kissed his daughter on her forehead. Mackenzie frowned.

"Seriously, Gid?"

He nodded. "It's fine. Just remember the holidays are about family and *friends*."

"You're right. it's settled. You two will be coming here," Mackenzie stated.

Gideon almost appeared to blush. "Really? I was just giving you a hard time. You don't have to have us here, you know."

"Gid, you're right. We're friends and you shouldn't be alone on Thanksgiving. You can come early and help." Mackenzie suggested and instantly regretted the offer.

"I'd love to." Gideon raised his beer and Mackenzie did the same. He clinked their metal cans and smiled at her. "Have you seen Molly?"

"I have. Poor thing, she looks worn out. They'll be here for Thanksgiving."

"How about Tiff and her husband?" Gideon asked as he got up and grabbed the pizza box.

"Of course." Mackenzie nibbled another bite of pizza while she balanced Azita in her arm.

"So the whole gang will be here. That's pretty cool."

Mackenzie winced. She'd invited Ian to join them as well and it hadn't dawned on her until now. She wasn't sure it was such a great idea to have her ex and sort-of-kinda new boyfriend under the same roof.

"What's with that look?"

Mackenzie blinked hard. "What look?"

"Oh, knock it off. There's something you're not telling me. You forget how long I've known you," Gideon said.

"Uh, well," Mackenzie began. She took a deep breath and grabbed her beer. She swallowed a long chug hoping it would calm her nerves. *Might as well get this over with.* "I invited someone else to join us."

"Like, a co-worker or another friend?" Gideon asked, though the expression on his face said it all. He'd guessed right away it was another guy.

"I'm sort of seeing someone," Mackenzie added.

"I see. You guys serious?" Gideon chewed his pizza without making eye contact.

"It's too early to say," she explained. "He's Colin's friend."

Gideon nodded again. "Mac, look. I don't want things to be weird or for you to feel like you can't date again. Would I love for us to being dating again? Absolutely.

I just want you to be happy. You know that, right? You deserve it and so much more." Gideon paused and took another long swig of his beer. "God knows I wasn't the one who was able to give you that."

Mackenzie grabbed her beer and looked away. *So much for this whole friend thing.*

Chapter Thirteen

Ian gave Mackenzie a sly grin. "You made it. I thought you'd never arrive."

Mackenzie lifted the bottle of wine. "And I even brought this."

He pulled her close to him. "You are more than enough." Ian kissed her full on the mouth. "I've missed you."

His apartment was everything Mackenzie had imagined — industrial-chic, very modern and contemporary. Lots of steel and smooth glass. The furniture was all hard angles and leather. It was masculine and edgy. Ian lived in the busy downtown area not too far from Blu. The upscale apartment lacked warmth and any kind of homey feel, but it smelled divine as Mackenzie followed Ian inside. He threw a small towel over his shoulder, and even in his home, he looked like a proper chef. He was just missing his infamous blue chef's jacket.

"It smells incredible in here," Mackenzie complimented.

"Thanks. You want to open that wine for us?" Ian peeked at something inside the oven then gave a steaming skillet a quick flip. "Glasses are up there," he instructed as he motioned to the glass door right in front of Mackenzie.

She grabbed two wine glasses and set them on the counter. The counters were polished concrete and gleamed with the hanging lights. She felt awkward in the cold space. Her home was completely different. Hers reminded her of the kitchen she'd grown up in — her mother's kitchen, where she and her sister had spent days baking and learning family recipes. After pouring the wine, she went to hand Ian a glass and instead he snared her. He looped his arms around her waist, kissed her neck then gently bit her flesh.

"I say screw dinner. I could just eat you. You smell delicious," he complimented her as he nuzzled her neck. She was growing more turned on by the minute. But, as usual, everything seemed to move so fast with Ian. It was as though they were a VHS tape with someone pressing fast-forward. Mackenzie didn't feel like she could keep up with him or catch her breath. Maybe that was part of his plan.

Mackenzie tried to gain a little space between them as she backed away. "So, what smells so good?"

"You mean besides you?" Ian winked. "I just threw a little bit of this and that together."

"Well, I'm starving," Mackenzie answered.

"Me, too." Ian stared at her as though he could devour every last inch of her right there in his kitchen.

Mackenzie shifted her weight and felt uneasy. *Is tonight going to be the night?* She'd gone through the ritual that just about every woman knew was a huge pain in the ass. She'd plucked, shaved and made everything—*everything*—smooth and sexy. *You know, just in case.* She wore a skirt, heels and had even bought a new bra and panty set especially for the occasion. Mackenzie knew that with fast as Ian moved, he wouldn't keep settling for kisses and heavy petting. Besides, they were grown-ass adults approaching forty, so it wasn't as though they were naïve or inexperienced kids. Mackenzie was still somewhat old-fashioned and hardly a slut. She believed in monogamy and had always been against one-night stands. She'd left that kind of crazy and reckless behavior to Tiffany and Molly, who were both settled down and married now. *Go figure.* If Mackenzie played her cards right, that very well might become her future with Ian. As she surveyed his apartment, she knew one thing for sure. They'd be living in her home.

"Want the tour?" Ian asked, interrupting her thoughts.

"Sure." She swallowed the white wine and begged her nerves to relax.

Ian led them out of the kitchen, which truly was the gem of the apartment. She knew that was why Ian lived there. It wasn't the incredibly tiny bathroom or the single small bedroom. As they stood in it, Ian snatched her up into his arms. He found her mouth and she let herself fold into him. He tugged at her bottom lip, causing her pussy to grow wet. *This man knows how to kiss.* She could only imagine what other things he was good at. "This is where dessert will be served. I believe you brought that as well, right?" Ian winked at Mackenzie, causing her to blush.

He kissed her again and Mackenzie ran her hand down the front of his pants. She could feel Ian's large bulge through his slacks and it turned her on that much more that he was already hard. Ian paused and sniffed the air. "Shit." He hurried out of the room with lightning speed.

She noticed the exposed brick in the living room as she went in search of him. *Why does it seem like something always stops us when things grow hot? It's as if the universe is working hard to keep me from getting laid.*

"Sorry, love," Ian apologized as rescued a smoky skillet from the range.

"Oh dear, is it ruined?" Mackenzie asked.

"You distracted me, you terribly naughty girl," Ian teased. "You hungry?"

Yes, but not for whatever now smells slightly burned.

Dinner was, of course, perfect. Ian had some of the best culinary skills she'd ever witnessed. He'd made a sauce in record time and Mackenzie had watched in awe as he created it. They discussed Thanksgiving plans. Ian joked that he wasn't too familiar with American Thanksgivings. Mackenzie felt ignorant at first and laughed as he explained that it was an American tradition. He offered to help her prepare it and told Mackenzie he was excited to see her in action in the kitchen.

"Dessert?" Ian asked after they finished the last of the wine. Mackenzie felt even more nervous. The wine'd had the opposite effect to the one she'd been hoping for.

Mackenzie swallowed the last small sip in her glass and rose from her seat. She was a little dizzy. She wasn't certain if it was from the wine or being around Ian. Mackenzie sashayed as erotically as possible over to him. Ian found her hip as she straddled him.

Mackenzie kissed him along his neck and worked her way past his goatee to his lips. He moaned into her mouth, which only turned her on more and encouraged her to keep going. A thought flickered in her brain. She still hadn't slept with anyone since Gideon. Being celibate for nearly two years except for that spontaneous fucking in her dining room… Gideon was all her body knew. She wondered what Ian would feel like inside her. The nerves tightened inside her stomach as she deepened the kiss and attempted to forget Gideon. Her heart felt like it was doing something very wrong.

Ian massaged her breasts through her blouse. He began to pluck at the buttons until he opened the silky top to reveal her soft pink bra. Everything was silent except for her heart that pounded in her ears.

"God, you're beautiful, Mackenzie."

Her brain almost expected to hear Gideon's voice, not the sexy Irish brogue that escaped Ian's lips as he nuzzled her cleavage. He tugged down the cup of her lacy bra to reveal a nipple that demanded attention. He obliged and took her breast into his hand and raised Mackenzie's nipple to his mouth. He moved his other hand up her thigh. His cock hardened under her, begging to be released from the confines of his trousers. Mackenzie shifted away from it and slowly slithered off him to the floor. She moved between his thighs and planted herself on her knees. Mackenzie looked up at Ian. He showed his approval of what she silently asked with a dreamy smile and an almost imperceptible nod. Mackenzie undid his belt and pants. Ian slinked back farther in his chair and granted her access to his cock.

Mackenzie freed his rigid cock and he released a loud moan. She gasped at the girth of it. It wasn't incredibly long but damn, it was thick. For a brief second, Mackenzie panicked as she contemplated just how she was going to fit that sucker into her mouth. She devised a plan. Her tongue would do most of the loving as it worshiped this monster and Mackenzie's hand would have to fill in where her mouth couldn't.

She flicked her tongue against the velvety head then ran it down the entire length of his shaft to where it ended. She delicately kissed the soft skin of his nearly shaved balls. Every inch of Ian was groomed and granted Mackenzie easy access. His fingers were in her hair as he guided her closer to him. Mackenzie resisted and wanted him to know who was in charge here. Blow jobs weren't exactly her favorite thing in the world, unlike Tiffany and Molly who simply loved giving them. Maybe it was Mackenzie's gag reflex or that she didn't like being put into a submissive role, but blow jobs were usually saved for special occasions like birthdays, anniversaries or when she really wanted to get her way. Mackenzie slowly fed him into her mouth. She tried to relax her throat muscles to accommodate his size. Her brain was so focused on not gagging that Mackenzie worried she wasn't sucking enough and tried to remember to breathe as she worked his cock.

"Come on, baby," Ian urged as he pumped into her mouth suddenly. She tried to keep in rhythm with him, matching each thrust, but she struggled to keep up.

She remembered to use her hand to work his stone-hard cock. Her spit created a slick surface to maneuver. As hot as this should be, Mackenzie found it wasn't really doing it for her and she tried to move faster with longer strokes. She sucked hard on his head and could taste the salty-sweet pre-cum that had begun to ooze from him. He was tensing up and she saw the light at the end of the tunnel. *You got this, girl. Just hang in there. Not much longer.* Her jaw began to ache from how wide Ian was. Not teetering over in the heels she'd worn was an acrobatic feat as Ian began to fuck her mouth. He grabbed his cock with one hand and pulled a fist full of her hair back with the other. His face twisted into torturous pleasure as he neared his orgasm and pumped. His hips bucked and Mackenzie braced herself on his thighs as she held on for this wild ride.

Ian cried out, "Fuuuuuck." He came inside her mouth and Mackenzie swallowed as much of it as she could. The thick, warm ribbons slid down her throat in a steady stream. She felt it dribble onto her chin and Ian looked down at her in a lusty daze and gently wiped the drop with his thumb. He pushed it past her lips and smiled. "I didn't want you to miss a drop of dessert."

* * * *

Mackenzie yawned and stretched in bed. *Her* bed. Last night had ended on a very weird note. She had wanted it to be so much more and had placed such insanely high expectations on how it should go that she found herself let down. Ian had gotten what he'd wanted. It wasn't as if he'd asked for a lot. Guys were sometimes simple that way. Mackenzie wasn't all that sure what *she* desired — to be wined, dined, then what? She had decided not to sleep with Ian, because if she had, a blow job wouldn't have been the grand finale. It was as though there was a wall keeping her from taking that final step to the bedroom. What they'd done would have to suffice until Mackenzie figured out just what in the hell she did want.

Maybe things were moving too fast. She needed to get to know Ian more, to spend quality time with him — like pizza and beer while laughing at a stupid movie. She pictured Gideon, his daughter on his chest and him laughing at something ridiculous happening on the movie they'd watched the other night. Her brain said to do one thing, her heart another. She was the one who'd insisted they were just *friends*. *So why am I struggling with the whole concept?*

Coffee. That would right her Sunday morning. *Screw men.* Well, obviously not literally from how last night had ended. Things had gotten a little awkward after her not-so-grand blow job. Mackenzie was pretty sure that was probably the worst one he'd ever received and she felt like shit for not putting her heart into it. When she'd finished, it had seemed like everything fast-forwarded again and she had soon been leaving his apartment. It had probably been for the best. With Ian, things moved at lightning speed and Mackenzie wanted to slow it down. With Gideon, it was all was confusing. He was everything she remembered but a better version of the old Gideon. *How in the hell is that even possible?* Even Tiffany was warming up to him. That alone raised concern.

Enough thinking about men. Mackenzie decided that after she ate and drowned her sorrows in coffee with tons of her new cinnamon-vanilla creamer, she was going to call her girls.

Mackenzie popped out of bed and set to work grinding dark roasted coffee beans. Her kitchen filled with the aroma. That was nothing compared to when the freshly ground beans were being brewed into a magical potion. She peered out the window and no surprise. The dismal gray skies matched her crappy mood. Fat raindrops pounded the cedar deck outside the dining room. Her potted marigolds were still brilliant oranges and yellows and seemed to be enjoying all the rain. Everything out there was muted and ugly except those fluffy flowers. Mackenzie smiled at the thought of their resilience. If only she were half as strong and tough.

She filled a jumbo-sized mug and doctored up her coffee with loads of creamer and sugar. The first taste practically kissed her soul. It warmed her to her very core and she began to feel better. Screw fairytales with knights on horses and charming princes rescuing princesses from towers. Magic beans — more specifically, beans from Columbia — were where it was at. They delivered on their promises...unlike stupid men. *Who needs them, anyway?*

Mackenzie was headed to the living room when she heard a knock at her door. She looked down at her Hello Kitty pajama bottoms and oversized and well-loved dark green Seattle SuperSonics basketball tee. She'd owned it back when Seattle'd had a team — the good old days when Shawn Kemp and Gary Payton had owned the court in the Tacoma Dome.

Mackenzie held her mug, her blonde hair in a nubby ponytail, and she answered the door. "Don't you have a home?" Mackenzie asked.

"I like yours better," Gideon answered. "Plus, I brought scones."

"Are you trying to buy my affection?"

"Is it working?" he asked as he shook the white paper sack.

"That depends," Mackenzie started. "Are those — ?"

"Huckleberry scones?" Gideon asked with a knowing smile. "There might even be a few lemon and pumpkin ones."

"Okay, just get in here." Mackenzie tugged him inside.

"Hey, easy, lady. I don't take too kindly to being manhandled."

Mackenzie rolled her eyes and peered into the carrier. "She's always sleeping."

"Car rides always seem to knock her out," Gideon replied. "Got coffee?"

"Just made some."

"Damn, I'm good. I tried to time it just right."

"Well done." Mackenzie grabbed a mug for Gideon and poured him some of the rich coffee.

"Dear Lord. More creamer?" Gideon announced as he peeked into her fridge. "What happened to the days when people just used half and half—or hell, just milk?"

"Gross. Try the cinnamon vanilla. It's super good," Mackenzie suggested as she motioned toward her mug. She hopped onto her counter and watched Gideon.

Gideon grabbed her mug and took a sip. He leaned against her legs and smiled. He reached for the container on the counter she'd just used only a moment ago for her coffee. "You're right. It's pretty tasty," he commented as he read the back of the bottle.

"You doubted me," Mackenzie said as she shook her head and climbed down. They milled around in her kitchen, getting plates for their breakfast. It felt natural with Gideon there, and in many ways, it royally pissed Mackenzie off. She wanted things to feel like this with Ian. Easy. Natural. Right.

"You ready for Thursday?" Gideon asked after they were seated the table.

"Sort of. I need to do some last-minute shopping," Mackenzie answered as she reached for a huckleberry scone. The buttery treat practically melted in her mouth. She could kill Gideon. He knew her weakness. He knew *her*.

"Want to go today?"

"Oh, it's okay. I'll go a little later."

"Come on. It'll be fun. I need more diapers, anyway," Gideon insisted. "After we eat, you can go shower and get ready, even though I find that shirt incredibly sexy."

Mackenzie looked down at the faded dark-green shirt and snorted when she laughed. She was anything but sexy.

Gideon must have sensed her unease and asked, "Did you already find the bird?" Mackenzie shook her head. "Then you can use my brute strength," Gideon joked as he flexed his biceps. Mackenzie had to admit he was her hottest *friend*. Not only did this man deliver scones but he also made her laugh. If Mackenzie wasn't careful she just might start falling for him all over again.

Mackenzie showered and dressed while Gideon fed his daughter. She entered the living room to see him stretched out on the couch with Azita sprawled out on top of Gideon. Both were asleep and Mackenzie felt an overwhelming tug in her chest. She'd thought he was hot before but seeing a man with his child did funny things to her. There was just something about witnessing the tender moment that both tore Mackenzie's heart and filled her with maternal urges.

"Gid," Mackenzie gently whispered to wake him.

"Hey, beautiful," he replied. His eyes had that sexy bedroom glaze she missed. Gideon used one arm to reach for Mackenzie. She didn't fight it when he pulled her down and he kissed her as though it were the most natural thing in the world.

She backed away as if she'd been burned. "We'd better get going." He stared at her, but it was different from the hungry stare Ian always gave her. This one was filled with a familiar depth and regret pooled in the soft color of his eyes. Mackenzie wished she could erase that look, kiss the hurt away.

Gideon insisted they take his SUV for the shopping excursion. He strapped the baby's car seat into place. He tugged on the strap a few times — the sign of an overly protective father. He truly was a good daddy. Mackenzie was clicking her seat belt and witnessed him tickle the baby, causing her to coo back at him. He whispered sweetly to her, explaining where they were headed and who they were with. Mackenzie sighed and Gideon looked up at her.

"You okay?" he asked.

She nodded. *What can I tell him?* Mackenzie couldn't relay to him that it gutted her now more than ever that they had lost *their* baby, that she'd lost *him*, and that *his* daughter should be *their* daughter. *How am I expected to move on from the past if it keeps pulling me back to a time I really want to forget?*

The ride to the grocery store was quiet. Traffic was light the entire way and Mackenzie pretended to be focused on her shopping list.

"You'd think by now you'd have that darn thing memorized," Gideon teased as he pulled into an empty parking space.

"I just want to make sure I have everything I need," she answered. Mackenzie was just so bothered by all the emotions taking flight inside her. *This isn't how today is supposed to go.* They weren't supposed to be going shopping like they some happy little family. She was supposed to like Ian.

Gideon removed Azita from the back seat and even opened the door for Mackenzie. They walked into the market, and after Gideon found a shopping cart, he clipped the carrier to it. He pushed the cart toward the produce section. Mackenzie began to walk ahead and searched for the items on her list. She welcomed the distraction and tried not to think too much beyond the food she needed to fill the cart.

"Damn, are you planning on feeding an army?" Gideon asked as the shopping cart was nearly full.

"You'd think, wouldn't you?" Mackenzie giggled as she added marshmallows to the growing pile.

"You going to make those candied yams with the marshmallows?" Gideon asked with a giant smile.

"It wouldn't be Thanksgiving without them."

"God, I love you," he said. Mackenzie turned around. Their eyes met and Gideon apologized, "Sorry. You know what I mean," he said as struggled to find his words.

"We better get the rest of the stuff on this," Mackenzie steered the conversation away and tapped her list.

"Mac, I do love you. I'm not sorry for saying it."

A woman peeked over at them and smiled. "What a precious baby. Hope you are both finally getting enough sleep. It's so hard when they're first born."

Mackenzie opened her mouth to explain when Gideon answered, "She's a very good girl and sleeps through the night."

"You two must've done something right." The woman continued to share some motherly advice with them. When she was done, the woman apologized. "Oh dear, I'm keeping you from doing your Thanksgiving shopping. You three have a lovely holiday. It's the early years when so many wonderful family memories are made."

Gideon wished her well and they said goodbye. Mackenzie began to say something and Gideon shook his head. His voice was rough. "Please don't. We were a family once, Mac. Let me just pretend that we still are."

His words splintered her heart and Mackenzie realized she was in way over her head. To see Gideon so vulnerable and open bothered her. She was used to him keeping his feelings guarded and protecting her by saying nothing at all. All those years when he'd leave to do his tour, he wouldn't say a damn thing. He would just hold her until it was time for him to leave again. Gideon had soldiered on and pretended that everything was fine. Mackenzie thought she's been the only one breaking every time he'd left. She'd bought into his tough-guy act. She'd thought that it had been her world that had imploded when they'd lost their baby. *What about his?* His world had been obliterated just as much as hers, and on top of it, he'd had to go back to that fucking awful desert.

Mackenzie suddenly felt like a selfish bitch and was disgusted. She was mad at Gideon but mostly herself. *Why did I give up on us so easily?* Mackenzie should've written to him. *Why did I leave all that up to him?* He'd suggested they break up because he was grieving, too. He was processing everything and had to find a way to soldier on. Gideon felt responsible for everything that they'd lost and was left with little way of fixing it. Now he was back and wanted more than ever to pretend that everything did work out just fine—to be the family they'd both wanted.

Gideon avoided her gaze and kept his eyes trained on his daughter. *His family*. Mackenzie did the only thing that felt right. She grabbed his hand and linked her fingers through his. She didn't have all the answers, and maybe that was part of the lessons she was learning in her life, but there was one thing she could do for him. They could pretend, at least for today, in this overly bright and crowded grocery store, that they were a family...again.

Chapter Fourteen

Mackenzie wrestled with the enormous raw turkey to remove it from the fridge. *Why did I have to get the biggest one at the store? Because Gideon insisted on it.* And now it sat on her kitchen counter, taunting her with the messy task of prepping him for dinner. Mackenzie peeked over at the green digital clock on her microwave. It was early. *Way too early.* She waited for the coffee to finish brewing. Hopefully it would be the jump-start she so needed. *Why do I subject myself to this kind of torture? Why do I always have to be the hostess?* Complain as she might, Mackenzie loved playing the role of Martha Stewart — not *prison* Martha Stewart, but the crafty one who could make fancy five-course meals out of three ingredients. Every wannabe Betty Crocker-type woman wanted to be a Martha. Mackenzie was pouring her coffee when her doorbell buzzed.

"Why don't you just let yourself in?" she said when she opened the door to Gideon.

"Where's the fun in that? This way I get greeted by the prettiest girl in the world," he replied as he followed Mackenzie inside. "It doesn't smell like turkey yet."

"Ha. Ha." Mackenzie leaned against her counter and stared at the center attraction of the day. Its pink skin would eventually be the perfect brown and its meat succulent. That was the plan anyway.

"I need to run out to the car. Can you keep an eye on her?" Gideon set the carrier on the ground. He returned with a ton of gear, a portable playpen and several grocery sacks.

"Moving in?" Mackenzie teased.

"I wish. I figured it might be a good idea for her to have her portable crib here today. And you'll thank me when you see what else I brought." Gideon began emptying the brown sacks. She spied orange juice then champagne. *Mimosas*. "Remember that one year you let me help on Thanksgiving?"

"I do." They had drunk mimosas and had had the best time in the kitchen together. Granted, most of the time Gideon had been snacking either on the food or her. Those had been the happy times. It had also been their last Thanksgiving together.

Mackenzie handed Gideon a mug of coffee.

"We ready to get him in the oven?" Gideon motioned to the turkey.

"I just need to rub him down with butter," Mackenzie answered as they both stared at it.

"Lucky bastard."

Mackenzie rolled her eyes and they soon got to work on Thanksgiving Day dinner preparations — chopping, dicing, peeling, stirring and basting. Mackenzie hadn't realized how long they'd been cooking. That was mostly thanks to the mimosas. She and Gideon laughed and worked together in perfect harmony. Gideon wasn't the best cook, but he was an enormous help and took instruction well. He was given simple tasks while Mackenzie took on the more intricate aspects of the meal. He made cooking fun.

"It smells amazing in here," Tiffany announced as she appeared in the kitchen.

Mackenzie hugged her and accepted the bottle of wine she offered. Mackenzie looked down and saw their precious bulldog. He wiggled and begged to be petted. Colin quickly hugged her and went to chat with Gideon, leaving the two women alone. The bulldog paused then followed the men out of the kitchen.

"So, how's it going with him here?" Tiffany asked as she watched the guys leave the kitchen.

"Great. Getting along is not the problem." Mackenzie walked to the oven and peeked on the picture-perfect turkey.

"Then what is?" Tiffany raised an eyebrow.

Mackenzie sighed. "I'm not sure."

Tiffany gave her a tight-lipped smile. "Ian still coming to dinner?" Mackenzie nodded. "Won't that be a little awkward?"

"Probably," Mackenzie answered. "Wanna peel potatoes?"

"Sure," Tiffany replied as she went to the sink to wash her hands. "When will Molly be here?"

"A little later. I told her she doesn't have to help too much. That baby is still keeping her up all night, poor thing," Mackenzie explained then yawned.

"I have no desire to be utterly exhausted. There isn't enough coffee in Columbia to cure that kind of tired."

"True. But, damn, their baby is so cute, isn't she?"

"And that somehow makes sleep deprivation worth it? I don't think so," Tiffany teased as she began to peel the potatoes.

"How are you and Colin doing?" Mackenzie stirred the mix for her pie.

"Good. Really good, other than this baby fever he's got. He's probably in there with Gideon plotting my pregnancy now," Tiffany said with annoyance. Mackenzie decided to take a peek and tugged Tiffany with her. They snuck against the wall as though they were secret agents and caught sight of the guys in the living room. "Just look at him, will ya?" Tiffany whispered. Colin was holding Gideon's daughter and the smile on his face said it all. "He'll be a hot dad someday."

"You'll be a pretty smokin' mom," Mackenzie reassured.

"I guess I'm not fully ready to share Colin yet," Tiffany admitted after they were back in the kitchen.

"The baby wouldn't be robbing you of him. If anything, it'll bring you guys to a whole new level."

"I like it just being Colin and me. I know it's selfish. I would miss going out with him, traveling and just our quiet time together. And what about Pauly?"

"He'd love a baby," Mackenzie replied.

"But *he's* our baby. Maybe I can convince Colin just to get a puppy." They both laughed and Mackenzie knew it was time to baste the bird so she called for Gideon's help.

Gideon smiled at her as he entered the kitchen. "You need my muscles again?"

"I didn't want to hurt your ego by doing it myself," Mackenzie joked. "Might as well take advantage of your services since you're here."

"I can think of other services I'd be happy to share," he teased with a sexy grin. She swatted him with a pot holder that he accepted to grab the giant tinfoil roaster from the oven. "The offer still stands." They worked together getting the turkey basted. The golden juices flowed over the brown skin. "Damn, this looks really good," Gideon commented as they covered the turkey back up with foil and closed the oven. "Need anything else?"

"No, you can go back to play with your new friend," Mackenzie teased.

"You should get a bulldog, Mac," Gideon suggested. "He's the coolest dog."

"Pauly's adorable, isn't he?" Tiffany added.

"Tiff, want to hold my little girl?" Gideon asked. "Colin's falling in love."

"I'd love to." Tiffany glanced over at Mackenzie and smiled.

Things were going too well. Gideon was fitting into this picture. *What will happen when Ian arrives?* Mackenzie looked at the clock. He'd be there in a few hours. She grew uneasy and wondered how the two men would get along. Mackenzie had told Gideon about Ian but they hadn't discussed it in too much detail. Ian had no clue about Gideon, other than this dinner would have her friends in attendance.

The previous weekend had left Mackenzie sifting through so many tousled emotions. It had started on Friday night, Gideon showing up with pizza and beer. He'd known she was lonely, probably because he too was all alone. He knew Fridays used to be spent with her girls and in the past that had caused strife between them. But last Friday had been fun and she'd appreciated the company. Then Saturday, she'd expected a sexy rendezvous with Ian, and in the end, it had turned out nothing short of craptastic. Sure, he'd gotten off, but Mackenzie had been too frozen inside to do anything more with him. Then leave it to Gideon to have shown up the following day.

Sunday had revealed more than she'd wanted, that had been for sure. Mackenzie had seen that Gideon hadn't been the only one to blame for their past and she'd witnessed a vulnerable side to him that had made her fall in love with him all over again. Maybe Gideon didn't realize the impact that shopping trip had had on her, but Mackenzie did. It wasn't anything super important, but when that woman had mistaken them for a young family, it had hit Mackenzie hard. She'd spent the entire week trying to ignore how it had made her feel. Part of her was tempted to cancel Thanksgiving dinner just so she didn't have to deal with Gideon *or* Ian. Now she stood in her kitchen staring at the closed oven and wondering how she'd gotten herself into this mess.

"Colin's trying to convince Tiff that it's baby time, but she's really pushing for a puppy," Gideon said from behind her.

Mackenzie turned around and smiled.

"Are Owen and Molly going to be here soon?" Gideon asked as he looked out her window. He wrapped his arm around her waist like he'd done hundreds of times before.

Mackenzie nodded. "Any minute."

"And that guy you're dating?" he asked in a low voice.

"A little while later, closer to dinner time."

"I promise to be on my best behavior," Gideon assured Mackenzie. "I won't make things weird."

"I appreciate that, Gid." Mackenzie stepped aside and pretended that something needed her attention.

Gideon didn't take the hint to leave and asked, "Does he make you happy?"

She wasn't sure how to answer that. *Does Ian make me happy?* He turned her on and was nice enough, but Mackenzie didn't know him well enough to say if he made her feel *happy*. She wished he made her feel that way, but if she were honest, there was only one guy who made her feel that way and he was standing right next to her.

Her doorbell buzzed and relief flooded her. *Saved by the bell.* Mackenzie left the kitchen to answer the door. Owen held an infant carrier that was similar to Gideon's. Molly raised a large bottle of wine and a bouquet of fall flowers.

"Those are lovely," Mackenzie thanked her. "Come on in, you guys. Tiffany and Colin are already here."

"Gid?" Molly asked in a whisper.

"He's been here since early this morning helping me."

"Mimosas?" Molly asked with a wink.

"How'd you know?" Mackenzie laughed.

"Because he's thoughtful and the last time you two hosted Thanksgiving, we all had them. Maybe there's some left over. Remember, I can drink now." Molly cheered.

"I'll see if we have some left."

Owen greeted Gideon and Gideon peeked under the pale pink blanket. Mackenzie joined him in looking at the gorgeous little girl.

"She's beautiful, you guys," Gideon said to them as they stood there. "My little one is in her portable crib in the living room."

"Really? Oh, let's introduce these girls," Owen replied.

Who are these guys? Molly looked at Mackenzie and laughed. "Future besties."

"Who Owen and Gid — or the girls?"

"Probably both," Molly answered. "It smells so good in here. I'm absolutely starving."

"You look amazing, by the way." Mackenzie noticed the color was back in her cheeks. There were no dark circles under her eyes, and best of all, Molly seemed happy.

"This" — Molly said as she waved her hands over her entire body and face — "is all thanks to makeup and finally getting a decent night's sleep."

"Well, you look great."

"What can I do to help?" Molly asked.

Tiffany appeared and nodded. "Me too. I'm done being pressured to get knocked up."

Mackenzie started grabbing veggie platters and other items from the fridge. "Here, we can set these out. You can't blame Colin for wanting a baby. Look at how adorable Ellie and Azita are. You two need to have a boy."

"We have a boy. His name is Pauly and he's already a handful," Tiffany countered.

Molly removed the plastic wrap and helped herself to a grape tomato. "So, when's the other one showing up?" Mackenzie sent her annoyed glare. "I'm sort of dying to see how that goes."

"He'll be here a little later." Mackenzie closed the fridge with her hip and brought more dishes to the counter.

"Do you think it was wise to invite him?" Tiffany asked.

"It's a little late now," Mackenzie answered.

Molly motioned toward the living room. "Gideon's in there right now making buddies with Colin and Owen. Poor Ian doesn't stand a chance."

"Ian's Colin's friend, so it'll be fine," Tiffany said.

"Gideon promised to behave," Mackenzie confirmed as she stirred some homemade dip to go with the veggies.

"He knows about Ian?" Tiffany and Molly asked in unison. The surprised look on their faces was priceless.

"Yes, and he's okay with it...I think."

"No, he's not. He may be acting like everything's all fine and dandy, but a man who shows up at your place at the butt crack of dawn to help cook and brings mimosas isn't just in it for the friendship," Molly explained.

Mackenzie knew she was right but that didn't change the fact that Ian was coming to dinner.

"He brought mimosas?"

"Yes. Why is that such a big deal?" Mackenzie asked.

"Because we all had those the last time you two were together for Thanksgiving. He's trying to remind you of the happier times."

"What about not living in the past anymore? Isn't that the same thing?"

Tiffany sighed. "Well, the past is the foundation of what you guys had before. It's where you built your relationship. That doesn't mean you need to keep living there. This thing you guys are doing now is sort of like the remodel."

"Remodel? Are you hearing yourself?" Mackenzie asked. "You didn't want me to see him at all and now you're totally good with it?"

"Let's just say that I'm warming up to the idea," Tiffany countered.

"You've got to be kidding me," Mackenzie huffed as she stared down at the arrangement of food. "You wanted me to date Ian."

"I wanted you to try and date *someone*. My hope was for you to move on and to at least get yourself back out there again—and you did." Tiffany smiled at her.

Molly patted Mackenzie's shoulder. "Tiff and I both see it, even if you don't." The problem was that Mackenzie saw it too.

The men were snacking on the food the women had set out. Mackenzie warned them not to eat too much. They teased that it was Thanksgiving, a day when they were expected to gorge themselves and that they were just keeping with tradition. The turkey was done and Mackenzie was waiting on the last pie to come out of the oven when the doorbell chimed loudly.

"I can get it," Gideon offered with a wink.

"Be good," Mackenzie reminded him as she removed her apron and went to answer the door.

Ian stood there with a lovely daisy and sunflower arrangement in deep reds and oranges. "Gobble, gobble," he said.

"You ready to experience a real Thanksgiving dinner?" Mackenzie asked as she let him inside.

"It smells lovely in here and I'm anxious to sample your culinary skills."

Mackenzie laughed and placed the flowers on a small table near the kitchen.

Everyone was huddled around the breakfast bar where the veggie platters, cheese and crackers plates had been set.

"There may be some snacks left, but dinner is basically ready," Mackenzie told Ian as they joined the group.

Gideon was the first to greet Ian and everyone watched in silence. *So much for this not being awkward.*

"Nice to meet you," Gideon shook Ian's hand. "Our girl has been hard at work all day. Hope you're hungry."

"Starving," Ian replied. His gaze shifted to Mackenzie then back to Gideon. No doubt they were sizing one another up, but true to his word, Gideon was behaving and acting more than friendly and cordial.

Colin hugged Ian and Owen introduced himself. Ian stood away from Mackenzie, which surprised her. Gideon remained close but within a polite distance. Mackenzie could feel Gideon's gaze on her and when she worked up the balls to meet his stare, he winked at her.

The men retreated into the living room and were instructed to wait until they were called for dinner.

"Wow," Molly said when they were finally alone. "First, he's hot as hell. Second, this is going to be one helluva pissing contest, let me tell you."

"There's no contest." Mackenzie removed the last pie to cool.

Tiffany grabbed a stack of white dinner plates to bring to the table. "You're completely right. There isn't."

"Thank you," Mackenzie appreciated Tiffany defending her.

"Oh, no. I mean, it's clear who has already won," Tiffany informed Mackenzie.

"Let's just get through this darn dinner, pretty please?" Mackenzie begged.

The table was set, candles lit and all of Mackenzie's closest friends gathered around it. This was what Thanksgiving was truly about — remembering to love those in your life, to share happy memories and to create new ones. She reveled in special moments like this and missed her sister, who should've been there with them. Gideon must have sensed her moment of reflection. He offered a kind smile to acknowledge who was missing from the table.

Ian now sat in her sister's place at the table. Mackenzie did her best to keep Gideon and Ian apart as a precaution. She just wanted to survive this dinner without any kind of drama. There were only a few small awkward moments when Mackenzie had briefly panicked. Carving the turkey was almost a biggie. She stood, prepared to cut into the bird but was unsure where to begin. Both Ian and Gideon had risen to help her. Ian had sat back down after Gideon explained in a very humorous manner that he and that turkey had been through a lot together and he felt he needed to see this to the end. Everyone laughed, even Ian, as Gideon retold the start of their journey together. He claimed they'd met in a totally cheesy-romantic-comedy kinda way, the supermarket of all places. It had been love at first sight. Then Gideon said the turkey had come home with him. He wiggled his eyebrows and explained how their love affair had continued with a buttery massage and lots of basting. Everyone loved his silly description of the turkey preparations and clapped when he was done with his monolog. Mackenzie could feel her heart smile as she listened to him command everyone's attention. He winked at her and bowed. Leave it to Gideon to save Mackenzie from what could've been an uncomfortable situation.

Mackenzie was seated at one end of the table and oddly enough, Gideon was at the other. Ian sat to her right, her sister's designated seat. Owen was at Gideon's right. Colin was seated across from Ian and they chatted among themselves about business. A lot of numbers and figures were being thrown out and she couldn't care less. Mackenzie ate quietly and listened on as everyone talked. Molly was determined to convince Tiffany to have a baby. Owen was asking Gideon for some baby pointers to which Gideon supplied what knowledge he had. Gideon's gaze kept finding Mackenzie's. *Is it wrong that I wish I was seated next to him?* Everyone was occupied and seemed to be enjoying their dinner. That was what she'd wanted. Her goal had been to create a successful Thanksgiving dinner and she'd done that. More wine was poured and Mackenzie heard something Ian said to Colin — something about London.

Ian must have sensed her curiosity. "I'll be opening another Blu in London."

"That's fantastic," Mackenzie said. *But is it really?*

"I'm very excited about it."

"When will you be headed over?" Colin asked. "We'll be visiting my family soon, probably over the holidays. My mum's been on my back for weeks."

"I'm torn between two properties at the moment and will be visiting to make a final decision, maybe in a week or so. I'll also be looking for a flat to rent as we undergo renovations."

This was the first Mackenzie had heard of this. *If we are dating and on our way to being a couple, shouldn't Ian have mentioned that he planned on leaving?* And by the sound of it, this wasn't a quick trip. Ian continued to discuss the details with Colin while the gears in

Mackenzie's mind began to turn. She'd known he was adventurous and always traveling, but Mackenzie had hoped she could instill some more of her homebody ideals into him. *Does he not see a future with us? Apparently, I didn't get the memo.*

The men retired to the living room to wait for pie to be served. Mackenzie was loading plastic storage containers with leftovers for Tiffany and Molly to take home. Molly was rinsing dishes as Tiffany arranged them in the dishwasher.

"Dinner was excellent, Mac," Molly complemented.

"Thanks," Mackenzie answered as she struggled to snap on a lid. "Stupid thing," she hissed.

"You okay?" Molly turned around and asked.

"It's just this damn thing." Mackenzie finally got it to close.

Tiffany threw her a knowing look. "I heard, you know."

"Why didn't he say anything?" Mackenzie complained.

"Wait, who and what? I'm a little lost here, ladies," Molly said as she turned the faucet off.

Tiffany dried her hands on a dish towel and explained, "Ian's opening another Blu in London."

"So?" Molly shrugged.

"That means he'll be leaving to set it up," Tiffany continued. Molly nodded as she understood what that meant.

"It doesn't matter, anyway," Molly said.

"It would've been nice if he'd mention it," Mackenzie fired back.

"But don't you see? He's not the right *one.*" Molly hugged her. Tiffany joined in.

"As much as I hate to even admit it, Moll's right," Tiffany added.

Mackenzie heard a sound and looked up from their circle to find Gideon with his cell phone. "What are you doing?" she asked.

"Just capturing a really cool moment between best friends," he answered while looking at his phone.

"Hey, that's my job," Molly teased as they broke their embrace.

"We all know you're the camera queen, but I just couldn't help myself. I promise I was just coming to ask if we were eating pie anytime soon." Gideon played it off, even batting his lashes at Molly.

She swatted him. "Did Mac call you in? No, which means we haven't dished it up yet."

"Can't blame a guy for trying," Gideon replied as he moved closer to Mackenzie and kissed the side of her head. "Dinner was fantastic, by the way, but us boys are ready for pie," Gideon whispered as he squeezed her ass. Mackenzie couldn't help but giggle.

"We'll call you when it's ready," she said as he left the room. "That guy... I swear."

"Look at her," Tiffany commented to Molly.

"Oh, I know." Molly laughed.

"What?" Mackenzie asked.

Ian entered the kitchen only a moment after Gideon had left. "Mackenzie, you have a minute to spare, love?"

"Sure," she answered and looked over to Molly and Tiffany, who pretended they were busy.

Ian led her toward the front door. "Thank you for wonderful dinner but I really must be going."

"Are you sure? You haven't had dessert."

He laughed and gave her a sexy grin. "I doubt I'll be having that anytime soon." Mackenzie tilted her head to the side and Ian kissed on the cheek. "He's a good guy, Mackenzie."

"When were you planning on telling me about the restaurant?"

Ian shoved his hands in the front pockets of his dark slacks. "Soon. I was trying to figure out a way to break it to you." He paused and looked at her. "I really like you, Mackenzie, but I don't think we're on the same page."

"We've only started seeing each other. It's a little early to make that conclusion, isn't it?" Mackenzie countered. *Why am I even bothering?*

"I wasn't looking for anything serious, but that bloke in the other room is. Don't you see the way he looks at you? Hell, you should see how you look at him. You two are in love. I think that's a very special thing," Ian explained.

He was telling her what she already knew. What everyone already knew.

"You're a wonderful woman and deserve to be with someone who wants what you want. I still have too much to do before I could give you that." Ian frowned as he moved a strand of hair off her cheek. "Maybe if the timing were better."

"They say timing is everything." Mackenzie felt an odd mix of emotions course through her—relief, sadness, regret and happiness all rolled into one confusing ball. "I wish you nothing but the best, Ian. I hope the new Blu is hugely successful." Mackenzie hugged him.

"Don't be a stranger. Feel free to stop by the restaurant anytime—or if you're ever in London." Ian kissed her on the cheek and opened the door to leave. His gaze gravitated to something behind her. "Goodbye, Mackenzie." She looked behind her to find Gideon.

"Well, he seemed nice," Gideon commented as he leaned against the wall.

"He is." Mackenzie closed the door and couldn't help but think that another one was opening — one that had been shut two years ago. Now Mackenzie had to decide if she wanted to cross that threshold again.

Chapter Fifteen

"I think we're going to head home," Gideon said after everyone else had left. He was stretched out on the couch with the baby curled up on his chest. "Thank you for today, Mac. I know she won't remember her first Thanksgiving, but I will."

His words warmed her. Mackenzie rose from her spot across from him and scooped up Azita. "I'm glad I was here for her first one. Just think, Christmas is right around the corner," she told Gideon.

"Well, maybe we can spend it together," he said and removed himself from the couch. Mackenzie didn't answer. She kissed Azita's cheek and handed her back to him.

"Let me grab those leftovers for you." Mackenzie raced to the kitchen and pulled a few containers of food from the fridge.

She loaded them into a canvas bag and followed Gideon out to his car. It was dark and chilly. Mackenzie inhaled the moist scents in the air. It smelled like snow was on its way. It didn't usually snow this early but it wasn't completely unheard of.

Gideon hurried to secure the car seat and closed the door. "Thanks again, Mac." Gideon kissed her cheek as she handed him the bag. "Goodnight."

Mackenzie watched him get into the SUV and felt her heart plummet to her stomach. She went back inside and the quiet began to bother her. She flicked off the kitchen light and decided that the day was officially over. She'd been on her feet for most of it and her body screamed with exhaustion. She'd been feeling run down the last couple of days and was beginning to wonder if she'd caught a flu bug from one of her precious students. Classrooms were like Petri dishes. Germs ruled the playground and it felt as though Mackenzie spent half of her paycheck stocking up on cold meds and preventive measures. The local drug store knew her on a first-name basis.

She let out a long yawn, kicked off her heels and began peeling off her dress. Gideon probably wasn't even down her street yet and she missed him. The thing with Ian was still running around in her mind. She truly did wish him the best and maybe if the timing had been better, they could've had a chance — or maybe if Gideon had never come back into her life.

Mackenzie had just brushed her teeth and was about to crawl into bed when she heard a loud knock on her door and the doorbell going off like crazy. The persistent ringing and knocking frightened her. Her adrenaline surged as she raced to answer it. *So much for going to bed.* Mackenzie was now wide awake. *Why can't coffee work like this?*

When Mackenzie flung the door open, not sure what to expect, she found Gideon standing there. Snow had started to fall and the white flakes floated behind him like the perfect movie backdrop. He didn't speak. Gideon stepped toward her and grabbed her face. He kissed her hard. The strength and power of their contact caused the world to stand still, at least for Mackenzie. She couldn't think, only feel the moment that surrounded them. It was as though she were suspended in space, a floating-like feeling possessing her. She could almost swear that her feet were not touching the floor. Gideon finally broke the kiss but his hands continued to hold her face as though she were made of fragile glass. Mackenzie was too stunned to move as she waited for him to say something, anything. He just stared at her with longing and pain.

"I love you, Mac," he said in a breathless tone. "I tried to be good. I swear I did — to play by your rules and do this whole *friend* thing. Shit, I was even polite to that guy, but I can't just hand you over to him or anyone."

Mackenzie blinked hard. Had he not heard Ian and Mackenzie speaking earlier? Did he still think she was with Ian?

"But we're—" she went to explain when Gideon covered her mouth with his again. The kiss was even more intense than the one only a moment before. This one was clearly fueled by desire and hunger, the need to prove his love and want. He was burning his signature onto her lips for every man out there to read.

"You feel it, too...right?" Gideon asked. His eyes were moist and Mackenzie trembled as she stood there. "I'm not alone in this, am I?" Concern became etched onto his handsome face. Mackenzie wanted to smooth away the worry and make all his doubts vanish. She got on the tips of her bare toes and kissed him on the mouth. Mackenzie nipped at his bottom lip. The muscles in his face relaxed as she slung her arms around his neck and he dropped his hands to her hips. *How could I not feel this?*

"Did you even make it down the street?" Mackenzie asked with a smile she didn't bother to disguise.

Gideon pressed his forehead to hers and peered down at her. "No."

"Good." Mackenzie wrapped her arms around his waist and rested her cheek on his chest. "I missed you like crazy, too," she admitted.

"I'm sorry it took me this long. I probably sat at that stop sign for twenty minutes."

"Get your butt back in here," Mackenzie ordered as she twirled around and headed inside. "I think I may still have some pie left and we need to talk."

Gideon gave her cheek a quick peck before he grabbed the blanket-covered carrier by his legs. Mackenzie watched him as he brought Azita and her diaper bag in. She extended her arms. "Give her to me." Gideon passed her the baby, who smiled up at Mackenzie. The gummy grin melted Mackenzie as she snuggled Azita close. "You should've told Daddy to turn around sooner, you little stinker," Mackenzie cooed to the precious girl.

Babies were hard work. Mackenzie hadn't realized just how hard. It took quite some time to get her to fall asleep. They had fed, changed, rocked and just about everything under the sun before Azita had finally closed her gorgeous brown eyes.

"I was beginning to think she didn't want me and her daddy to have any alone time," Mackenzie teased.

"Is it too early to ground her?" Gideon asked as they both stared down at the sleeping infant in the portable crib he had set up again.

"Don't you even think about it," Mackenzie warned him with a grin. Gideon circled his strong arms around her waist and rested his chin lightly on her shoulder.

"This is nice," he commented.

"It is," Mackenzie admitted.

"It just feels right, you know?"

"Trust me, more than you realize. I think that's what's been killing me," Mackenzie explained. "I've tried to ignore these damn feelings and I totally blame you."

Gideon twisted her around to face him. "It's *my* fault?" he asked with raised eyebrows. "Care to explain?"

"You know, by acting all sweet and wonderful, and for being a great *friend*. You've weaseled your way back into my heart, you bastard," Mackenzie teased as she slapped his chest.

"Babe, I don't think I ever left." They both knew that statement was true. Gideon had his lips on hers in an instant. Mackenzie moaned into his mouth as her brain went numb and her heart went up in flames. "God, I need you," Gideon's words were rough as he whispered them into her ear.

Mackenzie didn't need any more convincing. Her clit throbbed with intense need and she wanted him more than anything else in the world. She didn't want them to just fuck like animals as they had the last time. Mackenzie needed him to make love to her – the kind that would last for hours but still wouldn't be enough to quench the thirst she felt for him.

She grabbed him by the hand and led Gideon in the direction of her bedroom. Mackenzie left the door open, just in case the baby cried. She removed her top and Gideon reached for her. He held her soft flesh as he helped himself to her nipple. He flicked his tongue over the sensitive nub, then his teeth grazed it, causing a sharp zing straight to her sex. Mackenzie held him close to her chest and threw her head back as he feasted on her breasts, giving both equal attention.

"You sure about this? Things didn't exactly end so well last time," Gideon said in a low voice.

Mackenzie circled her arms around his neck and kissed him. "Look who's living in the past."

Gideon gave her a wicked smile and pulled her even closer. "Damn, I love you." His words were filled with raw but playful emotion.

Mackenzie traveled her hand down Gideon's hard stomach and rested it on the crotch of his khakis. She smiled once her fingers brushed over it—the best cock in the world as far as she was concerned. It whispered promises to her, ones that had been fulfilled in the past and ones that would be gifted to her tonight. Her pussy grew hot just thinking of the ways she'd been pleasured by it. Lost in the fantasies that played in her mind, Mackenzie realized he'd lifted her from the ground. In one powerful movement, Gideon laid her on the bed. A sinister grin played across his lips. He hovered above her and kissed her deeply. He parted Mackenzie's thighs with a knee as Gideon started to leave a wet trail with his tongue down her chest and belly.

Mackenzie swallowed hard when Gideon removed her pajama bottoms but that was nothing compared to when he removed her panties with his teeth. The man was a showman and the bed was his stage. *Does he even realize just how damn sexy he is?* He rested on his knees on the mattress and removed his polo shirt, revealing smooth golden skin with sculpted muscles. Desire flickered in his eyes and he managed to smile with her panties still between his teeth. It was beyond hot, watching him stare at her, knowing full well what was about to happen next. He tossed the panties to the side and pulled her thighs farther apart. Her pussy ached for attention — anything, a finger, his tongue...his huge cock. Forget slow lovemaking. She needed to be fucked.

Gideon waved his finger at her. "We rushed it last time. We're taking our time, sweetheart. I want to worship every inch of you."

"Can't we do that next time?" Mackenzie begged. He let out a laugh and shook his head.

"No. If you'd rather I go home?" he threatened with a wink. "Just be good and let me love you." Mackenzie lay back on her pillow and stared up the ceiling. "Don't pout, Mackenzie, or I won't let you come," he teased.

Oh, for fuck's sake. Mackenzie lifted her eyes to meet his. "Okay, I'll be good. I just really need you," she whined then rolled her tongue across her lips, hoping to entice him to speed things up a bit.

"I need you too, baby. I just want to savor this." Gideon crawled closer until he was inches from her face. "I want you to know how much I love every inch of you." He kissed her neck and sucked the skin. It made her body pool with heat. *Damn him.* He knew all her erogenous zones and how to drive her utterly insane with desire.

Gideon abandoned her neck for her breasts again, and once he'd had his fill, he moved lower. He paused to kiss her navel and trace her exposed sex. She grew antsy and squirmed beneath him. Mackenzie hooked one leg around his hip and pinned Gideon to her. He slid past her and moved the wet folds of her pussy apart with his fingers. When he touched her clit with his tongue, Mackenzie almost came right then and there. Gideon licked the delicate skin, exploring deeper and deeper as his thumb applied pressure on her swollen clit. He lavished her soaking wet pussy with tender nibbles and sucking.

Mackenzie raked her nails through his hair and hugged his head as her body grew tight. The wave built inside her, the pressure mounting and growing as it took over. Her body hummed as light exploded from behind her closed eyes and she found her release. Gideon lapped at her flowing juices. Her pussy grew ticklish as her orgasm ended. She panted hard and was desperate to catch her breath and calm her racing heart. Only Gideon could make her feel this way. She surrendered any feelings from the past and set them free. Mackenzie only wanted Gideon. No one could ever replace him.

"That was so fuckin' hot," Gideon said as he left his station. "I love when you come, baby. You taste so damn good." He licked his lips and dove back between her legs. She squeezed her thighs together. Mackenzie needed more. A throbbing desire deep inside of her ached to be penetrated and filled.

She sat up in the bed and pushed Gideon away from her wet and needy pussy. "Those pants need to come off." Mackenzie stared hard into his surprised eyes. Gideon smiled as he moved to kiss her neck. "Now," she ordered as she poked him in the chest

Gideon hopped off the bed and quickly undid the button and zipper. He shucked them and joined her back on the mattress. Mackenzie spied her prize and was drawn to it. The smooth skin was warm in her hand. She ran her thumb over the round, velvety head and smeared a drop of pearly pre-cum. Mackenzie was tempted to put his member in her mouth but she desperately needed it elsewhere. Mackenzie pushed

Gideon back onto the mattress a little more forcefully than she'd planned. "Sorry," she said.

"Don't be," Gideon said. "It's kind of hot when you get all bossy."

"Really? I'll have to remember that."

"Only in the bedroom."

Mackenzie climbed on top of him and straddled Gideon's waist. "We can discuss my bossy side later. Right now, I really need to feel your cock buried in my pussy," she said in his ear.

Gideon moaned as Mackenzie mounted him in one full movement. He was nestled deep inside her, filling her to the hilt. Mackenzie planted her hands on his chest and began to move her hips, rising and falling. The pleasure that coursed through her veins made her want to scream out. Instead, she quickened her pace. She rode Gideon hard and took hold of the headboard. He anchored her to him and lifted his pelvis to fuck her with long, deep strokes.

"I can't get deep enough inside of you," he growled. She missed the feel of him as Gideon turned and twisted them around in one quick, fluid motion. His cock re-entered her, taking Mackenzie from behind. She rose to all fours and backed into Gideon as he slid in and out. The deepness he pushed past drove her to the edge. Gideon rocked her as his hand cupped her mound. He located her clit and she saw stars as another orgasm raged through her. Mackenzie moaned his name.

Gideon picked up his pace and drove into her in a steady, primal rhythm. Mackenzie's entire body tingled and buzzed as she floated. Her mind was white, completely blank of anything but Gideon. It was the strangest sensation. Gideon growled as he gripped her mound with one hand and her hip with the other. He pushed in one final time and held steady as he came. He collapsed onto her back and kissed the side of her neck.

They slipped under the covers and Mackenzie rested her head on his chest as he played with her hair.

"Was it always that good?"

"Each and every time, baby," Gideon answered as he kissed the side of her head. "You were so tight."

"Thanks, I think," Mackenzie said with a slight laugh.

"It's not a bad thing. I thought the same thing the last we had sex."

"Sorry. Were you expecting it to be loose or something?" Mackenzie joked but there was a defensive edge.

"Fuck, no. I'm a guy. I can't help but wonder if you've been with anyone else since we broke up."

"The answer is no."

"No?" Gideon repeated.

"There hasn't been anyone else. I'm so lame." Mackenzie felt her throat tighten as she admitted the pathetic truth.

"Baby, no, I don't mean for you to feel like that," Gideon whispered. "Wanna know a secret?" Mackenzie looked up at him and nodded. "I haven't been with anyone else, either. I guess we're both lame."

"In over two years, Gid? There's no way." Mackenzie was shocked. Gideon had always had a healthy sexual appetite and she couldn't imagine him not feeding that want.

"Honest. After we broke up, I went on tour, as you know. I couldn't even look at another woman. I knew I'd never find anyone like you again. Mac, you ruined me for all women."

Mackenzie laughed. Her entire body shook.

"What's so funny?"

"Well, I've always said the same thing. Even Molly and Tiffany said it — that you ruined me for any other guy."

Gideon raised his eyebrows and asked, "So, you and Ian. What's the story there?"

He just had to go there. It was as though he needed confirmation that there was nothing going on between her and Ian.

Mackenzie wove her fingers through the light golden hair on his chest. "He was my attempt at trying to get over you. I obviously failed miserably."

"He seemed nice enough," Gideon said in an obvious effort to be polite. "But I'm damn glad that it didn't work out."

"He told me today he could see that you were madly in love with me. Did you say anything to him?"

Gideon shook his head. "I just wear my heart on my sleeve. And he's right, you know."

"About?"

"Being madly in love with you. I've never stopped loving you, Mac. God knows I tried."

Mackenzie kissed his chest.

"I used to dream about you all the time. Even like stupid shit — grocery shopping or watching a movie."

"That's so sweet." Mackenzie felt tears form in her eyes.

"It got me through some horrible stuff and I knew that when I got out, I needed to come back to you. I didn't care how much you hated me."

"I did hate you," Mackenzie admitted.

"You had every right." They were both quiet for a moment. "You know, I'd even hear your laugh in my sleep. God, I love that sound—that and when you scream my name as you come." Gideon moved his hand under the sheet that covered them. He slipped it between her thighs. "I'd think about this amazing pussy of yours all the time, too. Just thinking about it now turns me on. You almost ready for another round?"

What happened to that deeply vulnerable moment of sharing? Men.

Chapter Sixteen

Mackenzie leaned against the door jamb and watched as Gideon pulled away. None of the magical snow had stuck around. Last night had been incredible and she'd slept better than she had in such a long time. The morning had included a fun quickie in the shower. Mackenzie could get used to this. Gideon had left because the baby was nearly out of formula but he had invited Mackenzie to stay the night at his place. *Thank goodness for long holiday weekends*. She intended to enjoy every minute of it.

Coffee, then Mackenzie would tackle her day. She'd just ground beans and was pulling out some chocolate-vanilla creamer when her phone buzzed.

"Hello?" she answered.

"I miss you already," Gideon said.

"But you made it past the stop sign this time?" Mackenzie teased.

"Just barely. Can't wait to see you." This man caused all sorts of delightful feelings to bloom inside of her.

Mackenzie's cheeks hurt from smiling so much. They said goodbye and Mackenzie's phone rang again.

"I promise I'll be there soon," she answered.

"Really? I was just calling to say hi," Molly replied.

"Sorry. I thought you were Gid calling me again." Mackenzie poured the creamer and watched the dark liquid lighten.

"I was just calling to talk about him. Obviously, you guys have talked since dinner."

"He's just barely left," Mackenzie said.

"Damn, are you serious? Girl, you didn't waste a minute. I'm so proud of you."

"God, it was so incredible, and oh, Moll, I wish you could have seen it," Mackenzie said.

"Yeah, no, thanks. I'm not exactly a watcher."

"I don't mean that. Like, so he left, right? Well, he came back and it was so romantic," Mackenzie gushed as she relived their magical kiss.

"Would you shut it?"

"Excuse me?"

"Not you…Owen. He wants to know if his friend can come over and play."

Mackenzie laughed. "How about dinner tomorrow? I'll have to check with Gideon, but I'm sure it's fine."

"I'm scheduling your playdate," Molly yelled. "Okay, sorry about that. Men…I swear."

"I'm glad he likes Gideon. Gideon doesn't have a ton of friends — at least none that aren't in the service, you know?"

"Tell me about it. I need to find Owen more friends so I can get him out of my hair," Molly joked. "I'm sure Tiffany and Colin would love to come over. Mind if I invite them?"

"Of course not."

"Oh, by the way, you should see that picture Gideon took yesterday."

"How did you get to see it?"

"He sent it to Owen. Gideon may want to consider photography. He was able to make me look skinny and that takes some talent." Molly laughed.

"Just stop. Jeesh. He's thinking of teaching after the holidays."

"Art?" Molly asked.

"Yep. Sculpting, I think."

"Didn't he used to have a pottery wheel like in that *Ghost* movie?"

Mackenzie answered with a laugh, "Yes."

"Well, you tell him if he's interested in getting into the photography gig, Owen or myself would be happy to help him. He's got an eye."

"Even better, two of them."

"Go get laid again and call me later after you ask Gideon about dinner."

"Yes, ma'am." Mackenzie hung up and drank her coffee.

Her sister's paper turkey caught her eye. Life never ceased to amaze her at how it could change on a dime. Her mind wandered to the last week when Gideon had called when she was in the garage pulling out that very decoration. She hadn't even had to say anything. He'd just shown up. And only a week ago Mackenzie had been trying to convince herself that she didn't love Gideon and that they could just be friends. Mackenzie let out a little giggle. How silly had she been to think that there could ever be anyone else? The cherry on the top had been learning that Gideon hadn't been with anyone since her. There was a sense of satisfaction that he'd suffered as she had. Somehow it all put them on an equal playing field and made him that much more attractive to her.

She was feeling kind of giddy. All those rambunctious butterflies were taking flight inside her. Mackenzie was in love…again.

* * * *

It had been a while since she'd even driven by the small home in the quiet neighborhood about twenty minutes from her own. The last time she'd visited his home had been because of Azita. She had avoided that route after they had broken up and Mackenzie had been in such a panic the last time that it hadn't truly hit her. There had been no reason to drive by until Gideon had begged her to help with a crying newborn.

She'd never really spent much time at his home. In the past, they'd spent their lazy weekends together at hers. She'd figured after they'd gotten married they'd begin newlywed life in her house. Gideon had tried to convince her they should live at his place. Mackenzie loved her home with the quaint porch and sunny backyard deck, not to mention the kitchen and entertaining space hers offered. She knew, though, that the houses hadn't been the real issue. How strange was it now that she was coming to his place when only hours earlier he had been at hers?

Mackenzie parked her sedan in the narrow driveway of the neat-as-a-pin house. The front yard was perfectly mowed but the porch lacked the homey touches hers had. Flowers or maybe even a porch swing would change the look. She was frozen, stalling for no particular reason, and couldn't exit her car. *Am I moving too fast? Is diving head first into this with Gideon really the right way? What does the future hold? Will we be picking up where things left off? Should we slow things down and take our time?* An image of her sister popped into her mind and that was her answer. Life had tossed her a ginormous lemon on that day. Mackenzie had learned that time was a funny thing. *We always assume we have tons of it, but when it's up, it's up. Game over.* Her sister had always liked Gideon and she had been devastated when they'd broken up. Mackenzie knew she'd approve. Heck, maybe her sister'd had a hand in their reunion—a little divine intervention. Thinking about her always made Mackenzie a little teary-eyed and she felt more emotional today than she had in a while.

Mackenzie took a deep breath, held the air in her lungs then slowly exhaled. Her stomach was a mess, a sudden ball of nerves as she walked up the narrow cobblestone path to his porch. Mackenzie knocked on the door and was greeted by a very handsome Gideon. *How is it possible for him to be even hotter than a few hours ago?*

His slanted smile was welcoming and reminded her of all the naughty things that mouth could do—and probably would do to her tonight. "Damn, what took you so long?" Gideon tugged her against him. It felt amazing to be wanted this much by a man, but not just any man—*her* man.

Gideon led the way inside, down a small entryway that quickly turned into the kitchen. The house smelled amazing.

"Fajitas? Shouldn't we be eating leftover turkey or something?" Mackenzie asked as she inhaled the grilled beef and peppers.

"We're going with the 'or something'."

Gideon went to work on slicing lemons and Mackenzie quickly noticed a large glass pitcher. *Lemonade.* Mackenzie smiled. Tiffany had told her *'when life hands you lemons, you need the right guy to make the lemonade'*. And there he was.

"What's so funny?" he asked.

"Nothing. Just something Tiffany said," Mackenzie answered as he stirred the mixture.

"Here. I know it's not nearly as good as the lemonade you always made." Gideon handed her a glass and raised his. "To us." They clinked the glasses together and Mackenzie sipped the tart drink.

Instantly she wanted to throw up. It took all the willpower she had not to. She should've known better with how queasy her stomach felt.

"You okay, Mac?" he asked with concern as he took her glass from her.

"Yeah, I haven't been feeling a hundred percent. It's that time of year at school," Mackenzie explained. "I promise I'm fine."

Gideon frowned. "Can I get you a water or something else?"

"Water's good."

"Food's almost ready. I got chips and the salsa's in the fridge."

Mackenzie opened the refrigerator and noticed how orderly all the contents were arranged. "And here I think I'm the OCD one?"

"Hey, I'm military...was military."

"I didn't realize the military forces you to face all of your condiments and have them arranged alphabetically and by size," Mackenzie teased.

Gideon leaned over and kissed her. "You know it turns you on."

"Your organizational skills always have." Women usually complained about their guys never cleaning up after themselves or being messy. Not Gideon. He liked order. He used to say that everything had a place and perhaps that was why any time he came to her house, even after two years, he knew where to find things.

Mackenzie dunked a tortilla chip into the salsa and asked, "Baby sleeping?"

"She just went down like ten minutes before you got here. You wanna make good use of our quiet time?"

"Gosh, wine and dine me a little first, buddy," she teased. Gideon laughed then kissed her on the neck.

"I know this is going to seem really dumb, but I'll ask, anyway. So are we like dating again?" he asked.

"No, I'm just a slut."

"Who hasn't slept with anyone for two years. Such a whore." Gideon winked. "Seriously, I hate putting a label on things."

"That's not true. You love labels. You own a label maker, remember? I got it for you that one Christmas."

"Shit, you got me there. I guess I do like to label stuff."

Mackenzie grew quiet for a moment as she took what he really wanted to know and processed it with her own feelings. "What do you want us to be?"

"Short answer or long answer?"

"Well, short answer first, I guess," Mackenzie leaned against the counter and waited for him to say.

"Married and with a dozen kids."

"Do I even dare ask about the long answer?"

"Mac, I'm not stupid. I know we can't pick up exactly where we left off. We're different people than we were then—or at least I am. The only thing that hasn't changed is that I love you."

Mackenzie gave him a peck on his cheek. "I think we need to just take each day as it comes. We both know that we love one another, so we're good there. That part is settled."

"And what about the marriage and kids part?" Gideon asked.

"A dozen kids is a lot. Not sure my lady bits can withstand that kind of wear and tear."

"True, and I do love your lady bits." Gideon nipped at her collarbone. He ushered her to chair at the small dining room table then brought chips and salsa. "I just want you to be happy. For us to be happy."

"I think we could be." Mackenzie dunked a tortilla chip into the chunky salsa and prayed her tummy would settle down.

"Me, too," Gideon agreed as he sat across from her. "What I would give to go back in time, though."

"You wouldn't have your daughter," Mackenzie pointed out. "Azita is worth everything we've been through."

"It's incredible to hear you say that. This is why I want you in her life — in my life. I still wish we could travel back to when we first met. I'd do so many things differently."

"Wasn't it you who told me to quit hanging out in the past? I think the future is looking pretty darn good."

Gideon leaned across the table and gathered her hands in his. He kissed her.

After a delicious and quiet dinner, they settled into the living room. Mackenzie played with the wiggly baby and fell more in love with Azita as each second passed. She fed, changed and cuddled the baby girl as though it was the most natural thing in the world.

She had been lying on Gideon's bed with Azita next to her while Gideon cleaned the kitchen from their dinner. Mackenzie stroked Azita's chubby cheeks and spoke softly to her. Exhaustion was starting to take over and Mackenzie rested her eyes for only a moment. She must have fallen asleep because Gideon was gently shaking her and whispering her name.

"Gosh, I guess I fell asleep." Mackenzie yawned and looked at the sleeping baby next to her. Azita's lips were pouted and her long lashes fluttered as she stirred.

"Looks like you both did."

"I better get home," Mackenzie said as she climbed off the bed.

"You don't have to. You could stay," he offered. Gideon entwined his arms loosely around her waist.

"Not sure I'm up for a slumber party," she replied while attempting to stifle a yawn.

"Want me to drive you?" Concern swirled in his bluish green eyes. They were the color of a harbor, darker than normal.

"I'm fine, but thank you." Mackenzie rested her cheek on his chest. It felt good being held by him. She inhaled the scent of his laundry detergent and fabric softener. She must have smelled it a million times. It brought back many memories of them doing this exact thing — holding on to one another, each scared to let the other go. "I think all the cooking yesterday wore me out."

"You better start getting used to it. What do you think feeding a dozen kids is going to be like?" Gideon teased and Mackenzie giggled.

"You're pretty dead set on that number."

"We'd have a baker's dozen. Azita doesn't count."

"Yes, she does," Mackenzie argued with a grin.

"You know what I mean. I want a dozen mini-Macs running around."

"You're crazy. You know that?"

"But you love me."

There was no argument there.

* * * *

Gideon hummed along to Cyndi Lauper's *Girls Just Want to Have Fun* and drummed his fingers on the steering wheel. Mackenzie couldn't help but sing the chorus. That brought back so many wonderful memories of the road trips they'd taken together. *Good to know our car karaoke is still alive and well.*

"I should put this on YouTube or something," Mackenzie threatened as she pretended to record him on her cell phone.

"Hey, I can't help it if this is *my* jam. Maybe I'm just a girl who wants to have fun," Gideon responded then began to sing louder. He even threw in a few sassy dance moves and Mackenzie erupted into a torrent of giggles. "You remember that time we took that road trip to that vineyard in Oregon?" Gideon asked.

"God, that was so much fun." Any time Gideon had been home on leave, they'd try to take a trip somewhere. Visiting the vineyard had been incredibly romantic and where Mackenzie had grown a new appreciation for wine.

"We should go somewhere soon," he suggested.

"Maybe when the weather is a little better," Mackenzie countered as large raindrops pelted the windshield of Gideon's SUV.

They were on their way to Molly's place for dinner. Mackenzie had slept like a log. Going home had truly been for the best. The second she'd unlocked her door, Mackenzie had made a beeline for her bed. She couldn't explain what had come over her but she had been consumed by terrible exhaustion. Today she felt much better and was looking forward to dinner with her friends...*their* friends.

"We live in the Pacific Northwest, Mac. We aren't scared of a little rain."

"Good point. Oh, turn here," Mackenzie instructed as they arrived at Molly's street.

"It's nice of them to invite us over," Gideon commented as he cruised.

"There's their house," she announced. Gideon parked along the curb.

"Nice place. And speaking of places," Gideon started.

Mackenzie was unclipping her seatbelt. "Yeah?"

"We may want to eventually start thinking about where we want to live."

She smiled. "Gid, I love my place and we've been through this once before." Mackenzie remembered several arguments they'd had when it had come to choosing. "That's why neither of us moved into the other's house."

"That's because we were both too stubborn."

"Probably. I'm sure we'll figure it out this time." Mackenzie leaned over and gave him a quick peck on his cheek.

They quickly got out of the SUV and Gideon did his best to shelter both Mackenzie and Azita from the rain. Mackenzie carried the diaper bag, one with wine in it and some brownies she'd baked earlier.

Owen greeted them at the door and ushered them all in. "You made it." Molly appeared in the entry, holding their daughter.

"There she is," Mackenzie cooed.

"Ellie is so ready for her nap, isn't she?" Molly kissed the baby's chubby cheeks. "She's been up all day and is a little fussy."

"You know, Azita was a little cranky too. Luckily, the car ride lulled her to sleep," Mackenzie explained.

"Listen to these moms," Owen commented. "All they want is for these babies to sleep. Where's the fun in that?"

"That's because she's always asleep when you're at home," Molly countered. "She thinks it's party time when it's just her and Mommy."

Gideon laughed. "Girls just want to have fun." He winked at Mackenzie, who could only shake her head. *Such a silly man.*

Mackenzie gently pulled Azita from her carrier and cradled the baby to her side.

"Someone is sure looking like an old pro," Molly commented as she carried Ellie into the kitchen. Mackenzie followed her and the guys ventured toward the living room.

"I'm not going to lie. I'm becoming more than a little attached," she admitted.

"No surprise there. You're the mothering type."

"True. I've spent the last ten plus years mothering you and Tiff," Mackenzie joked.

"And look how great we turned out," Molly added with an eye roll.

"Speaking of Tiff, where are they?"

"They'll be here soon." Molly rubbed Ellie's back and swayed side to side, obviously in hopes of getting her to fall asleep. "So, how are things going?"

"Good. You just saw us two days ago, Moll."

"Yeah, but in that time, you and Ian broke up."

"We weren't even together," Mackenzie argued.

"The next thing I know you're hosting a sleepover with Gid. Not that I'm complaining. I'm curious where you two stand now," she asked.

"We've been talking about that. He knows we can't just hit resume and pick up right where we left things."

"So, you two aren't getting married?"

"Not any time soon." Mackenzie mimicked Molly's actions and rocked Azita. "We know that we love each other, but I think we need to take things one day at a time."

"Shit, you had two years apart."

"I don't want to ruin this and lose him all over again."

"Oh, babe, it wasn't your fault. You're not going to lose Gideon. He's not going anywhere. Besides, he's got a new playmate and Owen would kill him if he leaves you."

"How are you and Owen doing?"

"Well, the honeymoon phase is wearing off but we've entered a new one. This whole parenting thing is not as bad as I thought it would be. Ellie is our everything and we've only come to love each other even more."

"I can imagine. Owen already adored you and now that you two created that precious little girl, I can only bet he is even more head over heels in love with you."

"And vice versa. Granted, I may tease that he gets to enjoy her when she's not being cranky, but Owen tries to help as much as he can. He'll cook dinner, help clean up and tries to make life easier for me."

"Married life is hard, isn't it?" Mackenzie asked. She peered down at Azita to see that she'd fallen asleep.

"It's not a cake walk, but I wouldn't go through it with any other man. Owen is my *one*." Mackenzie could the truth behind Molly's words. Her friend was absolutely happy and honest that marriage wasn't all sunshine and roses, but even in the nasty storms, she only wanted Owen there with her. That was how Mackenzie had felt about Gideon, and she knew that given time, she'd feel like that again.

"Hey, you sexy mamas," Tiffany announced. Azita flinched in Mackenzie's arms and Ellie started crying. "Oh shit, I'm sorry." Tiffany frowned. "I didn't mean to wake them."

"It's okay," Molly replied but her annoyed stare said otherwise. "She's been fussy all day."

"Isn't that what babies do?" Tiffany joked. "See? You should've just gotten a dog."

"Wow, you're really anti-babies," Molly commented. "It's only a matter of time before you change your mind."

"I don't know about that. I used to want one so badly and I love seeing you guys with babies. I figure I can live vicariously through you two."

"And Colin?" Mackenzie asked.

"He'll get over it. I'm not saying *never*, just not anytime soon. I'm still on the pill and plan to be for quite a while."

Mackenzie swallowed back a lump that had formed in her throat. A sudden onset of nausea hit her hard.

"Mac, you okay?"

"I'm fine," she managed. "I think I may be coming down with a flu bug. It hit the first graders a few weeks ago and hasn't visited my class yet."

"See? Kids are gross. Walking and talking little germs. Mac's always getting sick then she gives it to us. You just stay away, lady," Tiffany said and crossed her fingers as if Mackenzie was a vampire or had the plague.

"You're so dramatic." Molly rolled her eyes. "I'm going to lay her down really quick. Help yourselves to anything you want to drink." Molly carried Ellie out of the kitchen, leaving Tiffany and Mackenzie.

"Tiff, you really don't want kids?"

She shrugged. "I like how things are right now. Everyone always asks people who just got married when they're having kids. It's annoying. Like, let them be married for a fucking minute. Jeesh."

"Who had been asking you guys?"

"Colin's mom — and like every other member of his family. When we Skype or talk on the phone, it's like the first question. No, 'Hi, how are you?' or anything else — just straight away with, *'Is she pregnant yet?'* or *'Is something wrong with her?'*"

"I'm sure they mean well and are just excited."

Tiffany flipped her long, dark waves. "I just wish they would cool it."

"What about the wedding in the spring?" Mackenzie asked.

Tiffany shook her head. "I'm not sure about it anymore."

"Seriously?"

"It seems a little ridiculous now, doesn't it? Molly has Ellie, so traveling with her isn't going to be easy. And now with you and Gideon."

"What about me and Gid? That shouldn't impact your wedding," Mackenzie said.

"It's not that. I just think maybe I'm going over the top. Shit, we're already married. What's really the point?"

Mackenzie was shocked. Tiffany had been so determined to have the biggest and best wedding any of them had ever seen. "Yes, but you wanted a beautiful wedding, not a drive-thru Elvis in Vegas."

"I'm starting to think maybe that wasn't such a bad idea after all. His mother is sort of a Momzilla."

"And you're a Bridezilla," Mackenzie teased. "But we still love you."

Molly entered the kitchen with a confused expression. "I leave the room for five minutes and you guys start talking weddings. What did I miss?"

"Nothing, just Tiffany whining about her special day."

"I already had my special day—or night, or whatever," Tiffany rambled.

"Mother-in-law problems?" Molly asked.

"They want to know why she isn't knocked up by now," Mackenzie filled in. "Tiffany is still on the pill."

"Seriously? Does Colin know that?" Molly asked with a surprised expression.

"Of course he knows. I'm not hiding anything from him. I think it's amazing you had a baby," Tiffany said as she turned to Molly then to Mackenzie. "I think it's great you're stepping up to help with Gideon's daughter. I'm just not sure I'm ready to be a mom anytime soon."

"You know what, Tiff? You're completely right. The ink isn't even dry yet on your marriage license. Enjoy time being married to Colin, and when the time's right, you'll know."

"Thank you. It's hard enough being that man's wife. Don't get me started on Pauly. Between him and Mr. Sprinkles, that's about all I can handle right now."

The conversation at dinner flowed as well as the wine did. The guys all acted like long lost brothers, causing the girls to roll the eyes and laugh at their stupidity.

This is how it should be—fun and yet completely comfortable. Gideon would occasionally give Mackenzie a sexy grin or wink, a little something to remind her that he was still thinking about her, even if he was talking to the guys.

Eventually, all the fun needed to come to an end. Mackenzie had a lovely time but the feeling of being utterly wiped out hit her again. She planned on loading up on vitamin C and sleeping in tomorrow. School was back in session on Monday and she had a ton to do before the holiday break nearly four weeks away. There were tons of arts and crafts that needed to be made, a winter performance for all the grade levels at her school, then there was the actual Christmas shopping and decorating. Mackenzie needed to be a hundred percent if she was going to survive.

The drive home was cozy. The SUV was warm and Mackenzie snuggled into the large leather seat. The gentle feel of the road began to lull her to sleep. Try as she might, Mackenzie couldn't keep her eyes open.

She felt Gideon nudge her and was confused for a moment as he whispered, "Babe, we're home."

"Damn, I fell asleep."

"You both did." Gideon smiled as he looked in the rearview mirror.

"Boy, I'm some date, aren't I?"

"You said you weren't feeling too great. Maybe you're coming down with something. Tomorrow you stay home and rest. I can bring some soup by," Gideon offered as Mackenzie unlatched her seatbelt.

"I may take you up on that. You two get home safe," Mackenzie said after she kissed Gideon on the cheek. "Maybe text me that you got in."

"Still such a worry wart. I'll text you, babe," Gideon promised. "Go rest."

"And who is the worry wart?" Mackenzie shut the SUV's passenger door. "Goodnight, Gid." She hurried inside her house and Gideon drove off. *Damn.* Even in her purely exhausted state, she already missed him. *We may need to figure out new living arrangements soon.*

Chapter Seventeen

Back to the grind. Mackenzie smiled as each of her students filed into the classroom. They spent the next hour discussing everything each student ate on Thanksgiving. All the talk of food made her a little queasy. Mackenzie was worried she might need to call for a sub if she didn't start to feel better.

Her stomach settled down after all the talk of food was over and she managed to get through the day fine. By the time she'd cleaned her classroom and made it home, Mackenzie wanted a hot shower and to crawl into bed. She felt like total crap. Mackenzie didn't bother eating dinner. It was probably for the best since her stomach was still acting goofy. Gideon called to check up on her and after assuring him she wasn't dying, Mackenzie burrowed under her comforter. Her pillow had never felt so good.

The alarmed buzzed, annoying her, and Mackenzie slapped at it. She groaned when she realized it was time to get up. It felt as though she'd barely closed her eyes and had only slept for a little while when she had been sleeping close to eleven hours. Her body screamed for more sleep but her stomach had other ideas. She bounded from the bed and raced to her bathroom. Mackenzie raised the toilet seat lid and purged what little she'd eaten the day before. She'd been expecting this part of the flu to hit. It had been threatening her for the last few days. Mackenzie remained hunched over the toilet and begged that the dry heaves would cease. They did after a bit and she washed her face. The cold water felt like heaven. When Mackenzie felt that it was safe to leave the bathroom, she called for a sub to take her place at class. Mackenzie crawled back into bed and had no trouble falling asleep again right away.

Mackenzie slept soundly. Her body needed the rest and she almost felt human when she woke up a few hours later. Her stomach growled but she wasn't eager to put anything in it. Puking wasn't something she enjoyed — not that anyone did. She avoided it all costs whenever she could.

She sat up in her bed with her eyes closed and contemplated her next move. The sound of her cell phone interrupted her brief meditation. She fumbled to grab it off her nightstand.

"Hello?" she answered.

"Hey, lady," Molly replied. *Must her happy voice sound so…happy?*

"You on your lunch break?" Molly asked.

"I'm home. I got sick," Mackenzie explained.

"Ooh, not good. I'm sorry. You need anything?"

"I'm feeling better. I finally stopped throwing up."

"You poor thing," Molly said. "Go rest. I'll check on you later. If you need anything, just call."

They disconnected and Mackenzie closed her eyes again. For a moment, Mackenzie considered getting up to make coffee. She quickly dismissed the idea. *That's a first. Yeah, I am sick.*

* * * *

"You feel any better?"

"A tad," Mackenzie lied.

She heard Gideon sigh as if he knew she wasn't being honest. "I can't bring you anything?"

"I don't want you or the baby getting sick."

"I hate not helping you," Gideon argued.

"Well, I'll survive. Molly dropped off some soup and can vouch that I'm not nearly as bad as you think."

"I just might call her," Gideon teased. "I miss you."

"I miss you, too. I'll be better soon. I promise."

"Please call me if you need anything, babe," Gideon said. "Anything. Even snuggles."

"Gid, you don't want this flu. I just feel so run down and exhausted. I could sleep for days, I swear."

"And what about throwing up?"

"That's what's odd. It kinda just comes and goes. It's more that I feel queasy."

"Yeah, that's no fun. Well, baby, you just get better. I may sneak over and check on you. I can have my mom watch Azita," he offered.

"And have you become infected and bring that home to her? I don't think so, mister," Mackenzie said. "I don't want her catching this. You'll survive without seeing me."

"Will I? I'm not so sure," Gideon said with great drama.

"Absence makes the heart grow fonder," she countered then chuckled.

"It doesn't like being away from you. It is too fond of you already."

Mackenzie released a happy sigh. She enjoyed the sweet banter between them. They were like lovesick school kids. She was crushing hard on Gideon.

"I'll call you later, Mac," Gideon promised and hung up.

She knew that meant he'd call in like an hour or so. Mackenzie decided to take a nap until that time, then maybe she'd binge watch some television.

After several more days with little improvement, Mackenzie began to wonder if there was something more serious going on with her. Her brain had a few ideas, but she didn't want to jump to conclusions just yet. Mackenzie had missed the entire week of school, which was unlike her. It was now the weekend and she still felt sort of lousy. Waves of nausea would hit but it was the feeling of sheer exhaustion that worried her. She made a pact with herself—one more week—next Friday—and she'd confirm her suspicion. Mackenzie called to arrange a much-needed *Friendship Friday*.

Somehow, Mackenzie survived the next week. Being worn out and feeling sick was becoming her new norm. She did her best to hide it from Gideon. They had plans to go shopping for a Christmas tree and Mackenzie planned on forcing herself to feel well enough to decorate and enjoy what was truly her most favorite time of the year. She didn't want to be robbed of trimming the tree and going shopping for presents.

Mackenzie heard a knock at her door that Friday night and knew it was Tiffany and Mackenzie. They stomped the slushy bits of snow from their boots and came inside.

"How's the sick lady?" Tiffany asked. "You're not contagious, are you?"

"What she has you can't catch," Molly added with a smirk.

"Uh, what in the hell does that mean?" Tiffany looked at Mackenzie then back at Molly. "Okay, someone start talking now," she demanded.

Molly reached into her purse and pulled out a small cardboard box. "Look familiar?"

"Holy shitballs, are you fucking kidding me?" Tiffany cried.

"I don't know for sure," Mackenzie replied with a calmness she wasn't sure she felt.

"That's why I brought this," Molly added as she shook the box. "Your turn," she said with a mischievous smile.

"I need a drink," Tiffany said as they all filed into her kitchen. Tiffany reached into the cupboard and pulled down a bottle of vodka. Tiffany asked as she retrieved two glasses. "You got any lemonade or something for this vodka?" Mackenzie smiled as Tiffany poured the clear alcohol about halfway into each glass. "What's that goofy grin about?"

"You remember what you told me a while back?"

"No, I bestow so much wisdom that I forget. Enlighten me," Tiffany said as she filled the remainder with cranberry juice. Mackenzie almost asked why there weren't three. "You don't get one until we know for sure. I suggest you piss on that stick so we can either cry or celebrate."

"I think we may end up doing both," Molly said as she accepted one of the glasses and took a sip. "Ooh, yum. This reminds me of those Santa's Sleigh cocktails we had that one year, just missing the lime."

Mackenzie cleared her throat. "Anyway, Tiff, you'd said, *'When life hands you lemons, you need the right guy to make the lemonade'*. Ring a bell?"

"Kinda." Tiffany had her glass to her lips and looked as though she was trying to remember.

"Well, I was on my way over to Gid's and I started to miss my sister. I got to thinking about how shitty life can be sometimes. I've had a few lemons chucked at me," Mackenzie explained.

"I'll drink to that," Tiffany said as she clinked glasses with Molly and they both took a big swallow of their cocktails. "So, tell me more about how wise I am."

Mackenzie grabbed a small lemon from her fruit bowl and sliced it. "I went into Gideon's kitchen and sure enough, there he was."

"Making lemonade," Molly finished. A lovey-dovey glaze filled her eyes. "How perfect is that?"

"I know, right?" Mackenzie agreed.

"Damn, I *am* good. You're welcome," Tiffany said as she poured more vodka into her glass. "Go piss."

Mackenzie grabbed the box from Molly.

"Whatever the outcome, it will be okay," Molly assured her. "Gosh, I remember how terrified I was when you guys made me take the test."

"That was a pretty cool night, wasn't it?" Mackenzie said as she recalled how the three of them had been at Molly's downtown studio and forced her to take the pregnancy test. Mackenzie remembered being so happy and excited for Molly.

Molly nodded. "It completely changed my life."

"Okay, enough stalling. Go," Tiffany ordered. Mackenzie gripped the box and made her way to the bathroom.

She trembled as she tore the package open. Two plastic sticks with clear caps came out. Mackenzie didn't need to read the instructions. She'd been through one other time before. Suddenly fear gripped her, pinching her throat close. *What if?* She tried to ignore the thought in her mind, but she knew it was there. *Can I handle another miscarriage? Would Gideon leave me again?*

Mackenzie heard a knock at the bathroom door. "You do it yet?" Tiffany asked.

"Not yet," she answered. The stick dangled in her fingers. That one stark white stick could very well change everything and Mackenzie had never been more terrified in her life.

* * * *

"I think this one is perfect," Gideon announced as he stood next to a full Douglas fir. He looked like Hollywood version of a lumberjack. The red flannel, jeans and knitted cap screamed Pacific Northwest, but the beginnings of a beard Gideon sported nailed the outdoorsy look. Her wannabe mountain man.

They had been looking at trees for well over thirty minutes in the small Christmas-tree lot. Multi-colored lights, like the ones with the large bulbs from when they were kids, were strung overhead. Christmas carols were spilling from an old radio and the night couldn't be more Christmassy. Mackenzie was clutching a Styrofoam cup of hot chocolate and trying not to freeze her ass off.

"It's fine," Mackenzie replied.

"You hesitated," Gideon said with an annoyed smirk and put the tree back with several others that looked identical.

"They're trees, Gid. They all smell good, look good and will do their job. Just pick one."

"But it has to perfect." Gideon grabbed her cup and took a long sip of her hot chocolate.

"Hey, get your own," Mackenzie complained, smiling.

"Yours tastes better." Gideon winked at her. Mackenzie raised herself on the tips of her nearly frozen toes and kissed his cheek. The whiskers felt rough as they brushed against her. He'd always been clean shaven since they'd met, but now that he was a civilian, he wanted to see if beards really did drop panties. Well, her panties, anyway. It was working.

They started to walk the lot again. Mackenzie inhaled the clean and delightful scent of the trees. Gideon moved past her.

"Here it is. A Noble fir." Gideon sniffed the tree and almost hugged it. "It's perfect."

"Okay, so you found the perfect tree for your house. What about mine?" Mackenzie asked.

Gideon threw her a confused look. "This is for your house. It's *our* tree," he stated.

"Well, you better have them tie it up. We've got some decorating to do," Mackenzie replied.

After the beautiful tree was strapped to the top of Gideon's SUV, they set off in search of something to eat. Mackenzie stared out of the window and none of the fast-food places they passed appealed to her. Gideon suggested some egg drop or wonton soup to-go from their favorite Chinese restaurant. Mackenzie agreed that sounded perfect, especially after having been outside for so long at the Christmas tree lot.

They took their containers of soup and a few egg rolls back to Mackenzie's home. She'd enjoyed spending the day with Gideon and was excited to decorate the tree he'd found. This was the most wonderful time of the year, and now a grand looking Noble fir stood in her living room. The house was beginning to smell of forests and pure Christmas.

"How long are we going to let it be naked?" Gideon asked.

"I'm trying to think how we should decorate it." Mackenzie studied the tree. She wasn't sure if she wanted to go with an old-fashioned theme, like popcorn and cranberries. Or should she do something chic, maybe something fun and pretty?

"While you decide, you wanna get naked, too?" Gideon wiggled his eyebrows.

What better way to spread holiday cheer? She didn't want to be a Scrooge so she raced Gideon to her bedroom.

* * * *

Mackenzie was nestled against Gideon, her sheet covered them as they lay there.

"What you thinking about?" Gideon asked as he kissed the top of her head.

"How wonderful this is," she answered. They'd finished making love. "And how this is going to be the best Christmas ever."

"I think it might be, too."

"We need to go shopping for Azita. Have you thought about what you'd like to get her?"

"She's a baby. I don't know, diapers?" Gideon joked to which Mackenzie slapped his bare chest.

"Maybe your mom can watch her and we'll go sometime after work next week," she suggested. "Is it weird that you are now having to shop for a little girl? Bet you didn't think you'd be doing that anytime soon."

"No, I didn't," his voice grew low and quiet.

"She's lucky to have you for her daddy."

"Maybe."

"What's wrong, Gid?" Mackenzie looked up to see him biting down on the pad of his thumb, his eyes visiting someplace far away. She'd seen that look on his handsome face before, though this time it was much darker.

"I shouldn't be her dad. Her parents should be alive."

"I know, babe. You did the right thing by taking care of her," Mackenzie whispered.

"Mac, sometimes I feel like adopting her was a way to cleanse myself of the shit I've done," Gideon admitted.

"Oh, Gid, because of what we went through with our baby?"

"More than that. Mac. War is a terrible thing. Even more awful than you can possibly imagine," he began to explain. "You're taught to neutralize the threat...at any cost."

Mackenzie shifted on the bed and moved even closer to him. She stared at him and tried to follow what he meant. Mackenzie witnessed a dark pain cross his face. "Gid, tell me," she pressed.

"You'll think I'm the worst person you've ever known."

"I could never think that. Gid, I love you with all of my heart. I always have and always will. Nothing could ever change that."

Gideon let out a snarky laugh. "You sure about that?"

Mackenzie rested her hand on his chest. "Yes. You can tell me anything."

Gideon rubbed his chin and looked in front of him. He avoided her stare and she grew concerned. The heaviness he carried was crushing. That much she could tell. Whatever it was that Gideon planned to say, if he even opened up enough to tell her, was going to be rough. *But just how rough?*

"Promise me one thing, Mac."

"Anything."

"Don't look at me differently. I was only doing my job."

Mackenzie watched tears pool in his eyes. She'd do anything in that moment to make all the pain, guilt, hurt and any other horrible shit disappear.

"You have my word, Gideon."

"Several months before I'd met Azita's family, I was forced to do something that I will never forget," he started to explain. Mackenzie rubbed his arm, encouraging him to continue. He struggled to speak. "I was faced with something I'd only heard horror stories about from other soldiers." Gideon stopped and chewed on his thumb. Silent tears began to roll slowly down his cheeks.

"It's okay, baby, just take your time. You can tell me anything." Mackenzie kissed his bare shoulder. He turned to look at her. Gideon pulled down the sheet and exposed his torso, Mackenzie noticed a pink scar. It was round and ugly. *How have I not noticed until now?* She ran her finger gently across it. Mackenzie had no idea he'd ever been injured and felt her heart break into a million pieces for any pain he must have felt. She covered the scar with her lips and kissed it.

"You get shot and blown up all the time. You get used to it. But what they don't prepare you for is the moment when you have to make a choice that will haunt you for the rest of your life."

"Oh, Gid," Mackenzie said as she waited for him to speak again.

"I had to kill a kid, Mac. Those fuckers strapped this kid with a gun bigger than his skinny little body, and I was forced to shoot him. Neutralize the threat, remember?" Gideon choked out his words. "He couldn't have been more than four years old and I fucking killed him, Mac. What kind of monster am I?" Gideon broke down and sobs rattled his body.

Mackenzie couldn't breathe for a moment as her brain tried to process what unspeakable horror he'd been through. She was almost scared to touch him. Then rage filled her. Gideon should never have had to make that choice, nor should any of the other soldiers who no doubt had because they were just doing their job. What they had been trained to do. She wanted to throw up. Mackenzie sat upright, pulled Gideon to her chest and held him as tightly as she possibly could. She wanted nothing more than to protect this man who carried a demon inside of him, who hid it well from the outside world, but inside was being destroyed bit by bit. He cried like she'd never seen a man do. The moment would never leave her, just as the moment of what Gideon had been forced to do would never leave him.

Chapter Eighteen

She needed to see him, to smell his laundry detergent and fabric softener again. Mackenzie needed Gideon. The week of feeling like crap had taken its toll on her, both physically and emotionally. Add on the stress of actual work and Mackenzie was a mangled knot of emotions seeking some much-needed comfort and she hoped to find that in Gideon's strong arms. Mackenzie just wanted to be held. That was what she missed most about not seeing him lately.

A girl had limits and Mackenzie had hit hers. She drove straight from work to Gideon's house. She hadn't bothered to call and hoped he'd be there. *Where else would he be?* He was a homebody like her. They were a boring couple. *Couple. That's what we are now, right?* Doubt liked to creep its nasty little head in every now and again. *Out of sight, out of mind.* The past week had been spent working and being tied up with seemingly endless Christmas projects with her class. She barely had the energy to get through the long days. The worst part was how much Mackenzie missed him. *How in the fuck did I survive two whole years without him and all those tours of duty before that?*

Mackenzie pulled into his driveway and breathed a sigh of relief when she spotted his SUV parked there. Mackenzie couldn't wait for another second and raced up to his porch and knocked on the door. *How is it possible to miss someone this badly?* She tapped her foot and grew impatient as she waited for him to open the door. Mackenzie knocked again. Nothing. She tried the handle and found it was unlocked. She let herself in.

"Gideon," Mackenzie called out. *Where in the hell is he?*

She walked past the kitchen then caught the sound of something strange, but then she remembered what it was. Mackenzie picked up her pace and jogged toward Gideon's garage through his dining room. She opened the door that led out to what could only be called his studio. There he was, seated in front of the pottery wheel. Music played and his bare back was to her. She could see his foot pressing the pedal to move the wheel. As it spun, Gideon's hands manipulated wet clay. Mackenzie got turned on at the very sight of him in his private and creative space. The craving to touch him overwhelmed her and Mackenzie entered the garage. She stood behind him, taking in the sensual sight, and Mackenzie realized he had no clue that she was even there. Mackenzie peered over his shoulder as quietly as possible and watched him work the clay into something smooth and quite extraordinary. The muscles in his bare and very sexy arms flexed and she couldn't resist any longer. Mackenzie kissed his shoulder blade. Gideon jumped and dirty water splashed everywhere. The beautiful creation went limp and crumpled into a wad of yuck.

"I'm so sorry," Mackenzie apologized.

Gideon seemed stunned at first as he tried to clean the mess. "It's okay. I didn't hear you come in. I didn't know you were coming over, babe."

"I feel awful, Gid. I messed up whatever you were working on."

"Oh, that? It's nothing. I sometimes just spin it around. It helps me think." Gideon smiled at her and wasn't the least bit upset. "I'm glad to see you, though. I've missed you." Gideon pulled her against him. He didn't seem to notice or care that bits of clay were stuck on his naked chest. "How was work?"

For a brief second, Mackenzie resisted. She feared that her blouse would get stained. *Fuck it.* She'd come here wanting to see him. *Who cares if my blouse gets ruined?* That was a small price to pay. Then a better idea came to her and she began to undo the buttons. Gideon's eyes focused on her exposed breasts and he wore a pleased grin. His hands were filthy but that didn't stop him from taking one of her breasts into his hand then to his mouth. Mackenzie released a heavy sigh and her body melted into his. *God, this exactly what I needed.* She needed Gideon.

He tugged her nipple with his teeth then flicked his wet tongue over it. The cool air hit the sensitive bud and she felt her center grow hot.

"I recall you wanted to re-enact a certain scene from a certain movie a long time ago. We never did," Gideon said in a low, rough voice. "Sit." Gideon planted her on the stool he'd been sitting on. He grabbed another stool and sat behind her. He grabbed the clay and moved in front of Mackenzie. "Give me your hands," he instructed he added water to the clay. Gideon expertly guided her hands over the ugly mound.

The smooth texture felt incredible. She let the clay move under her fingertips and palms. Gideon kissed the back of her neck. He kept his hands on hers as the clay moved and began to shape into something other than a blob. She closed her eyes and enjoyed the touching of their skin. With Gideon's mouth on her back and the wet clay in their hands, the erotic sensations began to take over her body. He must have sensed this and backed off a bit.

He whispered, "Working with clay is much like working with life. We strive to manipulate it, to bend it to our will. We're always working on perfecting it, even when it's as close to perfect as it will ever get." Gideon slid his hands around the clay and guided her hands again. He then removed his and let her work the clay on her own.

Mackenzie felt as though she were forming the dirt into something. Then Gideon found the center of her back with his lips and Mackenzie let go of the clay. She felt the wet mixture splatter all over her. Mackenzie looked down to find the creation they'd made together was now folded into itself. It was ugly and destroyed.

"Shit," she muttered.

Gideon's hands returned as he said, "Life can change. It can get messy and seem impossible to repair at times, but it can be fixed if you try hard enough."

Mackenzie stared in awe. Within minutes Gideon had reshaped the clay into something beautiful. It was a valuable lesson in love. The truth of what she just learned resonated to her core.

"You're amazing, you know that? You're going to be a great teacher," Mackenzie said softly as she turned around on the stool to face him. She wrapped her arms his neck and as she kissed him, Mackenzie could taste the chalky clay that was splattered on them both. "But I want private lessons."

"I think that can be arranged," Gideon replied as his fingers dug into her flesh and the clay was soon forgotten.

* * * *

Gideon smiled at her and shook his head.

"What's so funny?" Mackenzie asked.

He reached across the table and smoothed his thumb over her lips and then promptly. "You're adorable, you know that?"

The damn eggnog latte must have left some foam on her. Mackenzie wiped her mouth again, even though Gideon had cleaned it off.

This moment, as normal and quiet as it was felt wonderful. Sitting in the small café, the noise of patrons ordering their coffees, cars splashing the already-drenched sidewalks were all the makings of a perfect Saturday morning in Seattle.

"I wanted to thank you," Gideon said softly as he raised his mug to his lips.

"For what?" Mackenzie asked as she studied him. He was as handsome as ever and seemed more at peace than he'd ever been when they were together.

"For not treating me differently after we talked about..." Unable to finish speaking, Gideon looked out the window. Mackenzie saw him work on steeling his emotions and calming the storm that was brewing in his eyes.

She reached across the table and covered his hand with hers. "I can't even begin to imagine what you've been through, Gid. But I want you to know I'll always be here for you and that you can tell me anything."

He looked back at her and nodded. "I appreciate that. Telling you about that awful shit was the best thing I could've done. I feel sorta free now, if that makes any sense."

"It absolutely does. I saw a counselor after my sister died. It helped telling someone how I felt," Mackenzie explained.

"Well, we have each other now and can lean on one another when the burdens get a little too heavy." Gideon winked at her and Mackenzie smiled.

Mackenzie gripped her coffee mug and enjoyed the spicy taste of the nutmeg in her latte. She was no stranger to life tossing lemons her way but whatever life decided to throw at them, she was confident that they would be there for one another.

* * * *

The next week flew by at record speed. Mackenzie and Gideon had gone Christmas shopping for the baby and all their friends. Shopping so late in the season was a nightmare. Usually, Mackenzie was on the ball and even had presents wrapped before October. Despite the crowded stores, spending time with Gideon was worth the torture. He teased that it would be utter hell to shop for all their future children, that baker's dozen he wanted so much.

She had even figured out what to get him and couldn't wait to put it under their very beautiful but naked tree.

It was Friday night. Molly and Tiffany had come over to help. Wannabe-Martha-Stewart-Mackenzie was a little behind the curve. Both of her besties had already decorated their entire homes for the holidays. She'd pulled out the totes that contained the decorations. *Does that count?* Mackenzie needed help and had called in reinforcements.

"Cocoa or eggnog? Pick your poison," Mackenzie asked Tiffany and Molly.

"You got any rum?" Tiffany asked.

"Yeah," Mackenzie answered.

"I'll go with the eggnog then." Tiffany winked.

Molly nodded. "Let's nog it up."

In their jammies, sloppy buns and no makeup, they worked hard at transforming Mackenzie's house into something rather spectacular. Her house now rivaled the North Pole. Her tree sparkled with white lights that bounced off the arrangement of silver and gold ornaments. Rich silky ribbons cascaded down the tree. It was stunning.

"Wow, you guys, it looks amazing in here," Mackenzie commented as she finished her cocoa.

"What did you expect? We're like expert decorators," Tiffany teased.

"It's so pretty. I'm totally jealous," Molly added.

"Why? Your tree is so fun," Mackenzie countered.

Molly cocked her head to the side. "Owen decided the theme this year."

"And it looks really neat. Wait until Gideon sees it. He's going to love it," Mackenzie said.

"A Seattle Seahawk themed tree isn't exactly my idea of Christmas, especially since it's Ellie's first," Molly complained.

"It's sort of awesome," Tiffany piped in. "I love the green lights with the blue and silver balls."

"The tree is a hot mess. What about the hodge-podge of Seahawk memorabilia that Owen has collected over the years and has conveniently strewn all over because it goes with his 'theme'?" Molly asked with raised eyebrows and using air quotations.

"You do have a point there," Mackenzie agreed.

"I mean the tacky blue, green and silver garland is like everywhere, but the football lights are overkill," Molly said with a giggle. "God, I love that crazy bastard."

"You must if you allow him to decorate your house like that," Tiffany added.

"Tiff's condo is pretty much the envy of every department store from here to New York. It's gorgeous," Molly commented.

"Yeah, and Pauly thinks the tree is from the dog park and is constantly trying to pee on it. I have to watch that little bugger twenty-four-seven. Don't get me started on Mr. Sprinkles." Tiffany giggled. "God, I must love Colin a lot to put up with that slobbering dog."

"I'm not sure who you love more, Colin or Pauly," Molly said with a serious gaze.

"You're right. It's a toss-up," Tiffany agreed and sipped her drink.

Mackenzie smiled at her besties who were both lounging on her couch just as they had on a million other Fridays. She knew that there were going to be fewer *Friendship Fridays* and that she needed to cherish the ones they did celebrate. Each of their lives had changed so over the last year and she wouldn't change a damn thing. Well, maybe a few hiccups here and there, but they had gotten through them together.

These chicks were more than just her best friends. They were her sisters. She would share many more of life's milestones with them, just as she had for the last ten-plus years. They had practically grown up together and she cherished their shared history. Life had taken each of them on a wild ride thus far and Mackenzie knew it was not even close to being over. She and her besties had witnessed love, loss and through it all, they'd somehow managed to survive being single in Seattle…together.

* * * *

"Here. Open this one," Mackenzie said as she handed Gideon a slender box. "But read the card first." She was nervous as they sat on the floor next to the Christmas tree.

They'd spent the entire day fluttering between the homes of their friends and family. Many gifts had been exchanged, but Mackenzie had been waiting for this exact moment for the last few weeks. It took everything inside of her not to spill her guts and let the proverbial cat out of the bag. She'd wanted to make the moment special because there were only so many of those in one's lifetime, and right now it couldn't have felt more perfect. The soft lights from the tree created a romantic glow around Gideon and Mackenzie. The baby was asleep and the house was quiet.

"You sure you don't want to open yours first?" Gideon asked with a sheepish smile. "I suppose we could open them at the same time?" he suggested after he handed her a large box with candy-cane striped paper.

"I want to see your face when you open yours."

"Same here. I'm dying to see what you think," Gideon said, giving her a wink as he cradled the small box in his large hands. He shook it near his ear and gave her a perplexed look.

"Just open it," she said.

Gideon obeyed, but took his sweet time, which drove her crazy. He painstakingly peeled away the shiny red paper and silver ribbon. "It's so light," he commented as he paused to weight the box in his hand.

"Wait. Open the card first," Mackenzie remembered and pointed at the red envelope.

Gideon slid his finger across the seam of the paper and ripped it carefully. He pulled out the small card and read aloud, "Only eleven more to go?" Gideon's brow crinkled with confusion. Mackenzie shrugged and had a difficult time sitting still as he finished opening the box. Gideon removed the lid and unwrapped the tissue paper. He stared down at his gift—the pregnancy test with its two lines that would change their lives—and he was quiet. "You know, this kinda trumps my present," he said with tears in his eyes. "But I guess our gifts sort of go together."

Unlike Gideon's careful unwrapping of his gift, her inner child demanded she rip her package open, which she did with gusto. But Mackenzie found another wrapped box inside. She retrieved it and tore into that one. It revealed yet another slightly smaller box. This continued for another three boxes.

"Seriously, Gid?" Mackenzie sighed in happy frustration and opened the final box—or what she assumed was the last one. Gideon moved closer as she lifted a very small box wrapped in the prettiest paper she'd ever seen. The design consisted of delicate, glittery snowflakes. Mackenzie took her time to remove the paper. A velvet box was now sat in the palm of her hand and her gaze found Gideon's. He covered her hands and he took the box. Gideon opened it to reveal a gorgeous ring. Six perfect diamonds sat on either side of a large, heart-cut one.

"Our baker's dozen," Gideon explained softly.

The wrapping paper with the snowflakes now made perfect sense. Thanksgiving. The first snow fall. The kiss. It had been the turning point in their relationship when Mackenzie's brain and heart had both agreed that Gideon wasn't just her friend but the *one*. Her *right* guy to make lemonade anytime life decided to throw lemons her way.

"I know I've done this before," he started to explain nervously. "I love you more than I thought even possible. I thought I loved you to the moon and back the first time I asked you to marry me, but I see now that my love for you stretches beyond anything in our galaxy."

"Oh, Gid," Mackenzie cried. Her hand trembled as Gideon slid the beautiful ring onto her finger. She broke into loud uncontrollable sobs that she couldn't hold back any longer.

"So, that's a yes, right?" Gideon asked. Mackenzie slapped his arm as he wiped away her tears. "You were right, you know."

"About what?" Mackenzie managed to reply as she attempted to regain her composure.

"That this was going to be the best Christmas ever." Gideon cupped her cheeks and kissed Mackenzie.

It reminded her of the Thanksgiving kiss. It silently spoke of the undeniable and immeasurable love they had always had for one another. She wished for this moment to never end, for them to remain suspended in this very second for eternity, but something told Mackenzie that the best was yet to come.

About the Author

Gloria Herrmann is a romance author living in beautiful eastern Washington. She is an avid reader and lover of words, and becoming an author has been a dream come true for her. She still pinches herself all the time and wonders how she got so lucky.

Gloria loves to hear from readers. You can find her contact information, website details and author profile page at http://www.totallybound.com.

Home of Erotic Romance